I love writing short storie.   ... get me wrong—I love writing novels too, and penning **Named and Shamed** (published previously by Sweetmeats) was a whirlwind ride of filthy delight for me. But there's a special pleasure in writing a collection of short stories, perhaps because of the technical challenge. I have to think about crafting variety across the whole book, not just in erotic action and plot, but setting and vocabulary and viewpoint. Each story is a different facet of the whole, and I want that jewel to shine. Male *and* female points-of-view? Emotion *and* outrageous filth? First *and* third person narration? Fantasy *and* SF *and* historical *and* fairy tale? Check, check, check and check.

I love a challenge, me.

And I love my erotica to be challenging in and of itself. I delight in skating close to the thin ice, and I want to make worlds that are as convincing as they are surprising. I hope you find these tales immersive and enchanting in their fierce way, but take my advice—*don't trust the narrators,* at least until they have earned that trust. Don't ever just swallow whole what they have to say.

Too Much of Water is based on Ivan the Terrible, Russian folklore and the fairy-story *The Frog Prince,* told in the coldest voice I could muster. **Bolt Hole** in contrast is burning hot—a post-apocalyptic zombie story drenched in sweat and despair and need, with just the faintest glimmer of hope. **The King in the Wood** is based on a the central myth in Sir James Frazer's vast speculative anthropology text *The Golden Bough* (1915), which I read decades ago in the college library when I should have been writing essays; Frazer's work is mostly discredited now but it was a rich source for my fervid imagination. **The Last Thing She Needs** is a story of traumatized vampire hunters and BDSM. I think there are far too few tales out there told from the point-of-view of the DS bit of that acronym, and I wanted to explore the paradox of the conscientious sadist. **Sycorax**, a re-telling of course of Shakespeare's *Tempest*, employs one of my favorite devices: the tale written from the eye-level of the monster, where horror lurks between the lines. **Knight Takes Queen** is an Arthurian story, set in a chivalric world where modern notions of BDSM have never been articulated and sex is never simply innocent fun. **At Usher's Well** is based on a ghostly Scottish ballad that I first heard sung by Steeleye Span. I'm not usually a huge fan of melancholic or downbeat erotica but it does have its moments, and I worked quite hard to keep the grisly details implied rather than explicit! **The Military Mind** is a riotous space-opera gang-bang, and all I'm saying here is that I adored the movie *Aliens* from the moment I saw it, my first adult-rated film. And after that brutal pounding, we switch to a gentler gear for the last two stories. **A Man's Best Friend** was inspired by the very old TV series *The Water Margin*, but my version of ancient pseudo-China is fantasy without any historical basis. And **The Merry Maid** is pure playful fun, a riff on the fairy tale formula of three brothers seeking their fortune.

This is my third collection of erotica tales (following **Wild Enchantment** and **Dark Enchantment**) and I'd like to thank Sweetmeats Press for believing my vision and giving me my storytellers' voice again. Pull a seat up to the fire and let's begin. Just remember, you don't have to believe a word I say …

xxx

Janine Ashbless

FIERCE

ENCHANTMENTS

Short Stories

◆ ◆ ◆

JANINE ASHBLESS

§

SWEETMEATS PRESS

A Sweetmeats Book

First published by Sweetmeats Press 2014

ISBN 978-1-909181-68-7

Typeset by Sweetmeats Press
Printed and bound by in the USA

Sweetmeats Press
27 Old Gloucester Street, London, WC1N 3XX, England, U. K.
www.sweetmeatspress.com

Contents

Too Much of Water   7

Bolt Hole   27

The King in the Wood   48

The Last Thing She Needs   71

Sycorax   99

Knight Takes Queen   119

At Usher's Well   146

The Military Mind   175

A Man's Best Friend   223

The Merry Maid   253

For Roland –
And about time too.

Too Much of Water

Too much of water hast thou, poor Ophelia,
And therefore I forbid my tears

—Hamlet, *Act 4*

"Once upon a time there was princess who had a favorite toy: a ball of shining gold ..." That's how the story starts, doesn't it? It's nonsense, of course. She wasn't a princess; she was the daughter of a wealthy *boyar*. And she didn't love the ball, which wasn't a toy—although it was made of gold, or at least gilt. She was given the ball by the Tzar himself, when he rode away west to oversee the war upon the Livonians.

"Take and keep this ball of gold," he said as he leaned from his saddle at the gate of her father's house, "as a constant reminder of the troth you've plighted me. Let your chastity remain as pure and unsullied as this gold until our wedding day."

She watched the Tzar ride away with all his retinue and then she returned to her father's house to wait for him, just as she'd been told. Her name was Anna, but from her earliest days her family had called her Zorya—a nasty pagan name, and who knows what her parents must have been thinking of. If they had stuck to a decent saint's name perhaps none of the terrible things that followed would have happened.

The golden ball, she swiftly found, was an object of admiration to everyone else but a nuisance to her. Being a betrothal gift from the Tzar, and one laden with such meaning in the giving, it was hardly the sort of thing she could leave in her room for safekeeping. On the other hand it was too big to slip into a purse, and if she put it into an apron pocket it bumped heavily against her with each step. Zorya grudgingly grew used to carrying it about in her two hands, setting it beside her plate at meal times and on her pillow at night when she slept. Its gleam was the first thing she saw in the morning when the shutters were opened, and in the evening the candles that lit her chamber shone still more beautifully in the golden depths of its reflection. No matter how she handled it, no smudge of dirt dulled its shine.

"Oh, my lady," her maids-in-waiting would sigh; "what a beautiful gift: the Tzar must love you very much." Or "When you are Tzarina, my lady, you will eat off plates of gold and cut your meat with a golden knife, and this golden ball you will roll to your firstborn son. You must be so impatient, waiting for that day!"

But Zorya only moved her mouth in a troubled smile and did not reply when they spoke like that. She was a contrary girl. It was true that the Tzar had seemed most enchanted by her when they met—but what man would not have been, since she had two thick looped plaits of hair the color of beaten flax, and large eyes of cool gray, and her lips were as ripe as the cherries in her father's orchard. As for the Tzar himself, he was hale enough and handsome enough, his thick beard still untouched by white, but she hadn't warmed to him in the brief moments she'd been in his presence. Ungrateful as only youth can be, it was not enough for her that this was the Tzar of all the Russias courting her. She had balked at his commanding air and stern manner and wished that he was a gentler, humbler man, to put her at her ease. Nor had it escaped her notice that he had had four wives before her, and that every one of those women had ended badly.

One day she wandered, aimless, from out of her father's house and across the grounds of the estate. It was spring and the young leaves were pale speckles on the birch-twigs. Zorya smiled to see the goose-girl driving her flock out to graze among the last stubble of winter, and the new calves lifting their oozing milky muzzles from the cows' udders. She walked down toward the river, tossing the golden ball idly from hand to hand, but she held it tight as she crossed the plank over the millrace. Then she wound her way among the coppice stools edging the millpond, stooping to look for frog-spawn among the bright new spears of the rushes. The bank was a little steep, but she kept her balance with one hand holding the willow branches.

Willow is a treacherous tree. A narrow stem snapped under her hand and, slipping suddenly, she had to snatch at another trunk to stop herself going down the bank. The golden ball dropped from her fingers and rolled down the slope, bounding into the millpond with a hollow splash.

For a moment Zorya could not believe what had happened. She slithered down to the water's edge and stared, trying to glimpse a gleam of gold beneath the dark surface. But in a moment even the betraying ripples vanished, and there was nothing to show where the Tzar's gift had gone. The pond lay like polished malachite, and the willow saplings only sighed.

"No," said Zorya to herself, pressing her knuckles to her lips. The second "No" built in her belly then came out as a long moan of pain. She hunched down, unheeding of the wet on her skirts, and dappled her hands in the water; it felt cold as ice and there was nothing but soft mud beneath her questing fingers.

Foolish girl. She didn't think to call on the saints to help her; she only folded her frozen hands to her bosom, sullying her bodice with mud, and burst into tears, rocking back and forth as she knelt.

"Why are you crying?" said a voice.

Zorya looked up and through her tears saw a man standing before her in the pond. She could only see him from the waist up, and what she could see was naked. Her heart clenched within her and crammed into her throat, but she was too frightened to scream. She felt the last tears roll down her cheeks.

"Well?" said he.

"I lost my golden ball in the water," she whispered. Her fingers twitched but she couldn't cross herself, despite being in no doubt as to whom she was speaking. This was a Vodyanoi: a water spirit. She'd heard that they could appear in human form, though more often they looked like sunken logs or moss-draped toads of monstrous size. This one wore the guise of a young man, and his long wet hair hung about his face and shoulders like drips of tar. His lithe body was pale, almost greenish in hue, each muscle visible under the wet shine on his hairless skin. He was very handsome. She wasn't fooled: the Vodyanoi are evil, and delight in drowning the unwary.

"Aren't you a little old to weep over lost toys?" he asked, his thin lips crooked in a smile.

"It's not a toy." She wondered if she could jump to her feet and dash away among the willows, but she was fairly certain he would catch her with a single lunge.

"What, then?"

"It was a betrothal gift from Ivan Vasilyevich, Tzar of all the Russias." It was the symbol of her faithfulness to him, and his public trust in her; to fail to treasure it would be counted an unforgivable insult. "He will have me buried alive for betraying him."

"Then I'll fetch the ball back for you." His black brows were wickedly arched, as proud as Satan's, and his smile was dagger-edged. "For a price, of course."

"What price?" The breath seemed to have deserted her

lungs.

His smile broadened. "An hour in your arms."

Zorya drew herself up, straightening her back. Acid found its way into her voice at last: "Then I might as well leave the ball where it is. If I'm not a virgin on my wedding night, the Tzar will kill me anyway."

The Vodyanoi seemed to find her ire engaging. "In that case, I will take my fee only after your nuptials," he suggested.

And Zorya was stuck then. If she didn't agree to his proposal she knew she would surely die, but if she did agree then he would likely betray her. At the very best it would be an act of treason and adultery which might buy her only a day or so's life. She wrung her hands and searched his face for some sign of goodwill, but found no comfort in his sardonic expression.

"Very well," she said at last—because even one more day seemed infinitely precious.

The Vodyanoi bowed his head and slid beneath the water's surface, his disappearance leaving a single slow ripple. Zorya took the chance to retreat up the bank a pace or two and crouch among the willow stems, wrapping one arm about the stoutest. The trees could not shield her, but she meant to cling on with all her strength if he tried to drag her into the pond upon his return.

He didn't take long. First the green water bulged, and then it broke around the peaks of his dark head and his pale shoulders. He lifted his face from the pool and smiled, showing her his outstretched hands cupped about the golden orb. Then he waded out of the pool, each step revealing more of his body. She feared at first that he would be naked, but there seemed to be something heavy wrapped about his lower half. As he mounted the bank, streaming water, she saw that it was a leathern sheet, secured by a knot of thong and all slick with water and algae, hanging low from his hips and so long that it brushed the tops of his feet. With every step his left leg flashed pale through the gap in the wrapped hide. He ascended the bank and then knelt down so that his face was on a level with hers.

"What's your name, Daughter of Eve?"

His eyes were gold, she realized—not the pure gold of her gilded ball but dark and flecked like those of a frog, and quite beautiful. Somehow thrown into confusion by this—was she not a foolish girl as well as a willful one?—she answered "Zorya," without thinking to lie. If she'd spoken a good saint's name perhaps, even then, it might have protected her; but as it was she was quite helpless. She didn't even recoil when he reached out a finger and drew it down the line of her throat, leaving a line of chill damp that made her shiver, before tracing a spiral upon the top of her breastbone just above the lip of her bodice. She couldn't wrench herself away, only drop her eyes before his impertinent gaze.

"You're quite comely."

"So they say," she answered through her teeth. A cold bead of water found its way from his fingertip into the cleft of her breasts, where it trickled down the slope of her warm flesh like a secret caress.

"And beloved of the Tzar. Such good fortune."

She clenched her jaw.

"Are you thankful?"

"Beyond words," she said in strangled voice.

The Vodyanoi smiled. "Here you are, Zorya," he murmured, pressing the ball into her free hand. Then he leaned forward and brushed his lips to hers, speculatively. His mouth was cold on her warm one, and her face grew even warmer as she flushed with shame. He chuckled at that. "Soon, my love."

Not, she thought, if she could help it. After all, her marriage would take place in Moscow, far away from this little millpond. How would a Vodyanoi find her at that distance? She would be safe from him, surely?

And yet despite her cold calculation she burned and squirmed inside.

Then he rose and left her, walking back down into the pool, his leather kilt dragging behind him, and she watched him go through the bars of her lashes: his narrow hips, his broader shoulders, his bare and muscular back, the slick of his hair as black and smooth as silt deposited after a flood. Those things burned themselves onto her mind's eye.

Then she took herself and her ball off back to the safety of her father's house. She dried and polished the Tzar's gift, and was relieved to find that it had taken no dint from being dropped. Only, now there was a smudge upon it that would not clean off: a tiny patch no bigger than a thumbprint, and luckily no more noticeable. She wrapped the ball in a silken cloth and did not let it slip from her grasp again.

❖ ❖ ❖

Shortly thereafter the Tzar returned and they married in the great cathedral in Moscow, and Zorya became the Tzarina. She lived in a great palace, far from the river, and she made sure never to approach any lake or pond. But as the pitiless heat of summer reached its height the Tzar decided to spend his days hunting in the deep shade of the forest, and he moved his court to the Royal Dacha there. Since he was well pleased with his new wife, he took her with him among his entourage.

The Summer Palace was built of wood from the foundations upward, through its beamed halls to its many-gabled roof and its carved shingles, so it was dark without and darker within. It stood upon a great rock in a forest clearing, and around the rock flowed a loop of a river—not the same river that ran through her father's lands to be sure, but Zorya's heart crashed within her breast when first she saw it. A window in the royal bedchamber opened out over a sheer drop down the rock-face to the river below. It ran fast and wild, and its music filled her dreams every night and disturbed her rest, leaving her anxious and fretful.

The golden ball was placed upon a shelf at the head of their walled bed.

The Tzar split his time between organizing the affairs of state and riding out to pursue wolves and boar in the endless tracts of forest, and Zorya was often left to her own devices during the day. She was never alone though, because when the Tzar was not about he set an old woman called Olga, who had once been his wet-nurse, to attend upon her. She was never left alone—not for a moment, not even to use the close-stool. It would not have been seemly.

Zorya, who did not dare set foot outside for fear of the river, would sit for hours at the window of her bedroom, looking out across the trees and down into the rushing sweeps of water. One day she let a tear fall. She could not tell if it struck the river below, but she saw the water suddenly seethe with foam.

"Vodyanoi," she whispered.

"What's that?" asked Olga, whose ears and eyes were still sharp, looking up from her sewing. "Did you say something?"

"Nothing," said Zorya, blinking back her other tears and swallowing hard.

As that afternoon drew on, the sky grew black with clouds and it began to rain. The gutters overflowed, and water ran from every eave, and the trees sagged under the weight of their sodden branches. Zorya, who was sitting with Olga in the great hall by that time, wondered when her husband would return. She ordered candles to be lit even though it was hours to sunset, but they didn't seem to dispel the gloom. It was as if they were living underwater, she thought: the air seemed thick and green.

"Ugh," said Olga suddenly. "There's water coming in under the door!"

There was; it was creeping across the floorboards. Zorya stood quickly, lifting her skirts. "Let's go upstairs!"

"Do you think the river has burst its banks?" Olga asked, hastily gathering up the embroidery frames.

Zorya shook her head; she didn't like that thought at all. They retired up the stairs to the royal antechamber. Up here, the rushing of the river sounded louder than ever. And in among it came a rhythmic noise, muffled but steady. Zorya's eyes widened as she first recognized it.

"What's that sound?" said Olga, cocking her head.

"It must be water dripping on a hollow beam," said the Tzarina rather desperately.

"It sounds like—"

"The drip of a leak in the roof, I'm certain—"

"—Footfalls." Olga frowned. "Perhaps the Tzar, God bless him, is home."

But the Tzar's feet had never made that noise on the stairs: that deep hollow knock, as if of a giant walking miles away, far beneath the earth. Zorya felt the wooden bench beneath her fingers tremble with each blow. Her heart seemed to be trying to climb out of her throat.

"What is it?" Olga got abruptly to her feet and advanced on the door to the stairwell. "Is there someone on the stairs?"

Zorya followed at her shoulder, though her legs felt like they were too weak to walk properly; she had the strongest desire to seize the lady-in-waiting and throw her away from the door.

"Who is it?" Olga called querulously as she pulled upon the latch. The door swung wide to reveal the wooden steps they had just climbed, descending into gloom—and below them on the stairs *something moved*.

For a second Zorya thought it was a snake, black and gleaming, that mounted the stairs; then she saw that it was water. A rivulet of water, that fell up from step to step as if it were finding its way downhill—and yet, impossibly, it was climbing.

Hollow footfalls echoed in their ears.

Olga fell back. "Witchcraft," she stammered: "it must be witches! We must … Guards …" Then she opened her mouth and filled her lungs to shout, and at that moment Zorya grabbed her braided hair and wrenched her head back, fumbling a hand over her mouth.

"Don't! Be quiet!"

Olga uttered a muffled squeal and for a moment the two women struggled. Then Zorya saw from the corner of her eye that the water was spilling into their room, forming a puddle on the red-dyed hides that lined the floor: it looked like a pool of blood. She froze, clamping the old woman in her arms, staring.

Step by step out of the puddle, as if he were climbing from his millpond, the Vodyanoi rose. His narrow eyes glittered. Without a word he advanced upon the women, and Zorya released Olga from her numb hands. For a second the old woman stared, her mouth and eyes round with disbelief. Then he put his hand on her face, casually, and she fell to the floor with water bubbling out from her nose and lips, and flopped about like a fish until the spill of water was joined by a white froth. But the Vodyanoi, most cold-hearted of spirits, didn't spare her another glance. All his attention was fixed on Zorya. She herself had no time to worry about Olga; she was too busy retreating before him.

Step by step she fell back into the furthest room, the royal bedchamber. Even there he did not cease his slow pursuit, until he had her backed up against the wall of the great boxed-in bed with its carved relief of Adam and Eve. He put his hands flat on the wood either side of her to pen her in: one hand on the Apple, one on the Serpent. His smile was full of ancient wickedness.

Then Zorya lifted her own hands and slid them about his bare neck, and lifted her lips to his cold mouth and kissed him, full and warm and breathless.

She didn't do it out of fear, you understand—although she most certainly was afraid. She did it out of nights dreaming of him and days remembering, out of the discontent of her greedy heart and her empty sex. She was under the spell of her own desire. The mortal flesh of womankind is ever subject to these fierce and foolish enchantments, and always they pave the way to trouble. But it took the Vodyanoi by surprise: he startled at her touch and hesitated a long moment, before pressing home to take full advantage of the kiss. His mouth, she discovered, was no warmer within, though his tongue was sweet.

When they broke the kiss she could see the question in his eyes and she lowered her own, unable to answer him. He was dressed just as she remembered from the first time, his torso bare and his flat nipples faintly blue. She took a deep breath and ran her hands down the cool hard planes of his chest, down to his waist and hips. It was her turn to be surprised: he winced at her touch and black bruises blossomed under his skin, like the dark soft fans of fungus that grow upon the branches of elder trees.

"Are you hurt?" she whispered.

He laughed, a little uncomfortably. "I had to fight the Vodyanoi of this river to come upstream and find you." He plucked off the kerchief that covered her bosom and looked down with approval at the twin swells of her breasts, pent behind the bodice of her dress. "He was a territorial old toad and he did not want me sharing his river."

"I'm sorry," said she faintly.

He put his hand on her head and pulled away the sheer white veil that covered her hair. "Well, you owe me now."

"For what?"

"For my pain." His hand brushed the stiff head-dress from off her scalp; the strings of pearls that had hung from it and framed her face fell suddenly apart. Pearls pattered and bounced upon the floor like hailstones. "It will cost you."

"You said you only wanted an hour …"

"My mercy is limited, as I'm sure you understand."

Zorya shivered, as he drew his finger down the tiny buttons that closed the front of her thickly embroidered robe. The loops broke and the dress split open, revealing the low-cut lawn shift beneath. "What will you do?"

"Guess."

"Will you drown me?"

His smile was cruel. "What do you think?" He took the front of her shift in both hands and it rotted at his touch like cloth that had been immersed in a pond for years, falling apart to gray shreds and then to nothing. The great weight of her robe fell from her as the warp and weft disintegrated; Zorya took a sharp breath and could not help looking down. Only the golden threads embroidered into the fabric were left, quite uncorroded; a fragile net that lay now against her goose-fleshed skin. The Vodyanoi chuckled. Then he stooped to kiss her throat, and his long wet hair hung upon the orbs of her breasts and clung to her puckering nipples, dragging at her when he raised his head. Zorya stifled a gasp.

"Please … What good will I be to you dead?" she asked.

"Oh, I think you will look very fair, down among the pebbles and the rippling half-light." His tongue lapped at her ear, his voice low and husky as his fingers explored her exposed breasts, playing amid the softness with the tightening halos of her pinkly-pale nipples. "Your hair will wave with the long weed, and minnows will chase around your pretty bones, and your soul will shine in the palace of my green dreams."

Zorya was unable to stop herself arching her spine, lifting herself to his hands.

"Just think how peaceful it will be," he murmured. "And how beautiful."

"But," she said, reaching down to the gap in his skirt and sliding her hand beneath the slimy leather, "while I'm alive, I can do *this*." She found his member. Substantial in girth and length, it was already all but erect, only the weight of his garment keeping it from standing—and though it was cold when she first grasped it, beneath the skin a warmth burned. She ran her fingers up its rippled length, and it jerked in response.

"Ah," said he.

Zorya raised her gaze to look him in the face. She read appetite there and a kind of twisted grudging fascination, and wondered if he could read the emotion in her own face. Wordlessly she sank to her knees and kissed his pale skin, the bruised flesh of his torso. She pulled at the wet thonging that held up his strange garment and it slopped to the floor in heavy folds.

He was not formed as a human man. Did I not tell you

that a Vodyanoi takes human shape only to trick the foolish? And we are made in the image of God, which such evil spirits may not mimic with perfect accuracy. His male member was not blunt and crowned like a man's: it came instead to a point, like the prow of a boat. Zorya saw this but did not recoil, though her heart hammered under her breastbone in trepidation.

What she did then not even the whores of Kiev will do. Such a thing is reserved for a husband alone, for the intimacy of the marriage bond. She took his pale bestial length, already oozing at the slitted tip with eager moisture, into her hot mouth. The Vodyanoi groaned at that just like a real man. She used tongue and lips to explore his girth and his strange contours and then worked him deep into her throat, sucking warmth into that chill staff. It gave her satisfaction in unexpected places to suck him like this, and she felt her own sex flutter as her fingertips weighed the heavy pouch of his stones, finding water still dripping from the black ringlets of hair at his groin.

Shifting his weight forward, he leaned into her. His legs were tense, almost as hard as the iron of his pike. His hips jerked as her head rose and fell in supplication, and he pressed his cock so far to the back of her throat that she gagged and tears welled in her eyes.

I could choke here, she thought, snatching her breath in the backstroke. It wasn't a new idea though—her husband had similarly used her. The Tzar was an older man and would sometimes take so long that she'd weep for the ache in her jaw—but that wasn't to be the case this time. She felt the Vodyanoi's rhythm grow fiercer, then become a stutter, and suddenly her mouth was awash with his slippery flood. Instantly—so copious was the flow—her fear of choking became a fear of drowning, and she jerked her head back with a gasp. His cock shuddered upon her tongue as the liquid, as cold and clear as mill water, overflowed her mouth and ran down over her chin.

He tasted of nothing at all: just like water.

The Vodyanoi withdrew from her open lips, glaring at her. Swallowing hard and struggling to get her breath back, Zorya nevertheless felt a strange bereavement now it was over, and a dread as to what would come next. Would he grow contemptuously indifferent now—or irritable—as her husband often did?

But her paramour was a Vodyanoi, and unlike a mortal man a single spasm of sin was not enough to sate him. Even as he stood back, his spend still drizzled down the underside of his rigid shaft, as if his balls were too full and now boiling over. He tilted his head, clearly weighing the options, as his gaze raked her kneeling body. "You have certain uses, alive," he admitted.

Then stooping, he lifted her, his muscles moving like waves under his skin. He turned her from him and thrust her toward the side of the royal bed—a piece of furniture so high that there was a padded bench to facilitate climbing into it. Zorya was pushed down to kneel upon that bench, her elbows on the bed itself. Then the Vodyanoi crouched behind her, lifted up the golden net that was her only garment, and spread her rump cheeks with his hands to reveal her most private parts.

Such shame! What man would do that to a woman? What man would thrust his face into that cleft and lick her, his tongue slithering over her pearl and into her well and then up between the orbs of her bottom to lap at the tight pucker between? It was as if the water spirit were trying to devour her earthiness. Zorya buried her face in the coverlet of the bed, rubbing her cheek upon the silver fox-fur as the Vodyanoi's tongue—longer and stronger than any human man's—danced and probed in her most private places, forcing entry into those treasure chambers that only her husband ought to access, and making her cry out.

Let us be charitable and say that it was shame that caused her to whimper and gasp and call upon God as the Vodyanoi's tongue slid in and out of her—for no woman is entirely devoid of shame, not even a headstrong wanton such as she. Let us assume that it was an attempt to dull the pain that caused her to thrust her fingers down between the smooth fur of the coverlet and her own rougher fur, as he rose up behind her and breached the portal of her sex with his ram. His hand was heavy between her shoulder blades, pinning her to the bed. His hard thighs slapped against the backs of hers and his scrotum bounced on the cushioning lips of her sex, so deep did he delve with each thrust. Zorya heaved her hips against his invasion, but if she regretted her witch's bargain it was too late now. He rutted inside her just as he had done in her mouth: swift and ruthless, taking his pleasure without regard for her delicacy of feeling. There was a minor difference, in that this time her throat was not stuffed with his meat and he could clearly hear her moans rising in pitch as he stretched her wide. But the result was the same: a great and sudden outpouring, flooding her to such an extent that when he pulled out it ran from her furrow and splashed upon the padded stool. Yet still his prick stood erect, quivering with eagerness, and he had one further use for it. Smearing his own issue up into her split with brazen-bold fingers, he redirected that slick and narrow tip to the juicy clench of her anus and pressed home his advantage, forging deep into forbidden territory.

Zorya felt every inch. His inhuman member was as slippery and muscular as an eel and it surged inside her as if swimming upstream. Under his touch she was becoming a river: everything fluid, everything falling. She could hear the rain drumming on the wooden shingles overhead and it was like it was falling into her soul. Her body gave up all resistance and yielded, unable to withstand the waves of sensation rippling up her spine and out along every limb to the tips of her spread fingers. She pawed the pelisse beneath her and sobbed into it, her heat soaking the fur. The Vodyanoi was laboring too, nothing like so swift or so casual this time—instead he bent low, his hair brushing her shoulders, and drew long and ragged breaths as he twisted into her. She saw his splayed hand braced on the coverlet, and the webbed skin at the base of his fingers. She felt his cold sweat splash upon her like the raindrops falling outside, and she felt the ripples radiate through her skin.

Then the river within her turned to gold as if the sun had come out from behind a cloud, and everything was transformed in the glory of it, and she felt him shoot through her like a fish, flashing silver.

It seemed a long time before she was Zorya again, flesh and bone, and the Vodyanoi's flesh was heavy on her, his arms sagging, his body no longer taut with passion but loose-limbed and clumsy. Slowly he lowered himself to rest upon her and for a moment they lay in silence, as still as a millpond under the dappled shadows of summer. She felt no desire to move, now or ever again. Then his lips brushed the skin between her shoulders and she felt him sigh.

He slipped from her without a word. Zorya turned her head. She was awash. "Don't go," she whispered.

The Vodyanoi paused in the act of picking up his leathern kilt. In his jeweled toad eyes there was no malice anymore, only a troubled wondering. But he did not reply. Fastening his garment about his hips he moved to the window, and as she raised herself from the bed to watch, he stepped through it into the void beyond, still looking back at her, still frowning as he dissolved into the rain.

◆ ◆ ◆

The Tzarina recovered her composure in good time before her husband returned that night. He was soaked to the bone and in a black temper suited to the overcast sky. She'd had time to wash and dress, to summon servants to take the body of poor faithful Olga—who, she pointed out, had suffered some kind of fit, as witnessed by the white foam plastered about her lips—and lay her out in the chapel for the priest to pray over. Zorya was ready with her hair combed out loose the way her husband liked it and a roaring fire and a flagon of mulled wine, when the Tzar marched in throwing his muddy coat and hat to the floor, grim with vexation. He dismissed the servants and downed the first goblet of wine, stripping off his clothes one-handed while Zorya hurried to fetch a fresh dry robe from the press.

When she turned she found him half-naked, staring into the dark recesses of their boxed bed.

"What's this?" said he.

"What's what, husband?" she asked uneasily.

Without a word the Tzar reached in to the top of the bed, and brought out her golden ball from its shelf, its pride of place, brandishing it in front of her. Only now it wasn't golden; the gilt had flaked off some base metal blotched with corrosion, and its metallic sheen was as eaten up as if it had soaked for years at the bottom of a pond.

"What," he said, in a low and horrible voice, "have you done, wife?"

"I—" she said, and then stopped, because there was no defense in the face of this inhuman witness, no lie big enough to mask her guilt. She went as white as the belly of a fish, her eyes huge. She felt quite sick.

"Who have you had in here?" he asked, then suddenly roared: "WHO?"

Zorya fell back, her hands clasped at her throat.

"Whore!" he bellowed, and turning to the fireplace he picked up an iron poker. Zorya hesitated only a moment: only long enough to see the look in his eyes as he hefted the implement. She turned and ran for the window: she had a foot on the sill before he could reach out to seize her: she was falling before his hand caught vainly in her long hair and snatched a few ash-blonde strands.

The full moon was reflected in the water below, as it broke through the clouds.

"Vodyanoi!" she cried as the river rushed up to meet her.

◆ ◆ ◆

That was the end of Tzarina Zorya. Her body, when they finally found it, was buried at an unconsecrated crossroads in the forest, and the Gates of Heaven were closed in her face. The Tzar remarried within the month. Let it be a lesson to you: wives must remain faithful, no matter what the temptation.

Like all girls who drown themselves, Zorya became a Rusalka. She haunts the river bend beneath the Summer Palace still, her pale form dripping with water. On summer nights she can often be seen cavorting in the pools with the Vodyanoi, their two slippery bodies entwined, but it's bad luck to watch them and the Royal Dacha is inhabited no more; its timbers are already rotting back into the forest from which it was hewn. Still, to this day, their laughter echoes among the trees. Remember her fate and learn from it: denied the sublime joys of Heaven she must spend eternity trapped in the grip of lust and sin, until the woods are hewn down and the rivers run dry and the world is turned to ashes.

B o l t   H o l e

She sees the deer as she comes out from under the supermarket portico. It's standing motionless between the carcasses of two cars and, as she moves into the open, it lifts its head and starts toward her.

The deer is surrounded by a cloud of flies, buzzing about the red mask of its skull. It has no eyes left, just empty sockets, but that doesn't seem to make any difference. They don't really *see* anyway—it's heat they detect, not shape or motion. Heat, and—more dimly—noise, and carbon dioxide. The exhaled breath of terror and exhaustion.

Looks like it's been hit by a truck, she thinks. *Wonder if anyone around here's still got fuel?*

She keeps an eye on the deer, but makes sure not to pay it too much attention at the price of the rest of her surroundings. One of its legs is smashed and dragging like a broken toy, and it isn't so fast that she has to worry. In life, the deer would be the epitome of grace in motion. Now, dead, it stumbles and lurches.

They aren't fast, any of them. Just persistent.

She moves lightly through the scattering of vehicles in the car park, knowing each one offers potential cover to an attacker. Dogs are what really scare her. Far more dangerous than human ACs—faster, and with teeth sharp enough to puncture her leathers. Checking a VW Golf for lurkers first, she hops up onto the hood. She likes to be up high for what's coming next. The spade she's got strapped to her back is heavy—that's the whole point of using it. She snaps the studs of the strapping and hefts it in both hands as the deer staggers up, its neck out-thrust grotesquely and its stained teeth snapping toward her shins.

Fallow deer, she thinks with the part of her brain that still belongs to the old days. *Dama dama. A hind.* Then she plunges the full weight of the spade down on the back of the animal's neck, and the sharpened blade shears through its spinal column. The deer drops like a stone.

"AC. Ay-Cee. NayCee," she says. Her voice sounds rusty. It's been two weeks since she had anyone to talk to but herself. She likes the sound of the words, though, and repeats them to herself, several times, in a singsong manner, before she breaks off in annoyance at herself.

AC was a grim biologists' joke, in the beginning. In lieu of other, more obvious nouns, they'd opted for the dry understatement of *Ambulatory Cadaver*. She can still remember the first time she walked into the abattoir, ready for another day inspecting and certifying the meat, and saw those carcasses squirming and twitching on their hooks. They only stopped when their heads were sawed off.

She's been vegetarian since that moment. It's mostly canned beans she took from the derelict supermarket.

It's nearly sunset now. She cleans off the blade but decides to keep the spade unholstered. The ACs are partially blinded by warm weather but grow active as the day cools. They are worst of all at night when the body-heat of their prey shows up in stark contrast to the ambient temperature. Lighting a fire or running an engine is the equivalent of sounding a dinner gong. She needs to get somewhere secure before the end of the day.

She's got a map in her pouch that claims there's a Safe House two roads over from this supermarket.

One road over, and she turns a corner and finds herself in trouble. There's a whole cluster of ACs standing around outside a gutted cafe. A few of them are chewing on each other in a desultory fashion—they seem to dimly realize that they're not getting what they want—but at the sound of her booted feet on the paving slabs they all swing round toward her.

Shit, she thinks, nervously, and breaks into a trot to scurry past them. A trot is all it takes to keep ahead—AC muscles aren't terribly efficient—but it does mean she's moving too fast to be properly cautious. She rounds another corner into a major road intersection and sees the Safe House. One of the old-fashioned ones. There's no mistaking it: a shipping container that's been dumped on the roundabout, with the big white "S" painted on its side and the stenciled logo of the Emergency Administration. It's been there a long time. Too long, she can tell, because there are ACs scattered all across the open area, standing quietly, waiting.

It's not like they learn where to find food … but they don't always wander away afterwards.

She sees them turn their blind and unbearable faces, slowly, in her direction. She thinks of ants clinging to the tips of grass-stalks, waiting—with the inexorable patience of their lancet fluke puppetmasters—for the cow that will eat grass and ant and all.

The steel door of the container is ever-so-slightly ajar. She grimaces. There may be some of them inside. It may be a rat-trap. She has to decide now: head for that dubious shelter or spend the night in the open, on the move. She slows, conscious that the pack is coming up the street behind her. The insides of her gloves are damp. It's been two years now, and somehow the relentless ebb and flow of danger has dulled but not yet washed away her fear.

At the corner of her vision something else moves—something too swift to be dead. A human figure, black-clad, emerging from the mouth of a building. *Living*. There's a moment of almost comic hesitation as the ACs vacillate between her and the other, and that makes up her mind. She launches herself across the tarmac, heading for the shipping container. She's nimble enough to dodge around some of the figures in her way. One she fells, using her whole body to swing her spade at its neck like a scythe; the blade is filed sharp on the edges too, and chops through flesh and bone. It jars her arms but she doesn't let go of the weapon. She doesn't stop. She keeps moving, barging and hacking, until she reaches the door. An AC pulls at her arm, bending to mumble at her with stinking jaws, but its blunt teeth are no match for her motorcycle leathers and it staggers backward as she wrenches loose and then plants the spade-edge in its face.

They're weak. Weaker than her, one-on-one. Slower than her. Stupider than her. But they have the advantage of numbers. She can't afford to wait around. Vaguely she hears someone shouting, but she doesn't listen. She heaves the container door open another few inches, enough to allow her to squeeze inside.

It's empty.

Thank fuck.

Dropping her weapon, she whirls round and grabs at the inner handle. Now she can hear him—a male voice shouting, "Wait! Wait!" She doesn't. She wrenches on the handle, pulling the door closed, shutting herself inside. There's a bolt welded to the metal and a swivel-brace that drops into a bracket. She rams the bolt home.

Safe.

Something heavy slams against the metal.

"Let me in!" he roars. "For fuck's sake—open up! Open up!"

She can imagine him brought to bay just outside there. She didn't see what sort of weaponry he carried, in fact she didn't get a proper look at him at all. But she can picture the ACs clustering around him, hands reaching, mouths agape. No matter how he fights, there are enough of them to overwhelm him by bodyweight alone. They'll bring him to the floor and pin him there. They'll find the gaps in his armor. They'll chew at any exposed skin, at eyeballs and lips.

"Come *on*, you bitch—help me!" The sounds of combat are more muffled than his cries, but they're there. Thuds and groans. She knows that eventually, inevitably, he'll start screaming.

She can't face listening to that. Not again.

She retrieves her spade. Her hand moves to the bolt and it rasps in its sleeve. She's already damning herself for her weakness as the crack of daylight breaks open and dark bodies occlude it. She can hear the bubbling moan of the ACs, and knows there must be dozens out there now, scores maybe.

He bundles in through the gap, whirls and hauls at the door. He's big, and heavy. A reaching AC arm gets caught in the gap but the metal edges crush the wrist flat as cardboard and the fingers are left spasming.

"Aaah!" he gasps, sliding the bolt home, setting the horizontal beam into place. "That was fucking close!"

She lets the spade-edge drop to rest on the back of his neck. "Just hold on," she says. "Kneel down."

He goes still. He can feel the metal, hard and heavy, pressing at the base of his skull. "Okay," he growls. "Whatever you say." The ACs are banging on the door now, but that's suddenly just background noise. The danger is in here. He goes to one knee, then both.

That's better. The spade is too heavy for her to hold up for long.

"Get rid of that weapon," she orders.

He lets it fall onto the metal floor of the container—it's a home-made pike of some sort, maybe more properly a naginata: four foot of shaft topped by a two-foot blade. The clang is horrible. Then he shoves it away, out of immediate reach. She wishes she could kick it right to the back of the chamber but she daren't ease the blade from his neck. She's looking at his crouched, black-clad form. His backpack makes him look hunched and inhuman.

"Right." Her voice is croaky. She rarely dares talk, even to herself. "Take your hood off."

Like her, he's wearing a tight leather balaclava that covers most of his head, with a zip behind the ear. Two years ago it would have been a pervy gimp-mask. These days, when even a small scalp wound can be a death-sentence, it's just armor. But he doesn't protest as he unzips and pulls the mask off. Underneath, his head is shaved down to all but bald, with just a stubbly ghost of his hairline. There's little light in their prison—two rows of airholes drilled around the top of the walls, that's all—but she can see his skin is shiny with sweat. She suddenly aware of how hot and itchy her own head is, and how much she wants to take her own hood off.

"Okay?" he asks. The metal walls rumble to the fumbling of dozens of hands on the outside.

"And the rest," she tells him. "Show me your skin's not broken."

"On a first date, darling?"

"Shut up and do it."

"Dominant type, huh? I like that." Carefully, he pulls off his gloves, shucks the backpack and unzips his padded motorbike jacket. Just like with her own clothes, there's a shiny silver lining on the inside of his leathers that keeps body-heat trapped, making him more difficult for the ACs to spot. The once-white shirt beneath follows the jacket to the floor. She sees the broad reach of his shoulders, and the hard, ridged muscle, and the scars. But they're old scars. If they've had time to go white then he wasn't infected. She gives him an inch of grace with the spade blade, because she hasn't cleaned it yet and neither of them wants that congealed blood on his skin, but she keeps it leveled at the back of his neck.

"Now turn."

He rotates, still crouched, and looks up at her. In her red-and-black one-piece, she must be nothing to him but a shape in the gloom, but she's got the spade braced, one elbow bent and the other hand stretched out on the shaft. One thrust and she'll have him. From that filthy blade, even a scratch would be enough.

His eyes, locked on hers, are deep-set in dark hollows, and his skin rough and grimy. He looks dangerous and desperate—but then, everyone left alive nowadays looks like that. His bare chest is bruised under a plastering of hair, but she can't see any blood.

"Interesting choice of weapon," he observes.

She doesn't answer. Sometime, long ago, she'd read that a sharpened spade was a favorite in the street-to-street battle for Stalingrad: silent and fool-proof. That was what had first prompted her to pick one from the trashed debris of a hardware shop.

"Want me to keep going?" he asks, popping the studs of his trousers with the exaggerated motions of a stripper. She's shocked to realize he's being sardonic. He mustn't see her as that much of a threat. She's suddenly aware of two things, above and beyond the bumps and bangs and groans of the besieging mob outside, and the creep of sweat down her scalp. She's aware that she's just locked herself in a metal box for the night with a strange man and no way out. And she can feel her arms starting to tremble from the strain.

I should kill him now. If it comes to a fight, that's my only chance of winning.

"I don't mind," he adds, with a lopsided grin, easing the waistband of his trousers. "It's like a fucking oven in here."

He's not wrong. The sun has been on the metal all day, and there's hardly any ventilation. The damn place must glow like a beacon to AC senses, but that's not's what bothering her. She's run and she's fought, wearing a suit designed to stop heat escaping. It's roasting hot, and the insides of her gloves and mask are sodden, and she can feel the sweat running between her breasts and crawling down the small of her back. She feels like she can hardly breathe. Suddenly, it's unbearable—the heat, the strain, the fear. The weight of his life in her hands. All of it. She wants to scream.

She's had enough fighting. Him … them … the world.

Without a word, she backs off, seven paces taking her to the far end of the container, where she puts her shoulders to the wall. The metal booms faintly. She rests the spade, upright, in front of her, glad to spare her tired arms. Her eyes must have grown more used to the gloom now, because she can still see his expression, and she watches the grin drop off his face to leave it horribly grim. Then he reaches into his discarded jacket and pulls something out.

The snickering levity was a front, she realizes dimly. A mask, like his leather hood. He's come within a hairsbreadth of death and he's as freaked out as her. And he's got something metallic in his hands.

Shit, she says to herself.

Silently, he lifts the object to his face and tilts it. It's a canteen.

"Water?" he asks, smacking his lips, then holds the bottle out toward her.

She would do anything for water—not to drink, but to pour over herself. Clean, cool, running water. She's cooking inside her insulated armor, like one of those old fish-in-a-bag dinners. But she doesn't answer him. Words seem too heavy to raise to her lips.

After a moment, he stoppers his bottle and scoots it right down the length of the chamber, almost to her toes. "What's your name?"

Still she doesn't answer. Maybe she should be trying to establish some sort of connection with this man, if only to mollify him, but the threat he poses is nothing compared to the discomfort she's already in. Panic is rising in her breast, like steam, as she tries to breathe deeper but finds she can only pant. There doesn't seem to be any oxygen in the metallic air. The room in front of her swells and billows and shrinks again. She catches her glove in her teeth and rips it off, then fumbles at the zip of her headgear. *I'm going to faint*, she thinks. *If I don't get this off I'll suffocate.*

The mask comes off with a foul wet dragging. She shaved her own head, weeks ago, but the hair has grown back somewhat. She can feel the air licking at that wet fur—an overwhelming relief. But still not enough. She tugs the zip that bares her throat then, bending, she snatches up the canteen from the floor. That motion almost undoes her. She can feel the blood running the wrong way in her veins, and she almost loses her balance. It's only her desire for the water that keeps her from pitching forward dizzily

Yanking the stopper out with her teeth, she tips the liquid over her forehead and catches it with open lips as it sluices over her face. It's tepid and metallic and it feels *wonderful*. Running down her chin and throat, some finds its way under her clothes into the secret valley between her breasts. Blinking stinging, sweat-tainted drops from her eyes, she glares at the man, daring him to have moved while she wasn't looking.

Maybe he has, just a little. She sucks defiantly from the neck of the bottle.

"What're you doing out here on your own?" he asks.

"I wasn't alone," she rasps.

"Huh." He grimaces. "Nor was I."

The water down her cleavage just feels like more sweat now. She can't bear it. She's got to lean back against the metal just to stay upright. Discarding the spade against the wall beside her, she wrenches off her other glove, then pulls down the zipper of her suit from collar to navel. The vest-top beneath is absolutely sodden with sweat, and plastered to her torso. She sees the pale flash of the man's widening eyes, and she knows her chest is heaving as she pants for breath, but it doesn't seem important. All she wants is to get out of these leathers.

She wriggles out of her bags and belts, frantic to shed the weight, and has to force herself not to fling down her most precious cargo. The front zipper of her biker all-in-one goes all the way down to her crotch, making it easier to peel off the arms and shoulders and drop the top half of the suit to hang from her hips. That helps. She sets her shoulders back against the corrugated metal, praying for cool, but it's warmer than she is. She can see the man staring. His torso is completely bare, and she envies that. She can feel the moisture flooding between her burning thighs. Her mind is a churning whirl. She wants to be naked. She wants to be cold. She wants water and a breeze.

He's gone very still. Outside, the living dead moan with frustration.

The trousers of her suit have zips up the outside of the shins, allowing them to be put on and taken off over boots. One leg at a time, she lifts her feet and looses the vents. Then she pushes the leathers down over her thighs and kicks them away.

She's not wearing anything but panties beneath. Panties and boots, and above that the tight, clinging vest. Even those last pieces of clothing disgust her. She wants to weep with frustration. Her singlet is like a second skin, and stained with wear. She pulls it away from her stomach, desperate for the tiniest breeze on her flesh, stretching her throat as she tilts her head back.

When she glances down again, he's definitely moved. He's still on hands and knees, but he's that tiny bit closer to her. She tries to focus her eyes, and registers the lift of one hand: a placating gesture, an apology for his entirely involuntary shift in her direction. His eyes are wide and his lips a little parted.

"S'okay," he mutters, not blinking. "Don't be scared. Nothing to be scared of."

She wants to laugh, but she's forgotten how. For the last two years there has never once been nothing to be scared of. Periods of calm or stultifying boredom, yes—many of those. But never freedom from fear. Not a single waking hour when the dread and the loss weren't there like a choking lump under her breastbone. Fear is the omnipresent guest at the feast, the mother of every decision she makes. It's the air she breathes. In a world where corpses move and speak and eat, fear is the one thing left that distinguishes the living from the dead.

She looks into the deep darkness of his eyes, searching for the fear. And it's there, that sharp and bitter edge. But it's only a glint. It's been almost driven out by something else, just as primal. He can't stop looking at her. At her tight and filthy clothing. At what's hidden beneath. Each heave of her chest seems to draw him in.

"What's your name, darling?" he tries again, in a throaty whisper.

She blinks hard, like a drunk trying to sober up, wanting to make sense of his questions and his haggard soldier's face and his muscled body. He looks strong. Bleakly handsome, perhaps—it's so hard to tell these days. She wants to know how she feels about him, but she's no longer capable of judgment.

"Zita." It's not her name, not her original one, but she's taken to shedding her identity every time she loses her companions. It seems too arrogant, to go on unchanged when so many of those she's loved and lived with have been slaughtered. Something of her has to die with them. Ben died two weeks ago, and she gave up being Evie.

"Well … Zita." He's shifting toward her, on toes and fingertips. Keeping slow and down on the floor, so as not to spook her. "It's a bit warm, isn't it? This box." The inanity of his words is not as important as the low, husky tone. He's got a voice that reminds her of some movie star's, though she can't think whose—she can't remember anything that far back right now—but it's oddly familiar because of that, and not unpleasant. "That top of yours, it looks … It looks a bit hot."

He licks his parched lips.

She wants more water. She wants the aching to stop—the ache that that seems to lie not in her muscles but under every inch of her skin, in her belly, right down between her legs. All she wants … is to stop feeling awful.

"Yes." Looking into his eyes, she takes the sodden vest

and lifts it to bare her breasts.

Oh God, that feels good.

"Ah," he says. Just that one syllable, a low vibration his chest. But it's a noise that sounds like profound relief. And for a long moment he just looks. She can feel the tickle of sweat-droplets running down her breastbone. They're beading around her dark nipples and slipping in arcs down the overhang of her breasts. Her whole body weeps salt tears. Like him, she's bruised and scarred and underweight.

Like him, she's alive.

Still on his knees, he closes the gap between them. She flinches at the last moment, afraid that his skin will be hot to the touch and only add to her torment—but in fact his hands on her hips feel cool. That's all he touches her with. Fingertips, and mouth. He brushes his lips to her belly and his tongue sweeps the skin, tasting her salt.

She utters a keening sob. It is the noise of the end of the world. It's been two weeks since she last saw a living being. Two weeks without human contact, without the press of Ben's body against hers, without comfort or pleasure or release.

"Ohhh," he groans into her stomach. She can smell the scent of his sweat, mingling with her own.

Then he floods her senses as he begins to lap and suck at her, his mouth craving her skin just as her skin hungers for comfort. He licks her from navel to ribs, and up the damp valley between her breasts, and over their twin mounds, across those pillowy swells that seem like the legacy of a former age, when softness and nurture meant something. He pushes her back against the metal wall and sucks ravenously at her nipples, drawing them out to swollen points. That makes her sob, dryly. He fills his mouth with her and guzzles, the snorts of his breath frantic, while she runs her hands over his bristly scalp and whimpers encouragement.

Then he hooks his thumbs in her panties and pulls them down over her thighs. She squirms—she doesn't want him to go there, she isn't clean, she can smell her own musk—but he doesn't care if she's been weeks in her leathers. He stoops to plunge his face to the juncture of her thighs, inhaling her greedily, lifting one of her legs to grant him access to her split and pushing her up on tiptoes in his eagerness. Then, almost perversely procrastinating, he laps the inside of her upper thighs with long teasing strokes, first one then the other. It makes her whimper more. Finally his mouth, hot and wet, closes over her clit and she bangs her head back against the metal, seeing stars.

He eats her.

He's like an AC, she thinks, half-terrified by the analogy and grabbing for purchase on the corrugated wall, on his head, anywhere that will help. There's the same inexorable appetite, the same obsession. Hunger is everything, and he eats without fear. She can hear her own gasping cries and the rising moans of the dead massed outside, on the other side of the wall. He lifts her up on his hands and wraps her legs over his shoulders, burrowing into her sex. His tongue lashes her clit and slithers into her deep wet furrow. Each motion of his tongue burns across her nerves. *He's eating me. He's eating me*, she cries in her head. Suddenly the heat and the stuffy box and the stink and the discomfort—none of that matters.

She always knew she was going to die like this: being devoured.

And, being eaten, she finally forgets to be afraid. She comes, arching and shaking and gasping, twisting in his hands and on his face, thumping her skull back against the metal. The dead outside take up the clangor and hammer their bloodless hands against the container wall. She tries to wriggle out of his grasp but he won't let her. He's going for it again, sucking her in, gobbling her up, forcing her into a second orgasm and then a third, without a break, until only the slamming of her palms against the metal anchors her to the world at all, and she's away somewhere else entirely.

Only after her fourth climax is his hunger sated.

"Oh fuck oh fuck oh fuck," she sobs, nearly witless, as she comes down at last. He lets her slip from his gasp and collapse back against the wall, pressing his hands hard against the tops of her thighs, sucking her juices from his lips as his gaze rakes her crotch and belly and up across her breasts to her face. The throb of her afterwash fills her. Panting, she drags her hands across her stomach and up to her breasts, as if checking that he hasn't torn her to pieces in his greed. The metal thrums against her spine.

"Better?" he asks.

Wide-eyed, it dawns upon her that, for a moment, she hadn't been able to feel the terrible heat.

His mouth twists in a smile. Then he glances aside, searching for the canteen she's managed to drop somewhere in the whirl of her pleasure. He tilts it to his lips but it's empty, so he reaches for the flask strapped to her own discarded bandolier.

"No!" she gasps, coming out of her sexual maelstrom with sickening abruptness. "Not that!"

Something in her tone gets through to him. "What?" he grunts.

"That's not water!" She puts out her hand for it.

He frowns at the flask, holding it just out of her reach. It's shiny and hi-tech, nothing like the battered military canteen he'd offered her. "What then?"

"It's a bioculture!"

"What?" Momentarily, he's distracted from his lust. But he still doesn't hand it back. Even kneeling there before her, he's somehow not remotely submissive. Her fear begins to creep back in.

"I'm a vet. I used to work for DEFRA—specialized in agricultural parasitology. That there's a bioactive culture. It might even be the cure."

"The cure?"

"For that." She waves at the walls of their prison, at the monsters clanging and moaning beyond. "Flukes."

"You what?"

"Flatworms. We've known for years that parasites can mess with animal behavior. Wasp grubs. *Cordyceps* fungi. *Toxoplasma* makes rats seek out cats. Lancet flukes make ants climb grass stalks at night and get eaten. Gordian worms make their insect hosts commit suicide by drowning. They infect the brain. That's how the parasite completes its life-cycle. Same with them out there."

"Worms in the brain?"

"Yes. Tiny ones."

"No shit." He doesn't look impressed.

"And we've found an agent—an even smaller nematode— that kills the flukes. We just need to find a vector for distributing it through the ecosystem. It has to be spread everywhere. We were taking it to Porton Down. They'll be able to work out a way."

"Hh. He tilts his head, considering her in the half-light. "D'you know where Porton Down is?"

"Yes. Sort of." They don't exactly print the location of government biological warfare research centers on maps.

"It's inside the Pale. How're you planning to get through

that?"

She shakes her head. "I'll find a way."

"Hh." He tips his chin, as if signaling to himself. Then he puts the flask carefully back in her hand. "Don't break it, now."

For a moment she's nonplussed. She's naked except for her boots, pinned against a wall by a man who's just eaten her snatch. She can still feel the pulsing slipperiness between her thighs.

As if reading her mind, he lifts his hand and cups her sex, and without letting go he stands. Now he's on his feet, he looms over her. His hand is big and calloused and warm, and it holds her wet pussy so snugly, with such intent, that she can feel herself softening and opening to him, her hips tilting into the nest of his palm in instinctive surrender. She can feel her pulse beating against his thumb. He stoops closer to brush his lips to her ear.

"Have you got water?" he murmurs.

She nods.

He licks his lips and nips the lobe of her ear. "I need a drink."

Slipping from his grasp, she puts the flask aside and finds the plastic water-pouch in the tumble of her belongings. He moves with her, staying in physical contact, his hand glossing the small of her back, then the curve of her ass, as she stoops over. His touch is a reminder that he hasn't finished with her, that there is something between them that is yet to be completed. It makes her heart hammer. It makes her clumsy and stumble-footed as she turns back to him with the flat plastic bag and offers it up.

Though he's sucked and sucked for all he's worth, she's no less wet between her legs.

Without a word he takes the bag and slurps from the

nozzle, drinking deep, his spare hand light but deliberate on her hip, his eyes watching her. The pressure on the bottle makes the water gush out, some escaping his lips, and it runs down his chin and over his chest just as his own water had spilt upon her body. In the half-light she follows the flow with eyes and fingertips, down over his sternum, across the ridges of his stomach, through the harsh, gathering hair at the base of his abdomen. His leather trousers are open, of course. The water slips into the dark V of tanned hide.

There. *There's* his cock. Waiting within, barely held back by the leather. Thick; hard; slippery with sweat just like the rest of him. Not nice at all. A rough beast impatient for its hour to come round.

When she strokes that red-hot length, that's enough to distract him from drinking. It's enough to tip everything into action.

He shoves her up against the wall again. Discomfort and delirious need are suddenly one and the same. The slick and the smell are both terrible and intoxicating. His skin slides over hers, the heat unbearable. They're slippery everywhere they touch. He's shaking now, perhaps because of their dreadful circumstances, perhaps with the strain of holding back. With frightening ease he grips her thighs and lifts her clear of the floor, and as she wraps her forearms about his shoulders he shifts her onto his hips, angling his big hot cock up into the open split of her sex. He effects entry in moments, sliding straight into the tight gap he finds there, making space for his bulk with determined thrusts. She gasps; the sensation is shocking. It's always shocking, like someone knocking on the door of her psyche. He's impaling her and pressing the breath from her and enfolding her, all at the same time.

"Oh fuck!" he groans, his voice breaking. And that's the noise of the end of the world too.

He's rough. Oh God, he's rough. This isn't a world for gentleness or delicacy. He pins her against the wall and fucks her fast and rough and deep, his face pressed against hers, his breath harsh and teeth clenched. She can't help crying out—and that's a release too, in its way. She's been quiet for so long, stifling her voice even in the brief and furtive throes of sex, in dread of being heard by the ACs. Even in the various Safe Houses, with Ben and with others before him, she's kept all noise down, fearing the resentment of the living almost as much. The taking of any pleasure seems like an insult these days.

But this man doesn't just take pleasure. He forces it upon her too. She tries, but she can't fight it. Every thrust nails it into her, deeper and deeper, and with every thrust she cries out in shock. Until her voice is just one ragged howl, and the dead lift their voices to howl along with her—but she can't hear them or herself, she can't feel the heat or the horror, she can only buck and scream as orgasm takes her like a storm.

Slowly her eyes regain focus. They are one slippery tangle of quivering limbs. Fresh sweat dews his throat. His pupils are hugely dilated in the gloom.

"Yes," she groans. "More."

Those eyes narrow. He drops her, turns her, takes both her wrists and slaps her hands against the wall. She can feel the metal reverberate. His hands descend on her ass cheeks, and then he muscles in from behind, rutting up against her. It turns out that he can thrust much more freely in this position, his cock sliding all the way in and then almost all the way out, on each stroke. His shaft feels huge. She has to brace her arms as hard as she can, just to stop him bouncing her against the metal, as he gropes her thighs and ass and grabs her hips, fucking her with immense thoroughness.

She lets loose, crying out with every slap of his pelvis against her. She's howling with pleasure, but also with defiance and grief. Screaming at the ACs massed outside, screaming for everything and everyone's she's lost. The dead yammer and claw the booming metal in frustration. The container is like a steam-room and everything within her is boiling up in an explosive seethe. Soon the man banging her starts roaring too, and—incredibly—she feels that big cock swell even further, spreading her wide as he bores in to her like a hammer-drill, all the way to his climax.

"Ah … Ah! I'm coming, you fucker!" she wails.

"Yes!" he shouts, his voice mingling with hers as he empties his balls inside her. He has a deep, rough voice, as thick and savage as his plunging cock. "Oh fuck yes!"

Loud enough to wake the dead.

❖ ❖ ❖

Dawn pokes gray fingers through the drilled air-holes of their shipping container, but they wait. They don't leave until the day is warm enough to blind the ACs. He slides the door bolt back, millimeter by painstaking millimeter, while she thumps the wall at the far end of the container to draw their besiegers away from the entrance. She pictures them like iron filings drawn in a dark swathe to the pole of a huge magnet.

Yes, ACs are that stupid.

They ease out into the open, treading softly, holding their breath so the taint of carbon dioxide doesn't give them away. They've both done this before. Stealth is as vital as speed and strength.

It's a whole block before he touches her arm. "That

way," he says, pointing down an intersection where a rusted sign indicates the route to a highway. "East."

She shakes her head. "I'm going south."

"East first, darling. We want the checkpoint at Reading. I've got clearance. I can get you inside the Pale, Zeta. If you stick with me."

She frowns. "Who are you, then?" she asks, realizing she's never asked so much as his name, never mind what he's doing out here on his own.

He grins. "Hang around and find out."

The King in the Wood

Those trees in whose dim shadow
The ghastly priest doth reign,
The priest who slew the slayer
And shall himself be slain.
  – Thomas Babington Macauley

It was the press of beggars that told her she was nearly there. The stones of the Via Appia were set so closely and evenly that Valeria's mule-drawn carriage hardly rattled as it drew her out of Rome, but as the road reached the long climb up the skirts of Mons Albanus the flags were cemented more roughly in order to give the laboring draft-animals some purchase, and the slow lurch of the wheels over each cobble roused her from her reverie on the cushions. She sat up, pulled open the wooden shutter to see what her surroundings were, and then slammed it hastily shut again. Outside, the way was flanked with beggars, and at the sight of her face in the little window several hurried forward from their positions among the roadside tombs with hands out. For a few moments she heard them knocking at the carriage, their muffled voices wheedling.

"Domina! Kind Domina! A few sestertii for a widow with children to raise!"

"Domina, I took these wounds in Illyricum, fighting for Rome!"

And then came a curse from the driver and a shout from the guards behind the carriage and the beggars gave up.

Brigit, the only female slave she'd brought with her on this journey, woke with a snort and looked around. "Are we there,

Domina?" she asked. Brigit was a Briton or a Gaul or somesuch from the far north; she was fat and middle-aged and, beneath her complacency, fearlessly loyal. Valeria had brought her along for comfort as much as for propriety.

"Soon, I think."

"Good." She settled back into the cushions with a snore.

They must be close to the sanctuary of Diana, Valeria thought. Beggars always congregated around temples, hoping that those seeking the charity of the gods would be generous themselves. Valeria opened her purse to see how many brass coins she had, but it was no more than a distraction for her fingers; her mind was elsewhere.

Because Valeria Prisca Secunda sorely needed the charity of the gods. She'd been married to Quintus Didius Messor for four years, and she hadn't fallen with child yet. She liked her husband very much; he might be more than twice her age and of common blood but he was liberal and kindly, and she wanted to stay married to him. If she didn't quicken with child soon though, she was afraid he'd divorce her—reluctantly, she thought, for he seemed very fond of her, but he wouldn't have that much choice. He was growing old and he needed an heir, for although he was of the plebeian class his wealth was considerable. That was the very fact that had persuaded her own patrician family to contract the marriage alliance. Valeria had to give him a son or both sides would be let down.

It was hardly an unusual problem among the women of Rome of course, and there were ways around it. Many women would have resorted to taking a lover or bedding one of their household slaves, but that was a risky strategy as slaves were all too prone to gossip. There were alternatives. There were places, sacred places, where a Roman matron might go and beg a child of the gods, conceiving with a little help from their earthly representatives. It didn't count as adultery. It wasn't much spoken of. But they were there, these temples. Juno Lucina or Tellus Mater would have helped her.

But Valeria had chosen to go to Diana, keeper of the mountains and virgin of the Lake of Nemi. While Quintus Didius Messor was away at their country estate she was taking a carriage-ride from their house in the city, with only six guards trudging behind the vehicle and a woman to accompany her. She intended to be away from home overnight.

And why Nemi? *Because*, she admitted to herself with a flush of shame, *there's a faint chance that Thoas might be there*. At that thought something inside her belly twisted—almost painful, but not quite. A little flip of the stomach.

Four years ago she'd been sixteen, and betrothed to Quintus Didius, but she was still living in her father's house on the day that he, Lucius Valerius Priscus, had died.

Four years ago she'd been in love with a Greek slave, her father's personal doctor. Oh—she knew now—it had been a silly girlish green love, as full of sap and as easy to snap as the stem of a narcissus. Thoas had been a darkly handsome man, well-educated and thoughtful—and with time to spare for conversation with an inquisitive and lonely girl whose elder sister had left to marry and whose brothers took no notice of her existence. And of course she'd never confessed her feelings to him. If anyone in the household had suspected her passion he'd have likely ended up sold or sent back to the army or just dead. The virgin daughters of the *gens* Valerius bore a heavy weight of honor.

So she had carried the ache hidden inside her, like a child that could not be born, and the day that Lucius Valerius

Priscus died was the last time she'd seen Thoas.

She'd helped her father back in from the garden when he began to spit blood and clutch his belly. He'd been pale and unsteady for some days, not his usual domineering self at all, but he hadn't mentioned that he was in pain. Complaint wasn't the way of a patrician of Rome and ex-officer of the legions, and she'd only guessed at the agony he was in from the look on his gray and sweating face.

"Fetch Thoas!" she'd called, supporting her father under the arm as he groped his way back to his own chamber. When the doctor ran in he'd taken one look and sent the other slaves out at once, and begun to prepare a tincture of opium in wine. She'd fetched a bowl and a cloth herself from the shelf, as if she were a servant, for her father to spit the blood into and mop his lips. But it had been like building a mud dam across the Tiber— quite suddenly Lucius Valerius Priscus had leaned over the edge of the bed and vomited blood in a bright gush, then fallen limp. His eyes were fixed and staring in death by the time they rolled him over.

Valeria's memories of the moments that followed were blurred. She was certain that she didn't scream; her father had added the philosophical precepts of the Stoics to the dignity of the patrician class and he'd brought his children up likewise. She'd just stared and stared. She'd been nervous of her stern father all her life, and now she didn't know how to react. Looking back on the scene from four years on, she was fairly sure she'd said nothing at all until she asked, "Was he poisoned?"

"No," Thoas had said. His voice was heavy. "The pain in his guts … he's had it for years. I've seen it before. There was a hole in his stomach, I think, and he bled from his entrails out through that."

"I should send for my stepmother." Valeria hadn't been able to tear her eyes from her father's still face. "She's sacrificing at the shrine of Juno Pronuba. For my wedding."

"Yes. Of course. She will want to know. Everything. She'll want to be sure."

There'd been something so horrible in his voice that she'd turned at last to look at him. He'd been sitting down on an ornately carved chest—which was forbidden—with his elbows on his knees, and was holding his head between his hands. He was wearing a brief tunic which left his arms and legs bare, displaying the strong frame he'd built while serving as an army doctor when her father was an officer—and Valeria had wondered with one small part of her mind why it was that she could still admire that at a time like this. But under his neat dark hair his face had been absolutely ashen.

"What …?" she'd croaked eventually.

He'd met her eyes briefly. "He died vomiting blood, Domina, with his doctor in attendance. It'll look like poison to most people."

"Oh," she'd said, slowly seeing what was only too obvious to him. "They'll …"

"Torture me for a confession, yes."

Of course, she'd realized, they'd have to find out whether Lucius Valerius had been murdered. Freeborn Romans took no chances when it came to the question of slave insurrection. And the word of a slave was not legally admissible in court, unless extracted under torture. "Oh," she'd said weakly, looking down at her blood-speckled hands and feeling sick. "Oh no. They can't …"

"They can. They will."

"I'll speak up for you."

"That won't help."

"Then you'll have to run away."

He'd lifted his face to hers again, as if seeing her for the first time, and for a long moment there was silence between them. Valeria had realized that she'd just promised not to betray him, and her heart had clenched.

"Yes," he'd said softly, "I'll have to. Though I doubt I'll get far." He'd touched his face, his fingertip brushing the old vertical scar that bisected his right eyebrow and ran down across his cheekbone: another souvenir of his military days. "A Greek with a scarred face—that won't be too hard for the slave-catchers to spot. Still, it's a chance, isn't it?"

"Go to Nemi," she'd said.

"What?"

"The temple of Diana the Huntress. You'll be able to claim sanctuary there. It's only a day from the walls of Rome, straight down the Appian Way."

"They give sanctuary to escaped slaves? Why've I not heard of that before?"

"They …" She'd hesitated. "It's only to one slave at a time. The King of the Grove there, he's an escaped slave. He dedicates himself to Diana by killing the incumbent King and taking his place. You'd have to do that."

"Kill the King of the Grove?"

"You could do that. You were in the army, weren't you?"

"I was a battlefield surgeon," he'd said, shaking his head. "Not a soldier."

"But you learned to fight. And you're young enough and strong enough, more than most slaves. You've got a chance."

Hesitating, he'd nodded. A smile—acknowledgment, not mirth—had pulled at the corner of his mouth. Then he'd stood.

"Half a chance, perhaps. More out there than I have here. My respects to your father and all the *manes* of your house, Domina." Then without another word he'd left, slipping out through the garden door. She didn't watch him go. She'd just sat there with her father's body and waited for the tears to come.

Now, four years later, Valeria had no more idea than that day what had happened to Thoas. She didn't know if he'd made it to the sanctuary at Nemi or even tried to, whether he could have triumphed in combat there or how long the reign of a slave-King usually lasted. Perhaps there were new contestants for the sylvan crown every day. All she knew was that he wasn't captured and returned during the time she remained in her father's house. And that now she was here, at Nemi, because of the wisp of a chance that he might be too.

◆ ◆ ◆

Lake Nemi, the Mirror of Diana, lay cupped in a deep hollow on the wooded flanks of Mons Albanus, close to the Via Appia but not visible from it. What could be seen was the complex of temple buildings on the lip of that bowl, with hostelries and inns and stables all waiting to cater for supplicants, and the droves of peddlers and guides and beggars waiting to greet them.

Lore had it that the goddess came to admire her reflection in the little lake on nights of the full moon, and that within the grove there was an even holier sanctum that none but the priests entered, where she was attended by her King. But entry to the grove in the hollow was strictly controlled. Behind the public temple was a wall of dressed stone that cut off from view everything but the treetops. In that wall was a low door with a single priest guarding it, and suspended on the wall over the doorway a bare branch, gilded so that its twigs shone. No worshipers seemed to be entering by that door; instead they all mounted the broad steps to the pillared portico of the temple. Valeria, after staring at the modest doorway and its idle keeper for a long moment, drew a fold of her mantle over her head and followed all the rest within.

Diana, she thought as she stood over the brazier of charcoal and watched a priest cast incense and olive oil and hemp seed upon the coals, was a perplexing goddess, as mysterious as the moon that invoked her. A huntress in a land of cultivated fields and proud cities: a virgin to whom women prayed for conception and for a safe easy birth, and who kept a consort imprisoned here in the sacred grove. A goddess to be found on the earth and in the heavens and in the underworld.

Even her marble statue here in the public temple was a contradiction. Wreathed in rising smoke, the image depicted the goddess wearing a dress as short as a man's tunic, revealing her smooth legs and boots upon her feet. With one hand she caressed the head of a stag. She looked both beautiful and kindly; her face was serene. But, Valeria thought, she was the goddess of the hunt. The stag she petted so tenderly was to be her victim—pierced by arrows or torn apart by hounds.

Valeria bowed her head as she listened to the priest's prayers, and wondered whether it was truly a good thing to be heard by the gods.

"I have a further request to make of Diana," she murmured as she paid the priest for the ewe that would be sacrificed in her name. "I need to ask the intercession of her priesthood in the conceiving of a child."

The priest looked her up and down, and she didn't like his expression at all. "Perhaps I might be the one to intercede on your behalf," he suggested, and Valeria forced herself not to recoil: he was almost as old as her husband and had wet, droopy lips.

"I've come to see the Rex Nemorensis," she whispered.

His eyebrow rose. "Of course. If you think you're up to that."

"What do you mean?"

"Only that such a meeting is considered an ... ordeal ... by some. Things could be arranged much more swiftly and simply if, say, I were to pray with you instead."

Valeria's heart thumped. *Ordeal* did not sound like Thoas. He'd always been courteous and mild when she knew him. Of course, then he'd been a domestic slave. Here—if he was here, if the priest-King were not some stranger, some rough laborer or bodyguard or miner who'd escaped from a life of brute toil— here he was the consort of the goddess, and a murderer. She bit her lip. "I will see the King," she said, in a voice so low the priest had to incline his head to hear it.

"As you wish. Follow this way."

◆ ◆ ◆

She made a substantial donation to the temple for the privilege of being washed—by priestesses, she was relieved to find—and dressed in a short linen stolla that came only to her knees, in the style of Diana the Huntress. Prayers were said over her head and incense burnt, and then she was left for an hour to pray in a tiny shrine all alone, preparing herself for the touch of divine grace. Valeria was mortified at the prospect of appearing in public dressed so immodestly, but when they came to fetch her she was led through private corridors to the back of the temple. A gray-haired priestess took her hand at the door.

"Whenever you knock here you'll be readmitted to the temple."

Valeria nodded, her throat dry. She could feel her

empty stomach churning. Brigit, who was hovering at her heels, whispered, "Domina—are you sure?"

"Shush, Brigit! I am under the protection of the goddess now. Don't be such a coward!" Telling the slave off made her feel a little braver.

Then they let her out through the door, into the sacred grove beyond the great wall, and suddenly she was alone—alone as she never was at home where there were always slaves in attendance, alone as she hadn't been in years. Since, perhaps, the day of her father's death when she'd sat on his bed and wept. Valeria had to grit her teeth to stop herself shrinking back into the porch. She was a Roman, she told herself, and she wouldn't show fear.

It was harder still to admit that under her chill nervousness there was a bubbling pool of heat. That her vulva was soft and swollen, fluttering with anticipation; that the fear and uncertainty did not diminish that ache, but inflamed it. Her heart raced beneath breasts that tingled, the nipples standing up stiff against her borrowed linen despite the warmth of the day.

She'd led such a sheltered life; her body's reaction to this risk surprised her. But then she'd been that way four years ago, whenever she was around Thoas: half-melting with desire despite the terrible consequences of her passion being discovered. She'd had to hide her hungry glances under cool lashes and disguise the quiver of her limbs with studied gestures.

Her own stepmother had been no better; worse, in fact. Thoas was after all an unusually handsome slave. But out of fear of Lucius Valerius Priscus—who most certainly would not have tolerated the slightest infidelity on the part of his wife—Drusilla had been too sensible to do anything other than cultivate an inventive list of ailments that required the physician to examine her at regular intervals. Always with her slaves present, of course.

The trees pressed up close to the buildings. Valeria had never been in a wood before either; she was used only to the tame trees of gardens and orchards and olive groves, and to the dark verticals of the cypresses that grew beside the roads. These were close-grown, gnarled, tangled trees whose canopies cast the ground into shadow, their leaves in full summer flush. She recognized green acorns on the branches of some, and there were spiky seed-cases littering the ground at her feet that got caught in her sandals and made her hobble as she picked them out. Although the air was fairly still down here, a breeze hissed in the high branches, masking even the distant hubbub from the crowds over the wall.

Nor was there any obvious road, just little spidery paths that wandered between the trees in no particular direction, though all sloped downhill. She supposed they descended toward the famous lake. Shivering, she set off. Her footfalls rustled in the dead leaves of a hundred previous winters.

Her stepmother, she recalled, had made Thoas perform for her amusement. She'd made him have congress with various slave-girls of the household while she watched, smirking but untouchable. Valeria had only been a direct witness once. That was when Drusilla had decided that since her stepdaughter was approaching marriage she needed to see what she was expected to do to a man. She'd summoned Thoas to the corner of their walled garden where stepmother and daughter were reclining under the pergola, one hot afternoon. Two or three slaves had stood in attendance too. Thoas, Valeria thought, had looked wary.

Take off your tunic, Drusilla had ordered him. *My daughter is ready to glimpse the nuptial mysteries*. He'd complied obediently, but with no visible enthusiasm. Valeria remembered her own pink-faced embarrassment, her terror that she would give away more than maidenly shyness, her pain at his humiliation—and her guilty pleasure at seeing him stand there in the dappled sunlight, his muscled body as glossy as the polished flanks of a horse. She'd been fascinated by the dark hair on his groin and the smooth dangle of his cock and the soft and oddly pale pouch that hung low under the weight of his stones.

Suck him, Drusilla had ordered one of her slave-women—a German, Valeria thought, with pale hair and big but low-slung breasts. She'd gone down on her knees before the physician and wrapped her full mouth round his cock and given Valeria her first demonstration of fellatio. And the Roman girl had watched mesmerized as everything changed: as that sleeping cock grew hard and erect, as his scrotum tightened like a fist between his thighs, as Thoas' studied indifference crumbled, as he'd taken that German girl's head in his hands, his fingers burrowing roughly in her hair, his face a mask of concentration. When he'd come he'd pulled out—on Drusilla's orders—to paint the woman's wobbling breasts with abrupt splashes of pearly ejaculate. Valeria had learned a lot from that lesson. Not least from the look in his eyes as his orgasm took him, because at that moment his glance had swept over them both, her and her stepmother, and there'd been nothing of the slave in that look.

At the moment of orgasm he was *free*.

Had he wanted to fuck her too, she'd wondered? Had he wanted to fuck the daughter of his master's household and show her exactly what her silly pink-faced shame and her insipid filial obedience and her privilege was worth?

Imagining that had warmed her marriage-bed many nights.

Thoas, she called in her head, her lips not moving: *Are you here?* If it wasn't him, then it would be someone else. The King of the Grove would be here somewhere, sword in hand, patrolling his tiny kingdom as he must do all day and every day, ready for the moment another slave came to supplant him. Valeria jumped as something rustled in the ground litter—but it was only a small brown bird.

Then a man stepped up from behind and put his arms about her.

Valeria shrieked, but the sound of her shock was trapped by a callused hand that clamped firmly over her mouth. She tasted wood-smoke and dirt on her tongue and she struggled frantically, but his grip only tightened, pulling her almost off her feet; the torso to which she was clutched was rock-solid, the two bare arms wrapped around her like bands of iron. Her sandaled toes kicking helplessly at the dead leaves. He pulled her head back and to the side, exposing her throat, and then he inhaled the scent of her hair and pressed his lips to her cheek and licked at her neck, his mouth burning.

"Pretty," he breathed. "A pretty little doe has wandered into my wood." Valeria had been hoping for a Greek accent, but she couldn't hear one in that unidentifiable hoarse whisper. She moaned in fear as the hand not pinning her head slid up to grope her breast, squeezing hard. "She didn't know the hunter would be waiting for her, did she? She didn't know she'd have to run for her life." His fingers slid under the linen to capture her nipple. "Can you run, little deer? Can you outrun me?" He caught her earlobe in his teeth, savoring the yielding drag of skin. "Meat always tastes better after a chase."

He let her go quite suddenly, and Valeria caught her breath as she fell forward. Whatever her intentions—speak to him, turn and see for herself—they disappeared as his hand descended on her rump with an almighty crack.

"Run!" he hissed.

She panicked. It was the unexpected pain; she couldn't think past the pain and the shock that flashed through her blood. She staggered away and began to run, and the gradient of the hillside caught her and pulled her onward, through brambles and under branches, twigs whipping her face and her raised hands, thorns scratching her bare legs. She ran because she couldn't slow without falling, and because her feet were tripping beneath her and because at her back she could hear his hoarse laughter as he followed.

Down through the cruel wood she fled until she saw a thinning of the trees ahead of her, and she ran toward that with a sob only to come to the shore of a lake: a round lake cupped by steep hills that walled it in and kept it in shadow. The water looked black, and hardly a ripple stirred on that obsidian surface.

Valeria randomly chose one of the many tenuous paths paralleling the shore and kept going: ahead was what looked like a patch of flatter ground and she thought she could see the gilded roof of a small building among the trees. But despite her desperation her strength was failing: she wasn't used to running and her legs felt as soft and heavy as lead, her breath was heaving in her throat and her heart thundered in her ears. And he was close behind her, always. She could hear his tread. He was right on her heels, keeping pace.

She stumbled. A hand caught the back of her stolla as she went down and hauled her right off her feet, spinning her onto hands and knees. Seams tore as she wrenched out of his grasp and tried to crawl up the bank, her hands digging into leaf-mold and grass. For a moment she thought she was clear, and then he gripped her ankle and pulled her roughly back down onto him, capturing her in his arms again.

It was over. Valeria had no more strength left to fight; she just gasped for air and sobbed with fear. The King of the Grove wasn't even out of breath. He pinned her to his shoulder again with a single hand as she sat in his lap—but this time he didn't cover her mouth, he just held her chin up tight, forcing her head back. She caught glimpses of long dark hair as he stooped over her; it fell in her eyes.

"Hey hey hey," he murmured: "Hush."

"Plea—" was all she could splutter.

"Quiet now." His other hand moved to stroke her breasts as if she were an animal that needed gentling, and she thought of the sacrificial sheep being held for the knife. "I'm not going to hurt you, little deer," he said, and somehow that promise was more darkly menacing than his previous threats. "I'm just going to …"

The hand slipped from her breasts to her legs. Her short skirt was no barrier. He lifted it aside as he stroked up the inside of her splayed thighs, searching her out. She was wet with sweat about her belly and thighs and groin. His fingers slithered on the shaven silk of her mons veneris, then parted her smooth cleft to delve into the heat within.

Valeria moaned then, and writhed in his grip. He shifted against her, tightening his hold, and she was left in no doubt that he'd enjoyed the chase very much: his erect penis was hard as a wooden rod and shoving painfully into the soft muscle of her rear.

"Oh yes," he said, almost to himself. His curled fingers invaded her, greedy for her heat and emptiness. He played with her wetness and she heard the noises he made there, like moist kisses. "That's nice." He spread two fingers, opening her. "I like that. I like that a lot," he groaned in her ear. Then he circled her clitoris with his callused fingertips, using her own moisture to smooth the path. There was a lot of wet to use. "And you do too, don't you?"

She whimpered. She could hardly speak, so tightly was her jaw held, so starved were her lungs after her running. But she could hear, now that he wasn't whispering. Hear the foreign vowel-shapes.

"Now, little deer, I'm going to …" he said, and humped her forward onto hands and knees so that he could lift her skirt at the back and set his aim, before pulling her back down into his lap—and onto the cock angled there like a spearpoint. She felt its blunt head surge through her outer defenses and realized he was far thicker of girth than her husband, and that he was going to demand things of her that she'd never had to give before.

"Thoas," she gasped.

"What?" He was finding her tight: his focus was on the next thrust as he squeezed her down onto his thighs, impaling her further.

"Thoas!" It was a squeal by now.

He heard her that time.

For a moment he froze, and then everything changed. He pulled out of her, dropped her forward on the sloping bank and rolled her over onto her back, pinning her there with his hand on her breastbone. As he loomed over her Valeria saw his face for the first time, through her blurring tears.

It was Thoas, but he was almost unrecognizable. Valeria's heart banged against her breastbone. The last time she'd seen him, he'd been clean-shaven with decently short hair, but now that hair, looking like it hadn't been combed in weeks, hung down to his shoulders and his face was swarthy with stubble. His skin was weathered dark and lined around his eyes and the corners of his mouth. He was wearing a worn tunic that was splotched and faded to the color of autumn leaves, and a sword belt that hung diagonally across his chest: the thin fabric of the tunic didn't disguise the corded muscle that packed his frame. The old vertical scar down his cheek had now been joined by one on his upper lip and a nose that had been broken out of its true alignment. He looked like a barbarian. He looked *terrifying*. And he looked older —quite considerably older—and it showed most around his eyes, which were undershadowed by patches black as blood-blisters and seemed almost unfocused, the pupils dilated wildly.

He searched her face for a long long time.

"Valeria Prisca Secunda," he said at last.

She nodded, and reached to touch his chest, like a plea for clemency. Her heart was pounding.

"You've changed."

"Not so much as you," she whispered. Was this even the man she'd come in search of, or just someone wearing his mask?

He nodded slowly. For the first time a faint smile tried to pull at the corners of his mouth. "Little Valeria, the pretty girl with the crush on me."

She inhaled sharply and her chest heaved. "You didn't know that!"

"Didn't I?" His gazed dropped from her face to her torso. The torn and twisted dress had been rent open when he rolled her, and one of her breasts was bared, her pink nipple pointing at the heavens. He lifted the hand holding her in place and ran it lightly down her body. As Valeria's gaze followed his she realized that he was kneeling over her spread thighs still, and that his erection, interrupted in its mission, was still standing from under the hem of his tunic, glossy and solid, sticky with her honey. And bigger than she'd remembered: Valeria's assessment of her own husband's equipment underwent a sudden terrifying downgrading.

"Are you married?" he asked, as if he'd heard her thoughts. His fingertips brushed the juicy slit he'd so recently assailed, and without being able to help herself she tilted her hips, moving her clitoris under his teasing touch.

"Yes," she said, trying to catch his wrist in her hand and stop him even as her vulva yielded to his exploration.

"Congratulations, Domina." His fingers gave her the caress she wanted, not for a moment believing her protesting hand. "And tell your husband from me he's a lucky man, whoever he is."

"Quintus Didius Messor," she whimpered.

"Ah. I remember. So are you childless—or just frustrated? What did you come here for, Valeria?"

Her eyes widened as his fingers stirred her fire, and she caught her lip in her teeth, but the words burst out anyway: "A child."

"Well," he said, moving over her and easing between her thighs, his prick nudging into the slippery path of her sex as his fingers bit into her skin. "I can give you that."

"Thoas!" she sobbed.

"What? Is this not what you were expecting?" His eyes were so glazed he seemed almost blind, but his cock was sure of the way. "Were you hoping for a little conversation, Domina—a little nostalgic reminiscence—before … this?"

"Oh," she said—then, "Oh!" as he retook every inch of lost ground, and no less demanding than before. He pushed into her with the implacable insistence of a man taking what was ordained to him by the gods, and Valeria cried out and arched her back, feeling as if her insides had to completely re-arrange themselves to accommodate him. "What's happened to you?" she groaned.

"Me?" He was moving slowly, taking the time to savor the roll of her hips and the quiver of her breasts with each thrust. "I've been King in this wood for four years, Domina." The honorific was subtly mocking. "I've killed men. I've fucked women. Many more women than men, in case you were wondering. Are you surprised I've changed?"

She reached up to stroke his face; he was braced on his hands and not close enough for her to kiss. When she was sixteen she'd wanted to kiss those lips more than anything in the world. Now they were scarred and cracked—but he caught her thumb in his mouth and bit gently upon it. She whimpered as he ground his cock deeper.

"Am I hurting you?"

"No," she answered, not entirely truthfully. And yet she didn't want that hurt to stop, because it was better than any pleasure she'd had from Quintus Didius Messor. She just needed to take it slowly, at a pace she could manage.

He paused, running his tongue over his lips. She wished he would lie down on her.

"Thoas …"

"No one's used my name in four years." A flex of his pelvis made her moan again. His eyelids sank almost closed. "I've been … not myself. Someone else."

She wondered that he was able both to talk and to plow her, even slowly, with long deliberate strokes and pauses. His voice was ragged with strain.

"I came here by night, you know. I thought it best. I jumped up … to touch the golden bough at the gate. You have to be able to unhook it. First time. That's how you prove you're worthy."

She ran her hands down his torso, feeling his muscles working beneath the fabric of the tunic. He was starting to sweat, the cloth clinging to his hips and sides.

"They gave me a sword … and I crept down here in the dark. To the temple there. It seemed the obvious place. I found him there. With a woman. A big plump Roman matron. He had her ankles up round his neck. Stuffing her good and hard. Maybe he didn't hear me. Or he was so close he couldn't stop anyway. I shoved my blade through his ribs … as he came."

"Oh gods."

Thoas clenched his teeth, his own rhythm rising to the steady powerful thrust of a man hewing wood, his face twisting. "When I rolled him away … she turned over on hands and knees. She stuck her cunny in the air. She said, 'Now you've got to fuck me too.'"

"Did you?"

"I did."

Valeria lifted her knees, letting him sink even deeper into her, wrapping her legs about his back. "You were such a good man … when I knew you," she said breathlessly. "So … Ah! Oh gods! … so kind to me, then."

His hands were slipping wider, his face dropping lower toward hers. "I tried to be," he whispered, as if it were a secret they were sharing. "The first few times, with the women, I was gentle and respectful. And you know what? They were *disappointed*."

She dug her nails into his thighs and hips, urging him on, pulling him into her.

"The women that come here … they don't want just a fuck. They can get that at home. They want something more, Domina. They want to be Daphne ravished by Apollo. Selene forced by Pan. Europa rutted by Jupiter. They want something they will remember forever in dread and awe. They want … a god."

She started to cry out, a sound like fear, and he bared his teeth.

"Is that what you want, Valeria? Did you come here to be fucked by a god? Filled with his ambrosial seed? Impregnated with divine life?"

"I came here … for *you* …" she wrenched out, and after that she couldn't talk at all, only cry out, because she was being taken up in orgasm and shaken limb from limb, dumb and deaf and blind to everything but the pounding of his cock inside her. And just for a moment she did feel like they were divine, that he was a god, that she was Danae being showered in gold—as she found one last breath to cry his name and he spasmed and roared and poured his seed inside her, and fell over her with a groan.

They clung together then, not like gods, but like children who'd gotten lost in the woods. She ran her fingers through his tangled hair and he buried his face in her shoulder.

But a moment later he dragged himself out of her embrace, though she tried to hold him. His face was so drawn that Valeria, glimpsing his expression, thought he was ill. A single drop slipped from his cheek onto her bare breast and she stared at the clear splash, wondering: it must be sweat, surely? By the time she looked up at Thoas he was kneeling up with his back to her, looking intently along the bank of the lake and through the wood.

His successor, she thought, trying to still her breath: *He must keep an eye out for the man who'll take his place.* She sat up too, tugging despairingly at her torn dress, feeling a lump swell in her throat and her face burn.

Thoas twisted to search behind them. Only when he was sure they were not being watched did he glance back at her and see the tears spilling down her face. He touched her chin.

"Why are you crying?"

"I'm sorry!"

"For what?"

"For telling you to come here. I'm sorry …"

She wiped at her cheeks with muddy hands, smearing her face, and met his gaze through wet lashes. For a moment in that wild rough mask she saw an expression that was almost familiar.

"Hey," said he softly. "Valeria. I'm alive, aren't I?"

She thrust out her lower lip, swallowing her tears.

"It's not so bad, believe me." His face moved into the semblance of a smile. "I spent two years patching up soldiers in a stinking tent on the battlefield, remember. At least I have as much to eat and drink here as I want. And the work's … relatively easy." His mouth twitched. "No one punishes me. No one tells me what to do any more. So don't feel sorry for me." He stroked her face. "I'm alive, Valeria—Oh gods, I'm more appreciative of that than I've ever been—and so much better off than many. And when I do get weary all I need do is remind myself it won't be for much longer. Somewhere out there is the man who'll finish it—someone younger and faster and stronger than me."

Valeria put her hand over her mouth to stifle her protest.

"I see her, you know," he whispered, his voice falling. "On moonlit nights. I see her between the trees. Or walking across the face of the lake. She *shines*, Valeria. She look and smiles."

She slipped her arm around his neck and held him, her face tucked in the angle of neck and shoulder, as he stroked her hair.

"I just wish I could sleep," he whispered. "I haven't slept in years, not properly. I can't afford to let my guard down. Not even for an hour. I would give almost anything to sleep."

Valeria lifted her lips to his. "Sleep now," said she. "I'll sit watch, Thoas. I'll wake you if anyone comes."

"Valeria …"

"I promise."

He looked her in the face a long moment, then kissed her. Softly. Hesitantly. "Anyone at all," he mumbled, and then laid himself down, pillowing his head in her lap. She shifted her position slightly to make herself comfortable, and laid her hand on his head. Her eyes scanned the empty shoreline. It was a warm summer's evening. Soon the sun would set and later the moon would rise, silvering the lake. This mountain hollow, this grove—it was a world to itself, and the one outside seemed unimaginably far away.

Thoas was asleep in seconds; she felt the tension drain from him and his bones grow heavy. Softly she stroked his hair, listening to the slow wash of his breath, and as he slept she held him safe, and watched.

The Last Thing She Needs

Shanna just hasn't been the same since we got her back from Appentak's clutches. Since I wrapped her up in the red satin bed-sheet and led her gently out from her prison, my arm about her shoulders, into the room where all the others waited around his open sarcophagus. She moved with tiny little steps that day, nothing like her normal confident stride, and I could feel her leaning against me for support. But when we reached Appentak's coffin and looked in, she shrugged off my arm and made sure to stand on her own two feet.

Everyone was staring at her, and no one knew what to say. I could see the hot relief and shame in the team's eyes. Desperate joy that she was still alive, but no words to express it without compounding our collective guilt. We'd found and freed her at last—but she'd been in the vampire's clutches for nearly two weeks. In her pale face and in the bite marks on her neck, we could all see the toll it had taken,

But I was the one who'd gone ahead into the bedchamber to release her from her chains. Who'd seen some of the other scars now hidden beneath the red sheet. I was the only one with a real guess at what her survival had cost her.

I took an ash stake from the holster at my hip and offered it to her. "You do it," I said.

She looked at the stake like she'd forgotten what it was for. Then down at the body in the stone coffin. Appentak lay with eyes shut. Out there beyond the brick warehouse walls it was mid-afternoon and that meant he couldn't move a muscle, but I was pretty sure he had some awareness of his surroundings, and if there's any justice in the world he would have been panicking inwardly at his helpless state. Certainly he'd have heard the gunfire as we took out his human servants. He might even have heard the screams as Rhiannon staked the two lesser vampires— both female, both no older than schoolgirls.

Fucking pervert.

That could have been Shanna, I'd thought as Rhiannon hammered the stakes between the girls' breasts. It really might have been. I wonder if she would've had the will to do if it if *had* been Shanna, if we'd arrived that bit too late.

"Shanna?"

She nodded. She only had one arm free of her bed-sheet, clutching it in place. "You hold it," she said, meaning the stake. "Give me the mallet." Her voice was hoarse and wispy, as if she'd spent long hours screaming.

I doubted inwardly that she'd have the strength left to drive the wooden point through bone and cartilage, but I didn't want to argue. My eyes found Rhiannon's in mute appeal— and she understood, thank God, stepping forward to help. She was flecked with blood-spatter from head to toe, but her hands were gentle as she took charge of Shanna's precarious sheet and tucked it in, holding in place.

"It's okay, Shanna," she murmured.

Shanna, who had never once in two years asked for Rhiannon's reassurance, didn't seem to hear her. But she held out her hand to me for the mallet.

I pulled open the vampire's ruffled shirt to make it easier for her, and aligned the splintery point where the furrow between two ribs met the sternum. The bastard affected a sort of retro Edwardian look in his clothes—I should have guessed from the red satin sheets that he had no taste whatsoever—and the skin beneath was gray as a corpse's. Which was what he was, after all.

Aside from that he was kind of handsome, I guess, in a gaunt and elderly way. Wavy silver hair.

I hated the fancy-looking fucker with a passion I thought I'd lost long ago.

Shanna hefted the wooden mallet. I hoped she had the strength to strike accurately, and not hit my hand. I watched as she bit her lip, seeming to hesitate.

Then Appentak's eyes opened.

He looked straight up at her.

I'd never seen a vampire with that much strength of will. They're usually inert during the daytime: just so much cold meat. His eyes were black, of course, without iris or sclera, but they seemed to look straight into Shanna's soul. I heard the intake of her breath.

Then she slammed the mallet down on the stake. It took four blows, each harder than the one before, to drive it through his unbeating heart. He spasmed and shook and screamed, but she didn't stop until he went still.

Cory came in then with the needles and drew off Appentak's blood into vials, just as usual. It's how we fund our project. Vampire blood is changing the face of medicine: not just kicking the ass of pathogens but with regenerative powers on top. They've used it to cure HIV and they're even talking about it being the answer to Alzheimer's soon. Well at least those parasites have made some contribution to the world, now … though it hardly makes up for the rest.

I cut off Appentak's head when it was done, and the corpse crumbled to wet ash.

Shanna hasn't been right, though, since that day.

We can't blame her—and not one of us would have criticized if she'd given the whole thing up then and there. We can only guess at what she's been through at Appentak's hands. But she's never voiced any desire to quit. Just the opposite in fact; she was out on a mission pretty much the minute she got her strength back, her face set like stone. She works out in the gym for hours each day, and she's first up and last to her bunk. I don't think she goes home to her apartment much anymore, just stays at Base.

But she's stopped talking. I used to like her sarcastic wit and her sassy spirit. She was always the one who could stop Lee dead with a barbed phrase when he went off on one of his look-at-me-I'm-such-a-badass-mutherfucka-you-all-just-watch-me-save-your-asses-again boasts. She never lost heart even when the odds looked impossible. And she never took any shit from Rhiannon, who was so determined to be queen bee in the team. Or from any of the guys trying to get into her pants.

I'm not included in that set. I never tried to get into her pants. Not that I didn't think about it, sure. But that's not what I do.

There's a time and a place for everything.

Well, everything natural.

Nowadays, it's like the light's gone out in her eyes. Or maybe just sunk to a tiny hot point like the tip of a soldering iron. We seldom hear her talk. Maybe me least of all—she avoids meeting my gaze, even, her eyes steely-set on some distant horizon. She goes out on hunts like it's the only thing she lives for, and she takes stupid, reckless risks, she's so determined to get the vampires. Because she's lost her own fear, that makes me scared for her. She acts like she's bulletproof, and that just ain't the case.

Nobody dares call her out. How can we judge? We've all got our own ways of dealing with the stress and the crazy. Lee has his back-to-back action movies and his crappy boasting.

Rhiannon does pills, I know for a fact. Cory has his shamanic meditation shit. Pretty much everyone drinks.

Me? I choose to fuck my way to mental health. Down to the bars and the clubs; a different girl every night. I rarely have a problem finding someone new. The others used to laugh at me, enviously, but nowadays they're thinking it's a bit too much, a bit weird. "You're so goddamn grim about it," Lee told me once, after a night out. "Isn't sex supposed to be fun?"

Maybe they're right. Maybe it is weird. I know what I'm looking for, and I know I won't find it there.

At least, I hope to God I never do.

But this isn't about me, it's about Shanna. She's on the edge. We all know this, and we're all starting to exchange alarmed looks when she kicks off and does something rash. But who's going to talk to her? Who's going to say "You need a break; you need to let it go?"

Rhiannon nearly lost her cool last week when Shanna shot a vampire's prisoner—not fatally, thank fuck. "This has to end," she swore. "I'm gonna tear her a new one."

I was the one who stopped her: "Leave her alone, Rhiannon. She's had enough shit to deal with, without you dropping more on her." There was an argument, but I stood firm. Because how do you *let it go* when you've been through what Shanna's been through? I'd seen …

I'd seen stuff in that vampire's bedroom I've told none of the others about.

It still keeps me awake at night.

So tonight, when it's been quiet for a week and everyone's taking time off and going home to get some proper sleep and some alone-time, or dropping in on their mothers or girlfriends or whatever it is that normal people do, Shanna is still at Base.

I've just called in to do some washing, and I find the place all but deserted. Just her and her laptop and her gun, in the vaulted, windowless bunkhouse. She looks up at me and nods without smiling. The computer lights her face from below, making her look as pale and shadowed as, well … a vampire.

"Kev."

"Everything good?" I ask. I make sure not to crowd her, not to face her straight on. Keep it casual.

"Quiet."

"That is good," I remind her, because she sounds peeved. "Looks like we might be getting on top of this thing."

"Yeah. I suppose." She pouts her lips, oblivious to the effect that has. "I was just going to take a shower." She's been working out again: I can see the sheen of sweat on her skin. It looks like it needs licking off. Someone else—Lee perhaps—might take her words as an invitation to make a pass. I don't.

After what she's been through, the last thing Shanna needs is some big dreadlocked guy in biker leathers pushing into her personal space.

"Well, I'm doing my laundry," I say, hefting my rucksack. The machine here is industrial-size: one of the perks of the job. "Don't let me interrupt your fun."

She eyes me coolly but says nothing, so I go off to load powder and fabric softener like a good boy.

When I wander back, she's in the shower cubicle and her laptop is still open on the table. I glance down at it with idle curiosity, and in one line I can feel hot and cold water running all over me.

She's logged into a chatroom, and she's talking to a guy. It's real ugly.

SHAZ103: When I get to the park youll be waiting in the bushes near the gate, watching for me. I wont see you but Ill feel someone looking and itll make me walk faster, feeling nervous. You wait til Im somewhere really lonely before you make your move. Grab me from the shadows. Ill struggle but youll be too strong. Youll take me into the dark off the path and when I beg you not to hurt me youll hit me to shut me up and then youll pull off my clothes and fuck me slow and hard.

UZI2000: Hell yeh baby Im going to fuck you good you dirtybitch youneed it youwant it bad Im going tomake you scream it hurts so good ,,, Im so hard now justthinking about mydick going into you raping you andyou trying to scream but my handon yor mouth stops anybidy hearing the noiseiwant to cum onyour tits and face and up yor ass and make you suckit shit and blood after,,, tonight you dirty bitch 10pm behind the burger concesion you get yours tonigth.

SHAZ103: Tonight 10PM

Jesus.

Jesus H. Christ, what am I supposed to do? What the hell is she thinking of?

And my second thought is *Why did she leave her laptop up and running?* Was it deliberate? Did she want me to see?

When Shanna comes out of the shower, toweling her hair, I'm sitting across the table from the laptop so I can't look at the screen. She's wearing cycle shorts and a lycra sports top, both black. My heart is going like a trip-hammer; I'm more scared and angry than I ever am on a raid.

"Shanna." My voice is loud and heavy—louder and heavier than I'd intended. I point at the laptop. "What the *fuck?*"

She stops in her tracks, open-mouthed. "What?"

"What the fuck do you think you're doing with that Uzi piece of shit?"

"You've been looking at my PC?" The towel falls to the floor. Her eyes are very wide.

"Screw that, Shanna. What are you up to?"

"How dare you!"

"FUCK THAT!" I roar, slamming my hand down on the table so hard the laptop bounces. I'm so freaked out I don't know what else to do with my distress. I see Shanna take a step back, eyes narrowing, and before I know it I'm on my feet. But I don't move toward her. I don't want to scare her.

I don't want …

"Talk to me, Shanna," I say through gritted teeth, dropping my voice to a low pitch. "Tell me what you're doing. Is this some sort of sting operation you're trying to set up?"

She shakes her head.

"Then it's for real? You're arranging to meet that guy tonight?"

She bares her teeth.

"Jesus Christ, Shanna." I want to tell her she's a stupid stupid *stupid* woman, but I've got enough sense not to let the words past my lips. "What the hell are you thinking of? Are you trying to get yourself killed!"

"He's in Baltimore." She practically spits the words.

"What?"

"Baltimore. That's where the park is. I looked it up on Google Earth. I'm not going to get to goddamn *Baltimore* in the next hour, am I? Like, it's not actually possible, Kev!"

That throws me. "So this is … what? A game?"

"Yeah. A fantasy."

"A fantasy where you get beaten up and raped?"

"Is that any of your business?"

"Jesus, Shanna. This is … bad shit."

"Screw you. I don't interfere in your ho love-life."

"It's not *safe*, Shanna! You're meeting these creep strangers on the internet and winding them up with promises … How do you know they won't try and find you? How do you know this prick really is in Baltimore, and not down the road? You're not the only one who lies on the Net!"

"Shut up!" She runs her fingers through her wet hair. "I'll deal with it! It's not your concern."

"You could get hurt—*really* hurt—and that is my concern!"

"What if I want to get hurt? Hey? What if that's what I want?"

Her shout rings around the bunkhouse, and the echoes fall into silence. I can see her trembling now, and blinking as she tries to force back the hot tears—and I'm nearly as shocked by that as by the fucked-up online conversation. My instinct is to reach out and hold her and make her safe. Not that I dare show it. Forcing my fists to unclench, I speak as gently as possible.

"Why? Why would you want that? Is it … shit, is it the Appentak thing?"

She throws back her head. "Say it; go on—why don't you. Tell me I'm crazy."

You're crazy. Appentak has damaged you but bad. "You're not crazy. But I'm thinking PTSD right now."

She's pale as milk.

"I saw …" I continue, uncertainly. "I saw … what he'd done to you." Oh Christ, I'd seen. The red satin, the black leather, the silver chains. The silvery flare between her beautiful …

I shouldn't have seen those things.

"Did you tell anyone?" she demands. "Any of the others?"

"No. Hell, no." *Is this why she's been avoiding me?*

Her lip quivers.

"Shanna, believe me. I've said nothing."

"Yes," she whispers. "It was Appentak." She stalks over to her laptop and snaps it shut, dousing its light. "But not him." Her voice is shaking. "All my life. All my life, these thoughts. Being whipped. Being held down. Being made to do things I didn't want."

I try to swallow. Shanna is one of the least submissive women I've ever met. Brave and self-assured and independent. Contemptuous of jerks who think they're any better than her— and rightly so. Sexy, but uninterested in sexual relationships. Or so it had seemed, anyway.

Maybe there's been a lot she wasn't telling us.

Maybe we all have things to hide.

"Do you know what Appentak did to me?" Her eyes are cold and hot, all at the same time, as she turns them scathingly upon me. "As soon as he had me back there, he bit me. You know what that does to you?"

I nod, reluctantly. The vampire bite is analgesic, psychotropic and causes addiction in 30% of victims. Those who've reported back describe it as an aphrodisiac of the highest order. It makes you horny, and it takes away all your inhibitions. It also gives you inhuman stamina: when I'd found Shanna in chains she must have been there for hours. Appentak would have retired to his coffin at dawn. If it hadn't been for the bite marks all over her body, she would have been in agonies of cramp.

"That was all it took: a bite. He bit me, and then he did all the things he'd threatened to do us." Shanna's smile is bitter. "And you know what? After that I *loved* it. The sex. The pain. The humiliation too."

I remember her throat, enclosed by a braided leather

collar, chained to a post behind where she knelt. Her nipples, tethered by twin silver clips on thin chains to the foot of the huge ornate bed. Every chain taut, so that she couldn't move forward without choking herself, or backward without tearing the clamps from her swollen flesh. Her wrists bound at the small of her back. The smell of wet, well-used pussy. The round peachy flare of her ass below the black corset, split by …

"That's not your fault," I say thickly.

"He fucked with my head, Kev, even more than he fucked with my body. He made me want it. He made me love it."

She had been blindfolded, with a scarf of the softest black leather. She hadn't known it was me, when I walked into the room, and I was too full of shame and pity to announce myself. But she'd heard my footfalls. And she'd turned her face toward me and wet her softly parted lips—in anticipation.

My own mouth is dry now. "I'm so sorry, Shanna. You know we got to you as fast as we could. I wish it had been faster."

She doesn't seem to hear the apology. It's only the latest of many, after all. She bares her teeth in a little snarl, defying me to judge her. "Now I need it. I want it."

"Need …?"

"I need someone to hurt me. It's like … it's like fire inside. Or hunger, chewing at my guts." She wipes her fingers down her torso, seemingly unconscious of the motion. "It's like all the demons in my head have slipped their chains and I need them to be whipped back into their cage."

"So you go online for … this?" I wave a hand at the machine as I circle the table end.

"What else do you suggest?"

"Jesus." I shake my head. "Not that. Not that, Shanna. If you want to get laid, get laid. Find a nice guy who's willing to spank your ass, if that's what you have to do. I'm sure there'd be plenty of volunteers."

Her lip curls. "I don't want a *nice guy*! Haven't you been listening?"

I grimace in apology. "Not nice, then—but someone you can trust. Someone who'll give you what you need, but know where to stop. Someone who'll take care of you."

"Where do I find that?" Her face is all twisted. "Who can *I* trust?"

"Well," I say, the knots inside me coiling and clenching. "There's me."

"You?" She laughs derisively, so contemptuous that she actually struts in closer, closing the gap between us. I'm much taller than her, but she looks up into my face like I'm a raw recruit and she's the meanest sergeant ever to walk the parade ground. "You couldn't hurt me if your life depended on it. You won't even kill female vampires, you're so squeamish. You look all mean, Kev, but you're a fucking *pussy*."

I slap her. Open-handed, across the face. Pretty hard too—not enough to stagger her but enough to knock her head sideways. When she looks at me again, her lips parted, aghast, there is a white handprint on her face that rapidly flushes pink.

And there's something else as well. All the twisted defensive scorn has dropped away in shock, and beneath that there is something so beautiful that I want to cup it and cherish it and keep it safe forever.

So I slap her again. My other hand. Her other cheek. A bit harder.

She's stopped breathing. Her eyes are enormous.

"That's better," I tell her, hoarsely. I tip her chin up, pushing her head back. "Lesson one, bitch." The word is a horror: it hangs in the air between us. "Now, go into the gym and put your hands on the wall-bars."

Then I let her go, pushing her away a little. For a moment she just stares at me, and I can hear nothing but the roar of blood in my ears. Her full, intensely kissable, lower lip is moist and trembling. Then, without a word, she slips past me—heading for the gym door.

I don't follow immediately, even though I'm depriving myself of watching the tick-tock of her fine ass as she walks. Instead I take a moment to draw several deep breaths and collect myself. My hands are stinging lightly from hitting her, and the vibration runs up through my body, making me quake. I'm sweating under my leather jacket, burning hot from the self-blame that's screaming in my head.

This is bad. Really bad. Shanna's got some serious baggage, by the looks of things. She needs care and comfort and probably a trained, experienced therapist. Whereas I'm … I'm a big gnarly guy with a well-honed talent for violence and no idea how to talk to her. The last thing she needs is me.

But I'm what she's going to get.

Even while I'm coruscating myself inwardly, I'm turning and walking to the gym door. My stomach roils, but my balls are heavy like a clip of ammo. I'm loaded and fully cocked.

My heart jumps as I step into the other room and see her. She's *there*. She's submitted to instructions. She stands with her back to me, her hands on the wooden climbing-bars and her long legs stiff with tension. Jeez: isn't this everything I've fought against?—but right now I have to bite the inside of my lip to stop the Neanderthal grin that tries to rise there. Instead, I turn and shut the gym door. Every door in the Base has a bars and bolts, just in case we're ever invaded. I slide them home noisily; I don't want any of the others wandering in and finding us here.

Then I saunter over to her, and as I walk I uncinch my belt so that the metal buckle hangs down and jingles. I stop within arm's reach, but I don't touch. First, I just look her up and down—from her damp hair that I know will be the color of honey when it dries, to her taut shoulders and the narrowing sweep of her back down from that muscled broadness to a silken waist; the concave of her spine that always makes me want to put my hand *just there* on the small of her back, and down again to the unwitting tease of her shamefully lush ass. Shanna never gives the impression that she wants to be sexy. She just is, even against her will.

She's quivering all over. Her hands squeak with sweat as she slides them nervously along the bars.

When I'd found her in Appentak's room, I'd said not a word. I couldn't burden her with the shame of recognizing me when she was trussed and bound like that. Leaving her blind, I'd stepped in and unclipped the nipple-clamps first, releasing her beautiful tits from their torture and seeing her gasp and writhe and whimper as blood flooded again into the pinched points of her breasts, swelling them to fat dark buds. Then I'd unclipped the collar at her throat. She'd fallen forward over her knees, gasping for breath. Revealing … everything. That was when I'd reached down to the ornate chrome below—

"Spread your legs wider." My voice comes out as a confident drawl, God knows how. But it's a test, sort of: a last-minute check.

She obeys. She's standing on the thin crash-mat below the bars, and her bare feet inch apart on the plasticized surface.

The rush of my relief nearly makes me groan.

"Good." Now I shuck off my leather jacket and cast it

aside. Underneath I'm wearing a white T-shirt, but it's not going to stay white for long. I'm already speckled with sweat, and this is going to be hot work. I pull the belt out from my waistband, double it over and crack the leather straps between my fists. Shanna jumps, her shoulders bunching like they're feeling the lash. I haven't touched her yet.

I take a risk. Dropping the belt over her head, I loop it around her throat and use the leash to pull her head up and back. My lips brush her ear, tasting the dew in her hair. I can *smell* the fear on her.

"What did you learn in Lesson One, Shanna?"

She tries to clear her throat but her voice is all hoarse. "You're not a pussy."

I chuckle. "That's right. Now." I swallow hard, because this is a moment I never dreamed could happen, and these are words I never thought I'd say to any woman. It's like giving myself the Pearl of Great Price that preachers talked about all those years back; it's like crowning myself with a golden crown. "Now I'm going to hurt you."

I have to close my eyes because I'm dizzy with gratitude.

Shanna whimpers. I feel it through the leather. My free hand is on her hip. I don't know how that happened.

"Feel free to scream, if you like. No one will hear you; no one will come save you. I've locked the door—you heard that, didn't you? Scream or cry or beg me, whatever. If you think you really can't take it anymore, you'll have to let go of those bars and crawl away from me, Shanna. Do you understand?"

She nods, tightly, constricted by the belt around her throat.

"Clever girl," I whisper sarcastically. Then I release her, pulling the long belt free. My hand on her ass has encountered a problem: with those black shorts of hers, brief though they are, I won't be able to see where I'm hitting.

I could pull them down … But something tells me that's a step too far, too soon. Too intimate. I signed up to hurt her, not strip her. So I take the soft cotton-lycra and I pull the panties up higher, right into her crotch, like I'm giving her a wedgie. Then I run my fingers round the hems, front and back, ease them up as high toward her hips as they will go, bunching the fabric into the grip of her ass-cleft, baring only the twin orbs of her butt-cheeks.

That sight takes my breath away. Her ass is so beautiful I want to cup and kiss it—but that's not in the contract. I take a step back.

"Arch your back," I order, folding the belt up in my hand again. I want a short, controllable length for what I'm about to do. "Ass out."

She flexes, just as she's told, and my cock surges. The blood is draining southward from my brain so fast that I'm in danger of losing control. I have to hit her. I have to hit her with the belt now, or God knows what I'll do.

So I do. The tongue of leather snaps out and slaps her right ass cheek, back-handed, with a crack like something breaking. It is the most beautiful, pure sound, followed almost before I can savor it by Shanna inhaling noisily through gritted teeth. And that noise—oh, that high pitched quavering yelp—wraps itself round my guts. I want to hold it trembling in my hands. I want to cherish and soothe it into peace. I want to make it happen again. And again. And again.

The strap leaves a pink stripe across her smooth butt, and then I swing the other way and lay down a matching line on the other cheek. The pistol-crack of skin on quaking skin is just as cold and keen this side, and my heart leaps.

She tries not to scream. She's proud, is Shanna. She squeaks and whimpers, she jerks and writhes, but she tries not to scream, at first. And I'm fairly gentle, at first, because I'm not sure what sort of punishment she can truly take. I've never done this. I've never hit a woman. Not even a vampire, except maybe in last resort when it's someone's life on the line. This is new to me, and I'm groping in the dark, my path lit only by burning, smoky need. But as I gradually pick up tempo and force, Shanna's cries become wilder, rising to shrieks. There are gabbled incoherent words in there too; words of protest, perhaps. It doesn't matter. I ignore them. It is her hands I have to keep an eye on; the white clench of her knuckles and then the spasming flex and furl of her fingers, spreading wide as if to thrust the pain away. Sometimes one splayed palm leaps off the bar: she is barely holding on. I know then to drop it down a notch, to slow my blows and eke out my cruelty.

That's how I reduce her to gasping and blaspheming and begging for mercy, crying, "Oh God no! No! No!" even as her ass thrashes from side to side. That's how she keeps me going, my desire focused into a lightning bolt of incandescent force that flashes down my arm, over and over, to earth in her soft flesh.

In the end it's me that quits first, because my hand's shaking so much that I'm starting to worry about my aim. But it's not muscle strain; it's adrenaline. I take a step back, panting hard, sweat running down my back, and I look at her. Shanna's still clinging to the bars, ass still out-thrust. There are crimson stripes criss-crossed down her long thighs, and her beautiful ass is scarlet and swollen. Any redder and that glistening skin would shine on a visible wavelength. She's making a soft keening sound, in and out on her breath. I can't believe she's still standing.

My admiration does not alter the fact that I want to

break her.

Nor does it make up for the discomfort of my turgid erection, trapped down the trouser leg of my leathers. I pop the waist button and slip my hand in, easing my thick length to the vertical where it nests behind my fly, and adjusting my rucked ballsack so it's not being ground by the crotch seam. I can feel the cum seething in my nuts.

"Get those fucking legs apart," I remind her with a growl, as I reduce the coiled belt to a lash less than a foot long. I close in to put one hand on her ass, rubbing my palm harshly over the tender flesh. She's burning like a furnace. I picture Appentak's poisons pulsing in her capillaries, making her crazy with need. You could heat the room with that ass. You could warm yourself through a Russian winter.

It's absolutely the most beautiful thing I've ever had my hands on.

She whimpers and complies. Legs open, shaking. The hot smell of her sex rising.

I hit upward, without warning. The leather belt-tip snaps up against her pussy, and all the shorts in the world couldn't save her from the sting on her clit. She screams. One hit and her legs buckle; two and she goes down, sobbing. Her hips jerk.

She's coming. She's actually *coming*. Fuck me, that is an incredible sight.

I have so much wood right now I could stake a goddamn vampire through the heart with it.

Yet she still hasn't let go. She's hanging at arms' length from the bars. I'm glad she can't see my face; she probably imagines my expression's stern and masterful. Far from it, Shanna. I'm fighting to control my breath.

I scoop her up bodily with one arm, pulling her back and

her ass against me. Her toes barely touch the floor. "You can let go," I whisper in her ear, dropping the belt with an ostentatious flourish.

She wriggles. The scrape of my fly teeth and buttons must be agonizing on her whipped ass. Her hands stay locked on the horizontal bars.

Oh Christ … *I shouldn't have touched my cock*. This is killing me. I have definitely stepped over the line now. I press my lips to her temple and slide my free hand around her throat, quieting her sobs. The bite-marks have long-since faded, healing with that unnatural quickness we know so well, so that her throat is slender and smooth and horribly vulnerable. Her weight is nothing in my arms. That ass of hers is a fucking miracle, yielding to the jut of my cock. And my need is a furnace, its roar filling my head.

"This," I growl, the words spilling from my lips as I rub my stiff cock against her: "this is why I don't stake female vampires."

And there. She knows. She knows my dirtiest, darkest secret.

This is why I don't get close. This is why it's a different girl every time, why I stick to the guarded, limited interaction of a knee-trembling quickie up against a wall, a blowjob in the back room, some frantic hand-action in the toilet cubicle. The strange sort of politeness to even the roughest casual fuck, because you're not intruding any further than the physical shell. You're not asking for trust or secrets or any of that shit. Keep it casual and you never have to let them see what's below the surface.

She lets go of the bar. One hand, anyway; it falls away to where I cannot see it.

Oh crap.

Reining myself in, jaw clenched, I let her slight weight

slip from my arms; I don't let her go exactly—my hands are still on her, her throat is in my grasp—but I let her feet take her weight again. "You understand, don't you?" I confess angrily. "The things that turn me on … they're not right. The things I want to do. To you."

And then I stop talking because her hand—I can't see it—her hand is sliding between us, up toward the small of her back: rubbing over my leather-sheathed cock, searching out my fly, tugging, wriggling, grasping my hot hard length. *Jesus wept*, she has it in her hand; she is measuring its length with each stroke. I am dreaming, I am dead and I have gone to a heaven so wrong it is perfect. I hear my own grunt.

"Fuck, bitch," I groan. "Do you know where this is going to take you?"

"Help me," she whispers, her throat thrumming under my tightening hand.

No. No, don't. I don't know the way out of this place. I'm as lost as you are.

"Fuck," I say. "You're going to regret that." I always carry a knife sheathed left-handed at the small of my back: a silver blade with a serrated steel edge. Whipping it out, I reach under her raised arm and slip the point beneath the stretched fabric of her sports top. "Don't let go," I snarl, and I feel her other hand tighten on my cock as I saw through the horrible elastic fabric, right up her breastbone. The cotton springs open and her tits bounce free. For a moment I let my blade lie along the valley of her sternum, while I contemplate the view.

Shanna doesn't trust her breasts: I can tell that from the way she always wears high necklines and sports bras to minimize their jut and their jiggle. She doesn't like what they might do, unfettered. Right now they're slippery with sweat. The last time

I saw her nipples they were haloed in vampire-bites and swollen from clamping; they don't look as big now, but exposure makes them pucker eagerly, like they're begging for punishment. I like that. If I was a vampire, I'd never stop biting Shanna's tits—except maybe to bite her pussy. Gently I prick her right nipple with the very tip of my knife.

"I could make you bleed, so easily." I whisper.

She doesn't answer, just writhes her big sore ass against me, whimpering, and squeezes my shaft. Her nipple, though, responds to the tease of the cold metal by standing bullet-hard. I imagine pricking her tit with the point, just a little—enough to raise a scarlet bead, that's all. Enough to remind her of what Appentak took from her, over and over again, as he fed.

I slam the knife, point-on, into the wooden support of the bar, and it sticks, quivering, just left of her hand. That gives me a hand free to grab that foolish nipple and roll it between thumb and finger, grinding it over my knuckles. I'm not gentle. She cries out.

"Yes!"

My other hand is still on her throat; I transfer my grip just slightly, to her jaw, and pull her face up and toward me. As I brutalize her willing nipple, my mouth searches out hers.

She hates that. I feel the change as her writhing turns to struggle. "No!" she squeals though her stretched throat, trying to avert her face. She doesn't want to be kissed. But I want it, and I know which of us is the stronger. I let her fight me, though. I let her kick and push and thrash and try to climb up my body, and even get one leg up on the lower bars to push back at me. In fact, that plays right into my hands; it gives me the angle I need to abandon her tit (with one last twist) and shove my hand down her shorts, forcing my fingers into the slippery chaos of her pussy.

Jeez. She arches and heaves and cries out, but her mouth is muffled by mine and when she parts her soft lips to shriek, my tongue is in there at once. I don't know what it is she has against kissing but I'm not taking *No* for an answer, and my hand knows exactly what it's doing with her clit in that steamy wet darkness, and soon she is taut and spasming, and moments later she surrenders her orgasm with a cry that I swallow.

And in all that time she does not let go of my cock, or the bar.

Her face is wet with tears, her sobs hiccuping in her throat. For a moment I hold her quite gently, my mouth gazing over hers, enjoying the territory yielded to it. She even kisses me back.

"That's better," I murmur. "Now, let go."

She goes limp, hands falling free. At last. Now I know I can do anything with her I want. *Anything.* I choose to turn her and set her back to the wall-bars, pinning her with barely any pressure, one hand holding her throat. She's nearly naked but for the rags of her bra and those useless, sex-and-sweat-soaked shorts. I allow her time to get her strength back, entertaining myself by tugging at her nipples until they are both swollen equally erect, the way I like them.

At last she opens her eyes. It's the first time we're looked each other in the face since I sent her in here. My breath catches in my throat. Shattered, flushed, trembling, Shanna has never looked more lovely. And my lust is howling now.

"Look what you've done to me, bitch," I tell her softly, searching out the most boorish, loaded words I can think of. I let go of her neck, drawing a finger down her slick breastbone. "Look."

She lowers her gaze to where my cock is spearing out

from my open leathers. Gratifyingly for me, her eyes widen.

"Well, it's not going to blow itself," I say, gravely. "Get down there and kiss it. Or am I going to have to hit you again?"

Her pupils dilate, but she falls to her knees. I take a step or two back across the mat, mostly because I like to see her crawl after me. When I let her catch up, she opens her mouth and tries to wrap it round my bobbing bell-end.

Shit, no. If I let her do that I'm going to come in seconds flat, and I haven't finished with her yet. The possibilities are still too various. So I grab her hair and pull her off, shaking her head back and forth with some roughness. "No! Were you listening to me? I said *kiss* it. Kiss my big dick like it's your boyfriend."

She gets the message. I push my leathers down until they're barely hanging from my hips, to give her proper access, and watch with satisfaction as she plants kisses upon me—my hairy ballsack practically blue now with compression; the thick underside of my shaft; all the way up to my glans and back down. She kisses with reverence and sincere enthusiasm, though she can't quite restrain herself from using a little tongue as well as those pretty lips; there's a viscid drip of pre-cum oozing from my cock-slit and she laps that up, nuzzling at the source. I let her get away with that; I'm not an unreasonable man. I put my hands behind my head and stretch my back as I revel in the feel of her mouth on my erect cock and her hot breath on my pubes. She makes the most charming little whimpers, almost below the threshold of hearing, and I'm half-conscious of the wiggle of her hips as she squirms her ass.

When I look down again from my pinnacle, it takes me a moment to realize what's changed. First thing I see is that she's got her hands behind her back, her wrists crossed as if bound. Second—her hands hide this for a moment—is that she's not wearing those shorts any more. Her hips and ass are both equally bare; she's wriggled the garment off as far as her thighs. So I'm looking down now at her big thrashed ass, and there's nothing between me and her open pussy anymore except my hesitation.

I step back from her worshipful lips, trying to think straight. Shanna tips gently forward, her eyes closed, until her face is on the mat and she is pointing her burning blush at the roof.

Shit.

When I'd first released her from her chains, that was how she'd fallen. Face down, butt up, her hands bound with soft leather behind her, her eyes swathed in darkness. She'd had no idea it was me. I should have revealed myself then. I should have pulled off her blindfold and told her it was all going to be okay. But I'd hunkered there, close enough to touch any part of her, close enough to smell her skin, breathing the perfume of her open sex; my hands nerveless and my heart pounding and my cock swollen in my pants. Just staring. Wanting so much to touch.

Wanting, even in my rage and pity, to fuck her.

Jealous as all hell of Appentak.

I walk a semi-circle on the crash-mat, so that I'm standing behind her. I can see the moist pink pout of her pussy-split between her abused thighs. I can see the dark crinkle of her undefended ass hole.

"Are you giving me this?" I ask. I sound gruff. "Are you offering me this fine pussy as a gift, bitch? Because you know you can't give a present and then take it back."

There'd been something sticking out between her cheeks, that day. A silvery chrome-plated flare of metal, finely crafted in the shape of an elaborate artsy fish-tail. The fish head and body, as far as I could tell, must have been wedged deep in her ass; I could see the pink rim of her hole stretched about the metal. There was one hole in the decorative fin that looked designed to slip a finger into.

Jeez. Was this a trap? Or just him keeping her prepped and open for business?

Tenderly, with great caution, I'd eased a digit into the metalwork and tried a gentle tug. I was poised to stop if she showed any sign of pain, or any hint that I was damaging her. But behind a narrow neck the metal was smooth, and it had slid out of her easily, all the way. Not fish-shaped at all: a curved, chrome-plated cock, heavy in my hand. I'd looked back at her ass and it had gaped at me, the sphincter fluttering like a little mouth.

I'd wanted so much to feed my stiff cock into that pleading, hungry hole.

Instead, I'd untied Shanna's wrists and wrapped her in a bed-sheet, and only when she was safely draped did I pull off her blindfold.

Now I'm standing in the gym and looking down on that same open cleft. On that same soft, splayed, juicy-wet pussy. She's kneeling over like she did that day; wordless, everything on offer. Just like she had done when she thought I was Appentak come to fuck her.

I crouch down behind her. One hand descends in a slap on her left cheek—more noise than force, but she's so tenderized she utters a breathy squeak. "So you'd better be sure," I growl, and my next slap is underhand and right on her open pussy. There's a splat from her wetness, and muffled yelp from up front. She pushes back against my cupped palm, panting.

Oh, yes. This is where I claim it back for the living.

I'm pushing my cock into her before I draw another

breath. Her slick hot sex is like a bull's-eye, and I strike home in three firm strokes. Christ, she's just *perfect*. So tight. So slippery. I grip her hips and I maul her hot ass and then I grab her wrists in my hands and uncross them, pulling them back toward her hips, like her arms are reins and I'm riding her hard. She squeals, her noise protest or pleasure—but how am I to know the difference, or even if there is a difference for her? Oh God, I'm going to come quickly. It's just too good and I've been wanting for so long and I've hurt her and *she's let me she's let me she's given me everything because she wants my hurt and my force and my cock*—

I feel the wave of my orgasm start to crest and I whip out, dropping her wrists. No matter how much I want to come inside her, that's not something we've negotiated, and I don't want to be a jerk. I grab my cock left handed and pump it in a slither of her pussy-juice, and the first convulsion of my nuts sends a great pale spurt up her back and over her red-hot ass. It's like time has slowed to a crawl: I see everything in high-def and bullet-time. The splat of my jizz right up the crack of her ass as the second jet slops out, heavier but just as copious. The reach of her hands behind her, grabbing her ass-cheeks and sinking her fingers into the reddened flesh: pulling them wide. The glistening pool of cum I've somehow managed to target right on the dusky pucker of her ass-hole.

I've got another pulse on its way and I shouldn't do it—I know I shouldn't.

I don't want to be a dick.

But I can't resist. I cannot fucking resist.

I jam my cock to that winking iris and push inside, flooding her ass with everything I've got left. For me it's bliss; a moment when I'm God Almighty. For her … We're lubed a bit with her pussy-juice and my cum, and she's tripping on endorphins, I know that—but I've done nothing to prepare her; no fingerplay, no waiting time. It must hurt.

And apparently that's enough to send her crashing into another climax. As I bear down upon her she lets go one more time, howling like a demon, juddering and thrashing and humping her hips.

It's just like impaling a vampire.

And afterwards she lies still. She even dozes off after a while, curled a little in the compass of my embrace. I hold her softly, and I stroke her hair and her flank and her thigh, trailing light fingers over the tender welts. I'm not scared to touch her, now.

I've claimed her back for the living. Not for me: for her.

At last she stirs and rolls over, rather gingerly, onto her back so that she can look up at me. Her eyes are calm. She smiles, just a bit.

I touch my finger to my lips, then brush the proxy kiss against her mouth. It's too soon, I think, to push for more—and shit, I'm never sure where I stand with Shanna. But she doesn't seem to object to the gesture; she only raises her eyebrows a little.

I sit up and reach for the bike jacket I dropped aside earlier. I'm a lefty, so I had to have my custom gun-holster sewn into the lining on my right side. Inside the original pocket is an object I've kept there over my heart for weeks. I draw it out now.

It's Appentak's chrome-plated ass dildo.

I put it into Shanna's hand as she lies there. Her eyes widen.

"The next time your demons get out," I tell her, touching the smooth silver tenderly, "you're going to put that in your lovely tight asshole—so you're good and open and ready—and then you're going to come to me. And I will fuck the living hell out of your demons."

"Will that hurt?" she whispers.

"It will. I promise."

Shanna nods. "Good. That's what I need."

Oh welcome, welcome, sweetling! Do sit down and talk with me; I feel like a chitter-chatter tonight. You're not afraid, are you? Is it the way I look that's got you staring? Oh, little man, don't be foolish … there are things out there in the dark that are far more likely than I to tear you limb from limb. Believe me!

There now. That's better. Comfortable, are we? Let me build up the fire and get a look at you.

Hmm. You're a funny-looking thing, for a sailor. I've seen a few of them over the years, washed up on the beaches. Leathery men, most of them. But you … you have such pale, soft hands …

Oh, not a sailor then? An *actor*? Well, that explains this book I found among the flotsam. It's a script, is it not? Is it yours?

Ah.

Famous, is it? Truly?

Well, I should be flattered. Perhaps I would be, if it were such not a tissue of lies.

Hah! Make-believe, you say? Tell me—which island did you imagine you had been wrecked upon, little man? Malta? Corsica? No—you are further off your course than you knew! Hee hee. What an irony. You have been blown all this way to bring me … Well. *This*.

Heh. Did you imagine, looking at me, that I could read?

Prospero taught me, little man. Well, strictly speaking, he and his whelp taught Caliban … but Caliban is my son, and I can see through his eyes. By the by, he is watching this fire from the trees yonder even as we speak, sweetling. If you were to stray too far from the light of the flames …

Shush. Sit yourself down. Panic will not save you. Tell me about this play. I want to know. Have you acted in it yourself?

And which part did you play?

Hah. How delicious a trick Fate has played upon you—wrecked upon these shores not once, but twice: first in make-believe, and then in the flesh. Tell me, did it irritate you to have to play out such a weak excuse for a story, night after night?

Magic and wonder indeed. That is some excuse, I suppose. Yet did it never occur to you to ask why, if Prospero was such a very great magus as he claimed, he did not haul his poor scrawny shanks off the island by magic? Or, indeed, why he let himself be exiled here in the first place? If he could raise the dead by his so potent command, and pluck up great trees by the roots—could he not conjure himself a boat and a fair wind? No? He must have told some of the tale when he returned to Milan, certainly—for the warp of this play is truthfully strung, even if the weft is lies. Yet there are holes in the cloth that even a sweetling fool such as you should have wondered at.

Well, listen now. Perhaps you will learn something. You know my name?

Yes, that's right. And that is the very first lie in the play, for it names me dead before the curtain lifts. Yet as you can see, I am not dead. This is my Isle, and I am of its earth—not of Algeria! How I laughed when I read that!—and I cannot be slain. I have been here ... many years. I forget how many. I am old, little man. I have mislaid many memories.

But Prospero I have not forgotten. No.

The Isle is mine. It is the Omphalos—the navel of the world. I rule from the earth, by night. The sky above and the day: they belong to Ariel. *Belonged*, I should say. I ... I think we had other names once, long ago. I do not remember them. It does not matter. All stories are leaves on one tree, and the branches may be long but they are all fed by the same roots. Names come and go, like dead leaves. It is perhaps better to forget them, in the end.

Are you hungry, little man? I have a haunch of meat here that is well-cooked and only a little gnawed upon.

Yes, it is from the wreck of your vessel.

Do not ask that. You are hungry, or not. And the night is long, and my story only just started.

Ariel ruled the Isle by day, and I ruled by night. At dusk and dawn we met, as husband and wife, to act out our carnal dreams. At sunset I would ride astride his long beam, and at sunrise he would pin me flat and plow my deeps. His seed came forth in great quantities, I recall—like sea spume, or like the white fluff of poplar-trees blown upon the wind. When I dug my long nails into his golden flesh, then the dawn would come up blood red.

I had many children by him. Have you not read that this Isle is *full of noises*? We are surrounded by legions; if you have not seen them yet, then it is because your mortal eyes are too dull. But this is the sorrow of it: Ariel let live only those babes I spawned that resembled him, that were of his delicate and airy nature. Those childer that bore my stamp—the dark and earthy, the heavy of flesh—those he hated, and devoured at first sight.

No. For years I bore this, until even I grew weary. And with age fewer and fewer babes were birthed at all. So when at last I whelped my youngest son Caliban, and saw that he favored me and not his father, I knew that I must hide him to preserve his life.

Oh, have you seen my boy then? Don't look so green. Think you he is ugly? I do not. Are not his teeth strong and keen?

Isn't his skin, hued with all the shot-silk colors of oil upon water, soft and smooth? The eyes that he opened upon me that first night, in such perfect trust, were as golden and beautiful as the eyes of a toad—and if two eyes are deemed lovely, must not *many* be even more enchanting?

I gave to Ariel a stone wrapped in blood-stained birthing cloths, and watched as he swallowed it whole. The babe I hid anew within the caverns of my body. And inside me, Caliban grew. But at last the night came when I could carry his weight no longer, so huge of limb was my child; so I birthed him a second time, half-grown. Even then, we both knew he was not safe. We went under cover of darkness to Ariel's crag, and as the first light of the sun touched the sky with gray, Caliban seized his sire and I split a great pine tree, and together we thrust Ariel into the cleft and closed it tight. It was over in moments: when it was done Ariel was entrapped and my child was safe.

You think I played my husband false? Don't bother to answer: I see it in your eyes. Well, you may be reassured to know that I have suffered great pangs over the years for my part in the betrayal. I missed his cock within me and his hands upon me; the ache of my loss brought forth great groans of anguish from my innermost being every dawn and dusk. For twelve long years.

That was when Prospero came to this Isle, with his infant daughter in his arms.

Listen well and mark this: the deposed Duke of Milan was no great sorcerer, however he styled himself afterwards. He was a second-rate alchemist—a mumbling book-wizard—a natural philosopher whose philosophy went no further than his own self-importance. But he was a man, and my cunt ached beyond bearing for the rough touch of a man. I saved his life, building him a cell in which to hide him from my own son; bringing him the fruits of the Island; fetching the contents of his leaky vessel from where it had foundered upon the rocks of the bay. I even let the girl-child live, though Caliban licked his drooling chops at the thought of such a tender mouthful. I forbade my boy to harm either of them.

In return I asked only that Prospero service my appetites. It was, I admit, not as easy for him as for my poor Ariel, for he was not so well-endowed. But he was a man of ingenuity and imagination, and where cock would not suffice, fist and forearm would. I demanded only that he persevere in his efforts.

In return for my mercy he betrayed me.

He must have found Ariel's prison while wandering the Isle under the foul sunlight. I sleep during the day, and Caliban hides from the bright day-eye and emerges only when it is clouded over, for he partakes of my nature. Prospero, as I found out later, made a secret compact with Ariel, to release him from his pinched torment in exchange for a vow of service. He had enough of the Art from his ridiculous books of gramarye to do that much. Perfidious mortal: he cozened Caliban too—my own flesh and blood!—by promising him the girl Miranda in marriage when she grew old enough, if only the boy did not interfere between Prospero and myself. Poor innocent Caliban—he had never known the sweet touch of a wife's love, nor did he have any idea how long he would be expected to wait. The thought of marriage was enough to turn his head.

I found this out one sunset, when I woke to find Ariel already had me in his grasp. I screamed for my son to aid me, but he did not appear. Then Ariel split an olive tree with a thunderbolt and wedged me inside before closing the trunk like a vice, leaving my head sticking out on one side and my nether quarters on the other. Outrage made me shriek and kick as he took advantage of my helplessness to ravish me above and below: outrage and, I confess, relief at last. He'd had more sense than me, to leave those parts he had use for free to the air. Oh, how I'd missed that golden cock stretching and pounding me! His service was swift and brutal; once again he flooded my cunt with his seed, and watched with satisfaction as it ran out over my thighs.

There I remained for twelve years: one for each that Ariel had suffered at my hand. Fair's fair, is it not, sweetie? Through sun and storm, night and day. Twice in each diurnal round my husband would visit to fill whichever of my orifices he chose. Sometimes Prospero would stop by too—whether from malice or frustrated longing for a female body I neither know nor care—and make furtive and wordless use of me, though that mortal man wisely eschewed my mouth and concentrated on my rear parts, flipping up his magician's robe to stick his prod into my holes and jiggle himself to the mystic revelation he sought. Personally, I could barely feel him. And Caliban—my poor son: as his new status upon the Isle became apparent, as his suffering grew, he woefully missed the loving shelter my body had afforded him for so long, and although he could not squeeze his whole bulk into my womb, he would repeatedly stuff his aching boy-parts back into my cleft, while he wept and called upon me to hold him. And so he afforded both of us temporary comfort.

That's a strange look on your face, little man.

You must surely pity Caliban, even after reading this lying play. The magician had the upper hand on this Isle, and the monster must obey him. He had been promised the girl Miranda, and then—poor natural—found he would have to wait a decade and more, even if Prospero intended to keep his word … which in all honesty I doubt was a notion that that man entertained for a second. And now his own father was free and taking every mean opportunity to torment him with cramps and urchins and blithering voices that would not let him sleep. Prospero at first tried to keep my son as a kind of pet, to tame and teach him. But that was not to last. There was too much hostility between Caliban and Ariel.

Nor was Ariel happy. He was free of the pine, but no longer master of the Isle. Now he was at Prospero's beck and call, promised to his service and held by the power of his own vow.

Was Prospero triumphant, then? No! He found himself in a cleft stick, as much as I was, and almost as royally fucked. He had power in the Isle, but only because he held Ariel on the leash of his promise. He could have almost anything he wanted within its physical bounds, but Ariel's influence did not extend beyond its coastal waters, and so he could not escape. And he feared Ariel, and Caliban, and even me, because we were all stronger than him and time was running out. Twelve years he had, and no longer: then Ariel's service would be complete. No, there was no trust between Prospero and any of the others.

Not even Miranda his daughter.

Little girls grow up into young women. Women want certain things. And she—this perfect child of Nature, unspoilt by the sins and coquetry of civilization—she took what she wanted without remorse or guilt. Nature is not tender, little man; Nature is not good. It is human society that teaches law, and restraint, and shame.

Prospero did his best, I am sure. He tried to educate her. But what child still listens to their sire or dam as they grow older? Alas … When they are small we are everything to them; when they grow up the opinions of their forebears wither in value, to less than those of the meanest stranger. So Miranda first loved her father, then laughed at him, then despised him. But for all that, she had Prospero's heart.

Oh, it would have done you good to see the girl, little man. She ran about the Island barefoot in whatever rags took her fancy, her knees scraped and her hair a tangled fleece. Her cheeks were not roses but brown as beech-mast, her eyes like the pale hazel eyes of a wild hare. Her long legs would flash, bare as the limbs of a hind, as she ran. And those breasts—so sweetly ripe, so brown, so berry-tipped like the very bounty of autumn! She would climb trees to rob the birds' nests and crack their stolen eggs into her mouth, licking her wet pink lips. She swam in the turquoise waters and caught fish in her quicksilver hands. She danced naked upon the yellow sands with the half-seen get of Ariel.

They taught her many things, my airy children. With touches and tickles, and with caresses soft and light, they burnished that tanned skin and brought her to giggling and sighing and shivering with pleasure. Autumnal fruits swelled with juices nigh unto bursting; berry-nipples flushed and stood proud upon ripe and quivering breasts. She was a cornucopia-maiden; a harvest begging to be brought in; a feast aching to be eaten.

Poor Caliban, prowling at a distance, did not know what to make of such a morsel. He wanted with all his heart to be close to her, this beautiful nymph, but he hardly dared. He knew that Ariel would most likely be watching, invisible, and that any hurt he did Miranda would be most sternly punished. They had grown to adulthood together, and she had never shown any fear of her father's strange pet—how was she to know any better?—but he had been trained by diverse tortures to restrain his great strength about her. He scarcely dared approach her, even when she summoned him to help her climb a crag or move a log.

So when she took to lifting her ragged skirts and flashing

her rosy cunt lips at him, he did nothing but watch, bubbling miserably, feeling his great member swell painfully fat. She liked to make water while he was in the vicinity, lifting her dress right up around her waist to reveal her bottom and squatting with thighs apart, smiling slyly at him over her shoulder as she let go and pissed into the dry earth. She could lead him anywhere, all over the Isle, and he would follow mutely at a distance, his cock so engorged that its tip trailed in the dirt between his feet.

What, my sweetling—haven't you seen his prick? Well I'm sure you will, sooner or later. It is not an easy thing to hide, being so big as it is, and more like the limb of a great octopus than the pizzle of a land-beast: tapered and rubbery. Miranda would giggle at it when it rose, questing toward her. She liked the way it responded to the sight of her pert bottom or her furry slit. She liked the way Caliban could not take his eyes off her, could not stay away; and his swollen cock was the testament to his discomfort.

One day she beckoned my Caliban to follow her down onto the beach at low tide, and into a sea-cave exposed there. The light inside was dim and the rock walls smelled of salt and weed, which lifted the poor monster's spirits. Seeking Miranda out in the gloom—he opens more of his eyes as the lack of light demands it—he found her sitting on the damp and silvery sand, her knees raised and spread wide. Between her thighs glistened the wet patch of her sex, pointing straight at him, and she was stroking it gently, holding her labia open with spread fingers.

"Have you seen one of these anywhere else on the Isle, Caliban?" she asked.

"My mother has one," he mumbled, falling to his knees, the better to contemplate the wondrous thing before him. "But hers is much bigger. Yours is … pretty."

"Do you like it?"

"It is beautiful," said he, poor simple thing, as his member crept toward her across the sandy floor like a sea-snake. Indeed, he could not imagine anything more bewitching than that secret pout, coral-hued as some treasure of the reefs. With all his being he longed for it.

"Look closer," she told him. And he, simpleton that he was, crouched down and crawled until he was between her ankles. His great nostrils flared and dripped, catching her wild and musky scent, and his breath gusted on her thighs. Shouldn't she have been afraid of that maw, those teeth? Yet she did not so much as tremble.

"Does it smell nice?" she wondered.

"It is the best smell in the whole world," said the monster who knew nothing of the world. He was drooling now: thick viscid ropes of slime.

"Kiss it," she ordered.

"I … I cannot kiss, Miranda." His lips were not designed for such delicacies.

"Then you may lick it. You know how to do that."

So he obeyed, and at the first lap of his tongue—big enough to cover the whole of her wanton sex—Miranda sighed and arched and closed her eyes. Encouraged, and dizzy with daring, he repeated the action. Each slippery lick seemed to send her further and further into her trance of delight, and as far as my son was concerned, each mouthful tasted of the nectar of Heaven. Soon he had her writhing at every touch, and clawing at the smooth skin of her thighs, and panting *Yes Yes Oh Yes* like one of Prospero's chanted spells. Then she bucked and squealed and thrashed, pulling away from him in spasmodic twitches and then sprawling to the sand with her chest heaving.

He's not overly bright, my Caliban, but knew he had not drawn blood, and he guessed that she must have experienced something like the gush of release he felt when he wrestled his own length, alone in his kennel. His need for release was very strong now—nearly overwhelming. He rolled the girl from her side onto her back, and when she spread her legs his member rose waving. Quickly, he pulled her dress off over her head. He wanted to see her naked; all of her. Those soft breasts, that narrow waist—she was slender as spring and ripe as autumn all at once, and the wanting of her drove him out of his wits. Hunching over her, he stooped and licked her from sex to throat, lavishing his tongue upon her breasts. The girl groaned with pleasure. And the slim tip of Caliban's cock inched forward into the tight wet embrace of her cunt, almost unnoticed at first … until it began to swell.

A shadow crossed the mouth of the cave then—perhaps no more than a gull in flight. Caliban, who would have normally flinched, did not look up, did not care.

So in the end, even Miranda betrayed Prospero. Ariel, all a-quiver with malice, brought news to the master that he *must come see*—and when he did come see, it was Miranda and Caliban writhing together in a sand-floored cave, the girl's ankles about her ears as the monster plundered her narrow slot with a glistening prick that one would have sworn was too bulky to fit in that virgin hole. Pulse after pulse of thick swell surged up its length, quite visible to the onlookers, and soup-thick seed squirted out around its girth with each wave, blue-gray and pearlescent, from a vessel already filled to overflowing. And all the while the girl sobbed encouragement.

Now, sweetling—you are all flushed. Perhaps you huddle too close to the fire.

So, you see, that was when Caliban the bestial pet

became Caliban the tortured, beaten slave. It did not matter that the girl had been willing and more—not to her father. Now Ariel was given full license to hound the poor boy.

You doubt me, I sense? Yes, I know all this, even though I was not there! As soon as I found myself entrapped in my tree, I sank my mind down through its roots and spread it through the earth of the Isle. I saw everything that happened in this small domain, for twelve years. All the vindictive fear and the arguments and the bullying and the rage. Trapped on our rock in the wide sea … Oh, we were just like a human family.

And I almost felt sorry for Prospero … His daughter a monster's whore, the sands of his power running through the glass day by day by day. Nor could he bring Miranda back into the fold of his fatherly authority. She simply fled him, inured to his exhortations and his imprecations alike, and he had no iron in his soul to set Ariel upon her. The girl continued to dally with Caliban whenever she could steal the opportunity. And yes, each time it happened Caliban would be beaten severely, but that never gave her pause—I suppose she thought that such a great strong beast must be created to endure pain and that this was the natural way of things. She had no other example in her life. No, neither did fear stop my poor boy. The temptation of her lithe young body squealing and mewling beneath his bulk meant more to him than all the punishment he had to accept.

Miranda did confront Ariel, I will say that much for her. "Why must you be so cruel to him?" she asked once, scowling.

"I hate him," said Ariel, hovering a foot about the earth. He was visible to her that afternoon, and wore the shape that Prospero preferred to see him in: a golden youth with a wicked, beautiful face and hair that crackled with lightning. For reasons of modesty—not his own—he was clad about the hips in a billowing cloth that somehow never slipped or floated away.

"Why?" she demanded, stubbornly.

"Because he is ugly." Ariel swooped up into a tree branch, and just as swiftly dived down again to stare into her face. Even human-sized, he loomed over Miranda. "I hate all ugly, creeping things. I love the beautiful and the dainty. The mere sight of Caliban offends me."

"Most of all when he fucks me, I think—you can't wait to tell my father."

"Such a thing is disgusting." Ariel's face twisted. "When I see him befouling your sweet flesh … it enrages me."

Miranda made an inspired grab into the baroque folds of his loincloth, and closed her fingers about a long cock, jutting and fully erect. She watched Ariel's eyes widen. "Yes," she said. "This is very angry—I can tell." She gave it a squeeze, finding it harder than even Caliban's blubbery muscular organ, and surprisingly thick. "I think it wants to hurt me."

"I would never hurt you," Ariel said hoarsely. "You are too fair."

"But if Caliban is to be punished," she said with a pout, stroking him from crown to base with long sure caresses, "shouldn't I take chastisement too? Should you not rain blows upon me with this big hard rod of yours?"

"Prospero would never let me punish you," he said, gasping.

"What if I *let* you chastise me? Just a little?" She released him suddenly, and as he reeled she stepped away, turned her back and pulled up her skirt to bare the beautiful round globes of her behind. Bending from the hips, she widened her stance, presenting him with a dusky split, a pink glisten, and an inverted smirk. "You do not have to tell my father."

As helpless as his son had been, Ariel was drawn forward, smooth upon the air, to touch that place where her scratched and dusty thighs met, and became Paradise. "You are wet," he whispered, sinking his fingers into her.

"Oh, you can make me wetter," she told him, wriggling upon his intrusion and trying to draw him deeper. His cock was as hard as a bone; it was an easy matter—indeed it seemed inevitable—to feed it to her slick entrance and push inside her.

"Where the beast fucks, there fuck I," he muttered. A hand on either hip claimed her so that he could thrust to the hilt, and when she squealed in delight every bird in the wood rose from its tree in alarm.

"Yes! Yes! Yes!" she cried.

From that moment on it became Ariel's dutiful custom to chastise her thus every time the girl disgraced herself with the monster. Indeed, he often could not wait until the trespass was committed and over with—as she knelt between Caliban's thighs, sucking upon his cock, he'd appear and swiftly pierce her with his golden dart from behind, and thus offence and retribution became a single thing. Any time of day you might find Miranda with her flushed face in the earth and her ass in the air, while Ariel crouched astride her bottom, thrusting wildly between her cheeks yet never touching the ground. Any time of night you might hear the girl's choking groans as Caliban slurped upon her coral garden while spilling his seed by the pint into her open mouth.

Sometimes Miranda would stagger to her bed drunk with exhaustion, almost unable to keep her shaking legs beneath her, her bare body painted from tit to thigh with pearlescent gray and creamy white semen that mingled yet refused to mix; more spunk glistening on her chin, and seeping from her well-used holes with each step to lubricate the cleft of her delectable bottom. And in her eyes—such gratification and triumph!

Caliban escaped with gentler punishment too, from that time onward. It was the nearest my husband and my son had ever been to truce.

And that is the point at which Alonso and Ferdinand and Antonio made their entrance.

Ah, you've been waiting for them to appear, haven't you? The melancholy King of Naples and his romance-addled son. The usurping Duke of Milan, Prospero's own treacherous brother. This is Prospero's moment; his big chance to change everything. The stage is set for confrontation and trickery and revenge!—and then the happy-ever-after of forgiveness and love. That's what you've learned from this play script, isn't it?

It wasn't quite like that in reality.

I don't remember the comic relief either. Certainly, there were other courtiers and servants wandering the Isle after their royal shipwreck … Caliban did meet a few, to be sure, but the encounters were brief, bloody, and short in witty conversation. Perhaps Trinculo and his like were there, perhaps not—they never did anything worthy of much note is all *I* can say, little man. Such clownish passages in the play I suspect of being naught but low amusement for the cheap seats.

Ferdinand though—his is a face I can still recall. A pretty youth with green eyes. And this verbose scribbler got it right that he washed up on shore alone, though I don't believe it had anything to do with Prospero's wiles. Our kindly magician was too busy directing Caliban to harry his brother across the Isle, picking off the foot-soldiers one by one.

No, Ferdinand came across Miranda by chance. The princely castaway, finding himself, as he thought, the sole survivor on a barren shore, showed a marked lack of wisdom—unlike the common sailors who had the sense to stay on the shore where there was fresh water from a river mouth, and fish to be caught from the rocks—and struck inland to look for food and water. Three hours later he was lucky enough to blunder across a shallow stream and slake his salt-parched mouth. It was as he knelt there, filling his empty belly, that he heard a low cry through the reeds, and managed to creep upstream and spy upon Miranda unseen.

Like all good nymphs of legend, she was discovered naked and bathing alone. Well … I say alone: Ariel was fucking her, but he was not visible to anyone's eyes but hers. What Ferdinand saw was a naked girl on hands and knees in the sandy shallows of the stream, her brown-tipped breasts underlit by the shimmer of the water, an expression of ecstasy upon her face as her hips jerked and quivered. It must have been quite an arresting vision, and I am not sure what he made of it. Certainly Ferdinand did not rush in to destroy the charming tableau—not until the participants (both seen and unseen) were done. Ariel took wing and flitted away. Miranda did not exit the scene but lay upon her belly in the shallow water to cool herself, a smile of satisfaction upon her plump lips.

I think Ferdinand suffered from too classical an education. He rose from behind his screen of reeds, his trousers tented by youthful enthusiasm, and waded toward the daydreaming girl. "What are you?" he asked as she opened her eyes. "A naiad? A goddess? Or some maiden of savage race?"

Miranda sat upright, water streaming down her breasts and belly into the wash about her loins. She made no attempt to cover herself, but stared him up and down. "I am Miranda," she said, laughing. "And what strange beast are you? I've never seen your like upon this Isle."

The young prince was not used to such bold looks or rude words, I fear. He flushed. "A savage wench, then, though you have been gifted with the tongue of civilization."

"Tongue of civilization?" Miranda asked, mocking his courtly turn of speech. She stuck her tongue out, looked down at it cross-eyed, then wiggled it at him. "Is this the one you mean?"

Ferdinand, alas, was not accustomed to such provocation. He stepped forward and made a clumsy grab for her, missing by some margin as she jerked backward. She splashed water directly in his face, causing him to stumble at the apex of his lunge and slip to his knees in the stream. "Missed," she announced happily, wriggling to her feet.

Ferdinand rose, aghast, held out his hands and made another grab for her, meaning no doubt to make her rue her impudence. Miranda skipped backwards up the stream-bed, laughing at the suddenly novelty. This strange man had come out of nowhere and now he was chasing her. She liked this game very much; it did not occur to her that his intent might be serious. As he staggered after her through the shallows, kicking water everywhere, she kept just beyond his reach, leaping far more sure-footedly than he. When she left the water and took to the river-bank he did a little better, twice managing to get a hand briefly on her bare flank, but she slipped from his grasp. Battered as he was by the shipwreck, his strength was at a low ebb, and at last he stood still, winded.

"Giving up already?" she mocked him.

"Come here!" he ordered her, angry and confused. As the heir to Naples, he had never in his life met a woman who did not treat him with respect. From the shyly blushing ingénues presented to him at court, to their ambitious and ingratiating mothers—and even more so the servants and the whores he'd encountered—not one had ever dared forget their inferiority in his presence. No one had ever treated him with the derision this naked wildwoman did now.

Miranda laughed. "Shall we play hide-and-seek next?" she asked, putting her fingers over her eyes. "Shall I count to a hundred and come look for you?"

He took advantage of her momentary carelessness and lunged, without a word, catching her about the waist and pulling her to him. Miranda shrieked with excitement and fought to wriggle free—but all her rough wrestling with Caliban had never taught her any caution, so impervious was the monster to any pain she could inflict. Her elbow smacked Ferdinand across the temple and he, poor youth, went flat upon the ground, stunned. When he opened his eyes the girl was straddling him.

"Harpy!" he gasped, but even as he reached to grab her shoulders she was yanking hard at the laces of his trousers, and all Ferdinand's righteous anger vanished in confusion as she bared his cock. His manhood had drooped with his tumble, but she fell upon it with her mouth and restored its wounded pride in seconds. The world, so far as Ferdinand was concerned, turned upside down. Then, as soon as she had him stiff, she rose and mounted him, staking her slick cunt upon his length with a whimper of pleasure. Her smooth hard thighs lifted her up and down with strong stokes, sending waves of delight through both of them at once. Her nails bit in to his ribs.

Ferdinand forgot to be angry. He thrust up into her as she thrust down upon him, and soon they were both glassy-eyed with lust and rigid with tension. She came to climax before he did—shocking him with her abandoned shrieks and pulled faces, but exciting him beyond measure too. He fucked and fucked, driving deeper into her, until he lost all control himself and let fly a plume of liquid fire into her belly.

He'd never known anything like it. Or like her.

Do you need to know more, little man? Prospero impressed his power upon Alonso King of Naples, through Ariel's tricks and torments (for once more-or-less accurately described in that play-script there). Enough to regain his title as Duke of Milan, and passage in the repaired vessel back to Italy. Ferdinand, besotted, begged Miranda to go with him. No, not as his bride: as his most privileged royal mistress. Such a come-down for his bloodline did not please Prospero, but he never could win an argument with his daughter, and the girl—being no virgin—was not suitable for marriage. Miranda was more than happy with her change in station. She could not wait to join human society in all its multiplicity and excitement. You've read what she said when she first laid eyes upon the motley gathering of men held captive in her father's cell, haven't you?

> *Oh wonder!*
> *How many goodly creatures are there here!*
> *How beauteous mankind is! Oh brave new world*
> *That has such people in't!*

That at least was reported truthfully … more or less. Nobles and commoners, old and young: such things did not matter to her. After her apprenticeship with the spirits of the Isle, fair Miranda was eager to spread her wings and partake of a little variety.

The wicked, usurping Duke Antonio … Did Prospero forgive him as this scribbler said? Of course not. Do you think the man such a fool? He didn't drown his books or break his staff either—what would have been the point of that? The magician had a reputation to keep up! No: he left his younger brother here upon the Isle when the ship rode away on the dawn, along with any members of the Milanese court who'd countenanced the coup all those years ago. Caliban, released from slavery at last, ate them all, eventually … one by one.

As for Ariel: Prospero freed him as promised. He was too nervous to do otherwise. But my husband left this place too. That was a surprise to me, I admit. Ariel chose to go with Miranda, and she was pleased enough to have him as her familiar spirit, though I do not know what her new lord thought of the arrangement.

No. I don't wholly understand that, I confess. But I'm sure she did well for herself thereafter.

And me? Caliban, grown to full strength, tore open the tree and released me from my prison. He was bitterly lonely without his wanton, you understand, and feeling contrite. I did not hold his part in my captivity against him. See—there *is* forgiveness in this story, even if it was bestowed by a witch upon a monster.

And now, it is told. That's the truth of it, sweetling.

The question is now, what to do with you? I'd not advise you to leave the firelight's reach. Caliban is prowling out there in the dark, and he has a taste for human flesh.

I'd suggest, little man, that you stay here and keep me company. There is an ache in my loins and a gape that needs filling. You may not have a sailor's strength of arms, but I'm sure you can apply that actor's imagination. Imagine that I am young and beautiful. Recall to your mind the emotions and urges of desire. Put them to use. Imagine I am Miranda, if you like. Are we not all but players, after all—pretending our parts?

Good.

I will look after you, sweetling.

Knight Takes Queen

The great wyrm had been dead a week by the time Lancelot returned to Camelot, dragging its severed head in a litter behind his horse, and more than a week before the occasion of his triumphal feast.

By the time the fifth remove was served, the reek from the head—which was displayed on a platter more usually reserved for serving up whole boars, in the center of the Great Hall—had crept up as far as the high table. The smell, reminiscent of rotting shellfish, turned the Queen's stomach, though she guessed that the quantities of wine and ale consumed had dulled the olfactory sensitivities of most of the Court.

"My lord," Guinevere begged, when she could stand it no longer. "Please, command the beast's head to be taken out into the courtyard."

Arthur raised an eyebrow at her over the top of his cup. "Is the sight too awful for your sensibilities, my Queen?" he asked.

It was the smell that bothered her—not the blood, or the head's fixed snarl of angled fangs, nor the sunken, cloudy eyes as big as rams' testicles—but Guinevere nodded. All Camelot loved her to play the role of tender-hearted queen, a Mother Mary upon Earth, interceding with her sterner King—compassionate where he must be just, and gentle where he was strong. That Arthur, moved by his love for her, gave way so often to her whims, offered them a picture of hope not just in this life but the next.

It was something Arthur had explained to her, soon after their marriage. "There must be justice," he'd said, "but also mercy. We are not barbarians, not any longer. And I must be seen to honor you, so that all men may honor their wives." Guinevere, who had come to him from a kingdom where older, rougher mores shaped men's lives, had been perplexed but obedient.

"Please," she repeated that night, laying her hand upon his. "Of your kindness, my King."

"Lancelot," said Arthur, turning to his right: "You are the hero of the hour and this trophy is yours, right bravely won. Will you suffer it to be taken from here, at my Queen's request?"

Lancelot stood to his feet. He was taller than the King— taller than most of the Knights of Camelot, except for oak-thewed Gawain—and the dark curls of his hair hung against skin tanned by a summer spent questing. Now that he was back at Court, every woman there looked upon his handsome features with desire. But the Queen's Champion had not publicly taken any leman at Court, and didn't even dally with the serving girls. His dark blue eyes were steady as they rested upon her, and she kept her expression serene, trusting to the candlelight to disguise the blush in her cheeks. "Whatever my Queen commands, that I will do," said he, lifting his cup to Guinevere. "My service is pledged to her."

Arthur nodded, visibly pleased. He signaled to the serving men. "Take it forth, and see that the skull is cleaned and mounted on the wall over Camelot's gate. For that is the greatest and foulest of dragon-kind that ever one of my knights slew single-handed, and all must remember."

Guinevere dipped her head to Lancelot, smiling a little. While the men bustled about with poles, preparing to hoist the stinking platter upon their shoulders, she excused herself momentarily from the table.

There was a private chapel upstairs, above the Great Hall, which was reserved for the King and Queen. It was a small chamber, but the window was of fine stained glass and the altarpiece was gilded and beautiful. It had the advantage that it was one of the very few places in Camelot that was not overlooked and where servants did not pass casually through. Guinevere made her way there from the garderobe. Habit made her dip a curtsey to the central statue of the Holy Mother and Child, even though she was unobserved and in dire need of shriving of her sinful thoughts. She knelt upon the hassock as if in prayer, and ran her fingers across the thick embroidery. Her hands were clammy with eagerness and anxiety.

What if he didn't come?

She was so overwrought that when the door creaked open behind her, she jumped in her skin. Turning, she saw Lancelot push the door to and lean back against it. Suddenly her heart was racing so fast that she felt that her clothes were suffocating her. She wanted to tear open her bodice and let her burning body stand before him naked.

Guinevere rose to her feet. She should let him come to her, she knew—she should make him kneel—but she couldn't restrain herself, and she closed the distance between them in a breath. The eager light in his eyes allayed every one of her fears. He reached out and caught her waist, pulling her into his embrace. His mouth was honey and wine, his kisses hot. Suddenly there was no breath in her lungs. She felt her whole body arch and mold into the hard press of his, her slender frame as fragile in his grasp as a bird caught in a mailed fist—but she was no innocent white dove; she was a bird of fire: burning, aching, blazing against him.

"Why did you not come to me yesterday?" she whispered, gasping, as they broke at last.

"I could not find time alone." He grinned, adding, "And it does you good to wait, my love."

She seized his face between her hands and kissed his lips bruisingly hard. He responded by catching her lower lip in his teeth and biting until she groaned, only then releasing her.

"Haven't I waited all summer for your return?" she gasped as he nuzzled her throat. Just the scent of his body made her brim with juices. "I thought I would die for longing!"

His voice was a growl in her ear. "What is closest to death tastes sweetest of all. Now you're as moist and ripe as bletted chequers, for me. And I have a great hunger to pluck that fruit."

She pulled back, holding his eye, trying to convey her rage. "I was afraid you were dead! You fought a wyrm! Alone!"

He lifted an eyebrow, his eyes shining. "Isn't that what a Knight of the Round Table must do? Slay dragons and rescue virgins?"

She'd heard the story he'd recounted to the whole court, and the mention of the girl made her bridle. "Was it as you said? Tied to a pillar, naked, to await her doom?"

He swooped to brush her lips again, but pulled away provokingly at the last moment. "Just so."

"She *was* a maiden, then?" she sneered.

His grin broadened. "Not by the time I'd finished with her."

"What?"

"But most grateful to be saved from both sources of her torment—the wyrm and her maidenhead."

Guinevere flushed scarlet. "You tumbled her, then!"

"You were many days away, my love, and my ball-sack bulged nigh unto bursting." His voice was light, but his heavy hands on the swell of her rump crushed her hard to his groin, and she could feel there the force of his argument. "Besides," he added teasingly, "she had the sweetest little freckled bubbies, and her nether hair was the color of new-cast copper. I could not resist plowing that field. Oh Jesu, but she was tight!"

"Shameless!" she snapped. "You boast to me of your whorings with peasant sluts!"

"She was no slut," he answered, with a delicate emphasis on the word "she."

Guinevere pushed herself away. "I am your Queen, and you should show me respect!" she hissed, and slapped him across the face with her open hand.

He didn't hesitate—he slapped her back. He put a lot less effort into it than she had, but his hand was heavy enough to stagger her. She clutched at her cheek, staring at him, and then he grabbed her throat and pulled her up so that they were nose to nose.

"You want me," he growled, "precisely because I do not treat you as a queen. Because I'm the only one who satisfies that base and sinful itch between your legs, my love. Your husband treats you with respect—so when have you cried for joy upon the thrust of his great weapon? When have you begged him to despoil you one more time?"

She couldn't speak, could barely breathe. His words, rough and intimate, made the wet run down the insides of her thighs.

"I treat you as my doxy, and that is why you will do anything for the feel and the taste of my cock. Anything I desire. I *know*. You would get down on hands and knees in the filth of a pigsty for me, wouldn't you, my Queen?" He watched as she lowered her lids in acknowledgment. Then he nodded. "Which is what makes my prick so hard for you, Guinevere. Day and night. Touch it now."

He opened the slash of his robe and forced her hand

inside. He must have freed his member from his breeches and hose as he walked up the stairs to confront her, she realized. It was bare and stiffly erect, as magnificent as a lance raised aloft. She wrapped her fingers around its hot, familiar length.

"Suck it," he whispered in her ear. "Kneel and suck it, my beloved strumpet. My beautiful whore."

The words made her knees turn to water. She slid to the floor, looking up at him beseechingly. His palm-print burned on her left cheek. "Here?" she said. "Before the Holy Virgin?"

His gaze did not leave her face. It was weighted with so much hunger that it could not rise from her to the statue on the altar behind. "Here," he ordered. "Now. Do you think your sins hidden from her eyes when we fuck elsewhere? Pigsty or church, it makes no odds to such shameless lechery."

He was right. She had listened to the Holy Word and knelt to receive the Host in this very chapel, picturing all the while Lancelot's hands mauling her pale breasts, or his cock plunging into her sex—or his mouth arising from between her open thighs, bruised and glistening with her juices, his eyelids heavy. The more she'd tried to stop those wild imaginings, the more they'd haunted her, more vivid than any vision of Heaven or Hell the priest had tried to invoke. Father Aldous' words had not been able to compete with her memories. She'd wanted Lancelot too much—hoped and prayed and wept only for his return.

Now he was here, his cock inches from her face, a thick, musky-scented pillar flushed darker than the veined and weathered hand he gripped it with. With the other hand, he guided her head to him. Those most sinful prayers of hers were answered. His heavy balls, usually well-defined in their loose pouch, were gathered now into a single corrugated clench, bulging with intent. She kissed it, feeling the tickle of wild hairs upon her lips and cheeks. She kissed the base of his shaft and felt it twitch with joy. Then she laid on kiss after kiss, ascending his length, each one a declaration of love for his heat and his hardness and his strength. By the time she reached the helm of his cock it was slick with an exuded oil like the Holy Chrism. She wet her lips upon it and felt the burn. One last, passionate, sucking kiss upon that warrior's helmet—and then she could resist no longer, and she engulfed him in her mouth, drawing him deep. She was so hungry for that bulk, that taste; now she swallowed him like she could eat him up and keep him inside her forever.

Lancelot made a deep and bestial groan, one that sounded like it had been drawn from his innermost being. His cock butted the back of her mouth and she adjusted her angle, pushing him flatter, straightening her throat. Sucking him deeper in, right down. "That," he gasped, wrapping his big hands about her elaborate golden braids. "That's what no virgin can do. Oh Christ have mercy. You are magnificent."

He'd taught her how to do that—or she'd learned herself, under his insistent tutelage—how to take him in her throat without gagging or resistance. Now that sensation itself was almost enough to send them both into crisis. Cut off from air and light, Guinevere lost all thought too; everything but the hunger that made her swallow deeper, deeper, deeper.

"Ah!" He pulled out, like drawing a sword from a mortal wound. Trails of thick wet hung between them, connecting turgid cock and open lips. Guinevere gasped for breath, wiping at tears and spit. She was still dizzy and unfocused as he pulled her to her feet, backed her up, lifted her, and dropped her to sit upon a hard surface. It was the stone slab of the chapel altar itself, she realized with a lurch.

"We cannot!" she gasped.

"Cannot? Can. *Will*." Lancelot rucked up her long skirts and pushed her thighs up and apart. There was no chivalry, no delicacy. They had not that luxury. His fingers found the slippery well-head of her sex and pushed within, gauging her readiness from the ease with which he entered, and the eagerness of her bitten-off cry. She had to brace her hands on the cold stone as he guided his cock to that target and rammed inside her.

This was the consummation. This was the moment of transfiguration. She wrapped her legs about his hips as he began to thrust.

"I would fuck you before the Holy Virgin," Lancelot grunted, as he piled on stroke after stroke. "Before all the Hosts of Heaven. I'd fuck you on the Round Table, in front of your husband and all his Knights." He looked down into her slack-jawed face, seeing the roll and flutter of her eyes. "And I'd make you climax in front of them all, my pretty whore. Just … like … that."

He did.

In the midst of her throes she felt him withdraw. He never spent inside her. He did not dare. She heard his stifled breath and she grabbed hold of him and pulled herself up to brace her head against his breastbone. She looked down between them in time to see him direct his cock and shoot his seed against the insides of her skirts, white pennons against the saffron-dyed fabric.

Reaching, Guinevere caught the last of his seed upon her fingers, cleaning it off his twitching cock.

"My Guinevere," he whispered, arms about her.

She licked it from her hand: wanting the taste, wanting him inside her. She wanted him so much that, even in the rush and glow of her climax, her heart felt like it was breaking.

◆ ◆ ◆

Arthur came to her room that night. He visited her three times a week, on the same days each time—unless it was a high holy day. Not often enough to look uxorious, not seldom enough to be accused of neglect.

Guinevere watched from the bed as he disrobed. He was a lot older than her, of course—there was gray in his brown hair and his close-cropped beard now, and the first brushing of silver upon his chest. But he was still a handsome man. In the days before Lancelot, she'd thought him the fairest-looking man at Camelot, with those clear eyes the color of gull's back, rimmed by curiously dark lashes that made his stare more intense than any other's. Maybe that was why he drew men to him so: that stare, that look. He'd been a warrior in the early days, but his prowess in the council chamber was far greater than that on the field. He had a way of making people listen to him—and more than that, to listen to sense. A way of making men think with their heads, not their bollocks.

When they first married, she'd been deliriously happy, and very much in love.

Now ... now, he was still handsome. Even as she sat there with the stains of her lover newly-washed from her thighs, she still felt that admiration and pride as she watched her husband. She still loved him, too. How could she not? Arthur was gentle and attentive and fond. He would put an arm about her warmly, or kiss her, even in public. He asked her opinion and listened to her answers. And he was the greatest king Britain had ever known—just and moderate, wise and peaceful. The land prospered. Hot-headed young nobles like Sir Mordred might chafe against his disinclination to make war, but who listened to them any more?

"Good even, my wife," he said with a tender smile as he

came to the bed.

His only fault—if it was his fault, and not hers—was that in seven years of marriage he had sired no heir. But the people had faith. God would not forever deny that blessing to a king so devoted to the Good.

Only Guinevere knew the truth: that a man without a little sin is not man enough. Arthur was too perfect. There was no lust in his loins when he looked at her, or at any woman. Three times a week he came to her and did his marital duty, but though his body obeyed his commands, his soul was too chaste. There was no fire, no desire, in his embraces. And so he had never kindled the spark of life in her womb, however much they might both wish it.

"Welcome, husband," she said, making room for him beside her. She'd sent her ladies-in-waiting away, as she did every night. She was ashamed to think of the women realizing how brief and passionless were their couplings.

It had confused her, at first, and it remained a torment. She would have loved for him to rut upon her as Lancelot did, all sweat and savage need. She would have wept for joy to carry his child. But she dared not show her disappointment, not to Arthur. She couldn't even let him know she realized there was anything missing. Why should she hurt his feelings? Her husband did not deserve condemnation; if anyone did, it was her.

Arthur's cock was semi-erect as he stretched out beside her, but she knew by now this wasn't from eagerness, but from him working himself hard before entering her chamber. If it were not taken care of quickly, the shine would go off the helmet he had buffed so assiduously.

"Would you like me to …?" she suggested.

"Please."

Going down on elbows and knees at his side, she took his length in her mouth. She wished it were Lancelot's cock—that always responded to such administrations with brutish enthusiasm.

Thinking about Lancelot always helped her slurp and suck with vigor. She remembered again their tryst in the chapel, and it brought a bloom of warmth to her lower belly. She pictured his great proud weapon presented in her face, the way it strained and leered at her as if it had a will of its own, like some demonic serpent. She remembered the way he plopped her on the holy altar and stuck his cock in, as if it were no more than a bar table in a squalid inn somewhere, and she no more than a farthing whore not even worth the time to take to his bed. The blasphemy made her flush all over. She would like to be his favorite whore—no, not a whore, for that would mean she would have to spread her legs for other men, and she wouldn't like that, would she? His doxy then; some lower-class girl he'd take to his bed for as long as it amused him, as other knights did. If she were not Queen, she would be able to sleep with him every night. She could sit on his knee in the Great Hall and serve him wine and eat from his trencher, and he'd grope her tits and slap her ass in front of all the other men and give her a shove in the direction of the courtyard, following her out with a swagger as they laughed and urged him on.

"What do you think about when you do that?" asked Arthur.

Guinevere surfaced abruptly, shocked. Arthur *never* spoke to her while they were in congress. "Your pleasure, lord," she answered.

"Is it the thought of my pleasure that does *this*," he said, placing his one finger in the open split of her sex and running it over her clit. "Or something else?"

She was sopping wet, and the touch on her clit, however accidental, was like the ember that ignites the phoenix fire.

"Sir Lancelot," she said, caught off guard. Her eyes rounded in sudden horror. She peered up toward Arthur, trying to judge his expression. "I mean," she stammered, "his tale of the rescue of that maiden from the great wyrm. I would like to be a maiden, my lord, bound like that to a stake. I would like you to ride up on your charger, all in your armor, and fight the beast for my sake, and rescue me from dire peril."

Abruptly, Arthur sat up. Guinevere caught a glimpse of his cock and realized, confused, that it was no longer couchant but rampant, before he turned her with a jerk of his head and a grasp of her hips into her usual position for sex: on hands and knees. He was behind her in a moment, kneeling up, boring his stiff length into a hole that was only too wet and willing to receive it. He felt, to her, bigger than he'd ever been before. The thrust of his shaft was pure pleasure. She realized she was so aroused that if only she were allowed to reach between her own legs and play with the pearl that nested in the oyster there, she would easily be able to climax.

But she couldn't do that. It would betray a lack of innocence, a sophistication of technique, that she couldn't possibly admit to.

So Guinevere dug her fingernails into the sheet and remembered the first time she and Lancelot had sinned together—the single memory that was sure to inflame her more than any other. She had been several years into her lukewarm marriage when Lancelot joined the Round Table, journeying to Camelot from his domain over the sea. That fateful day, she had been sitting with him in the rose garden, in a small pavilion among the blooms, and they'd been playing chess—a game he'd taught the Court and which had swept the nobility. A ferocious downpour had sent her ladies-in-waiting running for cover, terrified for their silken dresses, but the two of them had remained in their precarious shelter, cut off from the castle by a curtain of pouring rain.

Guinevere had already been aware of her strong attraction to the man who had claimed the honor of being Queen's Champion, having bested every other Knight of the Table at the jousting lists. She'd been both absorbed by the chess game and giddy with pleasure. It hadn't mattered to her that he'd been much the stronger player. In fact she liked that. They'd played three games, wagering small sums of gold to sharpen the interest, and she'd only won the first time because he let her. His fingertips had brushed hers on a number of occasions and she had been hard-put not to giggle.

Then he'd announced, "Knight takes Queen. Mate." He'd looked her in the face, and at that moment they had both *known*. Heat had flashed through her body like a lightning strike. She'd reached out to lay her king over in surrender, but her hand had shaken so wildly she did not dare touch the board. He'd seen that too. Suddenly, without a word, she was aware of the danger she was in.

She'd sprung to her feet and backed off, knocking over her stool like a child in a panic. He'd followed, instantly, closing on her as she backed up against a wooden pillar. Rain struck the back of her neck but she'd barely felt it. He'd loomed over her, his eyes holding hers, his intention implacable. But his voice had been pitched soft.

"I win again," he'd said. "You owe me a forfeit, my queen."

She'd nodded, running the tip of her tongue across her lip in a frantic effort to wet it so she might speak. She could feel her voice all bundled up into a croaky snarl in her breast.

"Lift your skirts. Show me."

Maybe he'd meant only as far as the knees—that would have been shameful enough, but it hadn't occurred to Guinevere until later that there might have been some escape. She'd bunched up the floor-length front of her dress, hand over hand, revealing the secret path of her thighs, all the way to her sex. He'd glanced down briefly, no change of expression visible on his face, then pinned her gaze again.

"Open them."

She'd obeyed. She hadn't questioned the necessity. His face was so close to hers that she'd been sure he was going to kiss her. But he'd put his hand down between her slightly parted thighs, and cupped the dark gold nest of her sex in his palm, running his fingertips into her cleft. He'd found her as wet as if she'd been caught in the cloudburst.

She'd nearly died of the pleasure and the terror of that touch.

All he'd done was stroke her. Stroke her soft and needy sex, caress her clit with one moistened, expert fingertip, back and forth, utterly patient, while his face hovered over hers watching every nuance of expression. She'd arched her shoulders against the wet post and gasped and quivered and shaken, completely in his power, until she spent with a gush and a helpless cry and a sudden rush of tears. It was the first time a man had ever brought her to climax.

And he hadn't kissed her. Not that time.

But from that moment on, she'd known she was his to do with whatever he desired. The more shameful, the better.

On hands and knees in the royal marital bed, her husband holding her hips and thrusting into her from behind, Guinevere relived her adulteries until she blossomed, opening up, a shudder of pleasure running through her from head to toe. Arthur kept it up for a few more strokes, then withdrew from her and lay down, turning his back as he rolled into sleep.

That was her secret. Nine times out of ten, her husband didn't even spend when he swived her.

Lying next to him, Guinevere dreamed that night that she was knight in a tournament joust. As she charged down the lists, her lance set, she saw her opponent bearing down upon her on a huge stallion. His shield bore Lancelot's coat of arms and, as she recognized that, the tip of his lance struck her straight beneath the ribs and ran her through. The spasms of orgasm woke her, shaking and sweating, and she lay for a long time next to her oblivious King, her face wet with tears.

◆ ◆ ◆

"Are you still angry about the freckled wench?" The hawk on Lancelot's wrist flapped its wings suddenly, restless despite its hood, and Guinevere's palfrey caught the movement and made a nervous sidestep. With her own wrist occupied by a falcon, it took her a moment to bring her steed under control and calm it. At least this gave her an excuse not to dignify his question with a response. She turned her horse away, arching her neck. There were dozens of people around them in this hawking party, but no one close enough to overhear, so long as they were careful.

Lancelot was not put off. Wheeling his own horse in a circle, he cut her off and passed back alongside her to speak under his breath. "Let me show you exactly what happened, my Queen. They tied her to a stake, naked, to await the wyrm. Her hands over her head. That's how I'll expect to find you tonight, when I come to your room. After they ring Compline."

She widened her eyes at him in what was close to a glare, before she remembered not to draw attention. Lancelot smirked.

"What, my Queen? It's not the King's night tonight, is it?"

She bit her lip, and for a moment almost told him that he could not come to her room, that it wasn't safe. But he'd done it before. The man was ridiculously bold, and telling him wouldn't prevent it. It was simply up to her to make sure that they weren't witnessed.

A pulse beat low down in her belly, and she was acutely aware of the press of the padded saddle against her sex. With a slight dip of her chin she acknowledged his instructions. Then she rode away toward the King.

That night, alone in her room, she prepared with some nervousness for her paramour. First she stripped off her night robe, shivering a little in the cool air. Her bed had four great oaken pillars, and the heavy curtains hung from iron hooks on the crossbeams. She partly unhooked one of the drapes, from next to a pillar at the foot of the bed. Then she carefully measured the length of her woven belt, knotted it about both her wrists with a long loop between them, and caught it on one of the hooks. When she stepped down from the mattress to the floor, she had only enough length on her bonds to stand flat-footed, her hands held above the height of her head. She could feel her nipples rising and hardening with the exposure. Servants had left her with a fire in the hearth, but it was still cool enough to raise a prickle of gooseflesh across her pampered skin. She was not used to any hardship in her life, except for that dealt her by her lover.

She thought of the sacrificial virgin left out for the wyrm, awaiting her death in abject terror and then—at the last moment—seeing a Knight of the Round Table riding to her rescue. How heroic he must have seemed then, like an angel of deliverance—like St. Michael casting the Dragon himself into the pit of Hell.

She heard the bell toll for Compline. The watch on the walls would change now. Father Aldous would be reciting the office in the Chapel. Lancelot would be on his way. A draft caressed her skin. Her nipples were so stiff now that they seemed like pebbles of pink quartz. She had bathed and perfumed herself, but she could smell the warm tang of her sex rising in anticipation. She closed her eyes, imagining herself exposed upon a barren hillside. Had all the ealdormen of the town brought her there? Had they stripped her at the last moment, or walked her there naked? Had they looked at their scapegoat victim with lust as well as pity? Guinevere imagined freckles scattered across her shoulders and breastbone like tiny constellations. She imagined herself with copper-colored hair instead of gold. She imagined Lancelot looking upon her in fascination, his lust goaded not just by her nakedness but by the novelty.

The door creaked. She opened her eyes, surprised how deeply she had fallen into her reverie. There stood the Queen's Champion, already divested of his robe and boots, down to shirt and hose. No one seeing him in the corridor could have mistaken his intent. His expression was dark.

Guinevere squirmed in delicious shame.

"The offering awaits," he mused, closing on her. "So fair. So vulnerable." He ran his hand, feather-light, over her body, evoking shivers, testing the quiver of her flesh and the resilience of her jutting nipples. "Her flesh is succulent and juicy. But am I the rescuer or the serpent?" His blue eyes looked black in the dancing firelight. He scratched a nail down her underarm, making her spasm in ticklish terror. "Perhaps I am both."

"Please," she breathed.

"Please? For what do you beg?"

"Save me."

"From the Great Wyrm? He feasts only upon the most innocent and unsullied of virgins. Yet I sense sin here." Lancelot trailed his hand up between her thighs, as he had done that first day in the rose garden—and just like on that day, he found the parted lips of her sex dewy with moisture. But this time she bucked her hips toward him.

"Oh!" she moaned, closing her eyes as he stirred her secret flesh. "Oh yes!"

"Is this concupiscence, fair maid? Is this lust? You told me you were without stain. Yet it seems to me you need no rescuing."

"Oh, I do! Please! Sir knight!"

"Are you innocent?" he breathed, brushing her lips with his own. She turned blindly to his face like a flower following the sun.

"I am!"

"Perhaps you are, at that." His finger circled her clit. "Do you know what happens to innocence, fair maid—every time?"

"No?"

He stepped back. "It is broken." And through the open door into her chamber walked Arthur.

Guinevere convulsed as shock tore through her. "No!" she squealed—first at her husband, and then, incredulous, at Lancelot. She didn't understand, but it was clear that he had arranged this: the whole display. She yanked wildly at her bonds but the belt just cut into her wrists. She wanted to cover herself: her face, her breasts, her sex. She was Eve discovered naked in the Garden. She realized she had to climb back on the bed to unhook her hands, but when she turned Lancelot grabbed her shoulder and whirled her back again, pushing her against the bed pillar and pinning her there. The breath left her lungs.

"Guinevere," said Arthur, sorrowfully.

"Please!" She looked from face to face as they stood there side by side, the cuckold and the cuckolder. She could not read either expression—there was something dark and complex there in both, but she couldn't read it. "Why?" she squealed at Lancelot. "Why did you tell him?"

He shrugged. "We have been close friends, my love, for a long time. We met on campaign in France, after all, long before I came here."

She was aghast. She wanted to scream that he was insane—that adultery with the King's wife was high treason and they both faced execution. But he knew that. *He knew that.*

"My wife, with my closest friend and sworn liegeman," said Arthur. He looked grim.

"Please! My lord!"

"Your lord? You call me that, and yet betray me and set your flesh on display like meat, for another man's appetite?"

"Have mercy!"

"I thought you loved me, Guinevere."

Something cracked in her throat and when she cried, "I do love you!" It came out as a sob, tears running down her cheeks. "You are my husband! My King!"

"But you love him too, do you?"

She glanced wildly at Lancelot, whose face was a dark and heavy mask, whose hand between her breasts still pinned her in place. She felt like she did not know him. "I …" she started, and then fell silent. Anything else she might say would only condemn her further.

"It is not love she comes to me for," said Lancelot. "Something more bestial, I fear."

Arthur shook his head slowly. "Perhaps the fault lies with me too. If I had given her all she desired …"

Guinevere met his eyes, and her guilt felt like it would choke her. Amidst the betrayal and outrage, she saw the gleam of understanding—a hurting pity. Her heart twisted and tore within her breast.

"Be not so certain about that," said Lancelot. "There are depths to her appetite that even I have not sounded."

"So does love turn to sin, if unshriven." Arthur put out his hand and cupped her cheek. "You must be punished—you understand that, Guinevere? Both of you. You have broken the laws of the realm, and even the Queen is not above the law. You betrayed me, both of you. There must be justice, or I am no King of Britain, only a tyrant."

She tried to swallow her sobs, and failed. He let her gasp.

"But not in public. There will be no execution block for him, no stake or flames for you. We will not shame Camelot and destroy all we worked for, for so long." He wiped away a tear from her lashes with his thumb. "There will be punishment, but it will be meted out in private, here."

She stared, not sure what to think. No stake? Her heart hammered under her breastbone.

Slowly, Arthur untied his belt. It was no fancy accoutrement for state occasions, but a plain leather strap, wide as two fingers. He doubled it over in his fist. The hiss of her breath sounded loud in the suddenly silent room. "Lancelot tells me that often you provoke him to strike you upon the buttocks and breasts, and that it brings you release. In your heart of hearts there must be a great need for contrition, my Guinevere."

Her jaw wobbled. It was true. Sometimes Lancelot used her roughly, slapping her hams as if she were a stubborn mule, pulling her hair and smacking her tits. And she loved that, in a dark and vertiginous fashion. Once he had held her nipples in an agonizing pinch and fingered her snatch until she came, sobbing.

"Do not worry." Arthur stroked her face again, his fingers lingering. "I will not harm you. But you must be punished. You do understand?"

Gulping, she nodded. She deserved punishment, she knew that. Her guilt at betraying her husband was like a great stone carried inside her. She deserved punishment—and she wanted it.

"Hold her still."

Without questioning his liege-lord, Lancelot climbed up onto the corner of the bed, and from behind grasped Guinevere's throat in his big hand. It did not constrict her breath much, but it did constrain her view, keeping her head up. She caught the briefest of glimpses as Arthur brandished about a foot-length of doubled-over strap, showing her the instrument of her torture as was proper. And then he struck her smartly upon her right breast, and she gave up worrying about anything else. The red-hot strike seemed to boil up through her skull and down through her body. She cried out, and Lancelot's other hand muffled her mouth.

Six strokes in all, Arthur laid upon her breasts—three to each orb. He took it slowly, with great deliberation, pausing between each blow to examine her, drawing his fingers tenderly over the marks. Guinevere did not remember any time previously when he had paid such attention to her breasts—or indeed, touched them much at all. In moments she could feel the sweat running down her skin, greasing his fingertips. Her breasts felt like they were swelling up like inflated bladders, burning hot.

After the first six, he whipped her twice across the tops of her thighs, which made her struggle and writhe even more, but he lost interest there quickly. "Turn her," he instructed. Lancelot swung her in her bonds to face the pillar. He kissed her tear-streaked cheek. She could feel the panting strain of his breath.

That was when Guinevere realized that the punishment meted out to her breasts had been very restrained indeed, because when it came to her rear, the blows Arthur rained down on her were far harder. Perhaps because they were somehow easier to take there—they hurt, certainly, with the same fiery agony, but the pain did not terrify. Perhaps because he realized that Lancelot had mitigated her suffering by plunging his hand between her thighs and taking a tight grip on her clit, grinding the nubbin of flesh. That helped take the edge off the pain certainly, even if it was a weak mercy in the long run. It just made Arthur hit harder and longer, as she danced on Lancelot's hand and ground her body against the wooden post and shrieked, forgetting all discretion.

"Too loud," said Arthur abruptly, stopping. "Get her down."

Lancelot knelt up on the mattress, lifted her bodily and unhooked her from the overhead beam. She sagged into his arms, sobbing.

"Bring her here."

Guinevere found herself being half-carried across the room to the fireplace. There, on the stool before the flames, sat Arthur. He'd stripped off all clothes except his hose, which were unlaced, and though her sweat-bedraggled hair she saw the effect the exertion had had upon him. The King loved justice so much, she realized, that the meting out of her punishment had charged his member to full erection.

She'd had no idea it could get so *big*.

"Over my knees," he ordered. There was a sheen of sweat on his shoulders and chest, as if he were oiled slick, but in contrast his voice sounded hoarse.

She whined in protest, briefly—it was a posture of utter shamefulness that she thought she'd long outgrown—but Lancelot was unmerciful this time. He forced her face down over Arthur's lap as if she were somehow that brattish child all over again, caught stealing candied figs from her mother's comfit box. The sheer disgrace distracted her momentarily from anticipation of further pain.

Momentarily.

Thank the Lord and all His angels, Arthur had given up on the belt by this point. He intended to use a more intimate instrument of justice: his open hand. He ran it all over her inflamed, swollen buttock cheeks first, mingling the most intense pleasure with the burn of her recent pains. She couldn't help whimpering and lifting her ass to his palm.

"Such unseemly wetness," he complained.

"A sign she's prepared to receive the rod of your justice," said Lancelot with relish. "Punish her further. You'll see."

Arthur's hand descended on her rump with an almighty slap and Guinevere shrieked.

"Keep her quiet, Lancelot," the King grunted.

The knight scrambled to obey. He came in to view suddenly at Guinevere's head, where she hung face-down over the bearskin rug. Kneeling, he pulled his cock from his hose and shoved it into her mouth. It was hard as wood already, and its implacable bulk was strangely comforting—strange because she could hardly breathe, and Arthur was pinning her thighs and walloping her backside, and though it didn't hurt as much as the belt it certainly hurt enough—but that thick length surging down her throat, and the familiar taste of his musk, and the grip of his hands … it somehow felt as if she were being held tight, inside and out, and that she could let go and take the pain and surrender to the panic. She could thrash and struggle as much as she wanted because there was no fear of escape, not now that they both had her.

So she fought and she spasmed, over and over, pain and pleasure crashing into and through each over like red and black waves, indistinguishable in the end. Until the black won at last and she went limp, shriven and sinless.

Then they tumbled her gently to the bearskin rug.

She opened her eyes to see Arthur standing in silhouette against the glow of the fire. Sir Lancelot knelt before him with head bowed as if at his knighting ceremony—except that the King's weapon did not descend upon his shoulder; it was instead sheathed to the hilt in the knight's mouth.

Guinevere blinked the last tears from her eyes, astonished. She had thought Lancelot was rough with her, but that was nothing to the vigor and brutality with which Arthur fucked the knight's throat, his hips pumping in a savage rhythm. Lancelot's hands gripped his lord's thighs, but only pulled him closer. There was no fumbling uncertainty here; she realized with wonder that the knight must have done this before. Many times.

Lancelot's eyes rolled sideways at her. He pulled free, gasping, and held out his hand. "Come and kiss the King's scepter," he said with a grin.

She crawled in, but then hesitated. Her skin burned and stung, and her limbs ached.

"Thus Queen Esther obtained the mercy of Ahasuerus," said Arthur with a growling laugh. She remembered the Bible lesson preached from the pulpit only that week: to approach the Persian King unbidden was death, but when Esther dared he extended his scepter to touch her, in show of forgiveness.

Guinevere found herself tugged in to kneel with her lover at her husband's feet. To kiss and lick and mouth that spit-slick rod, and fight with her lover's lips for the honor of swallowing the crowned head. She could feel the heat and sweat of Arthur's groin, and guessed he must be on the edge of eruption. She had never tasted his seed, but now she desperately craved that completion, and absolution, and rest at last.

"Wait," groaned Arthur, pulling away. He wrapped his hand in Guinevere's long hair and eased her to her feet—not cruel, but not kindly. "Has he spent his seed inside you, my Judas?" he asked her.

"Never."

"Then now." He pushed her toward the bed. He sounded drunk with arousal. "Fuck the girl. Fuck her for me. Get her with child. What does it matter? Camelot needs an heir. Do it for me."

He shoved her on her back across the bottom of the bed, and she saw Lancelot rising, stripping off the last of his clothes. As he loomed in over her and Arthur backed away, she saw too, for the first time, the welts all across the knight's body—chest and thighs and arms. He'd taken his punishment already, and Arthur had not held back on him or shown him the mercy he'd shown Guinevere. But he showed no sign that he felt pain anymore; his lean face was lit with a wild and hungry light. Pushing Guinevere's thighs up, he mounted her in a few swift, clean movements, bearing down on her with all his weight.

She groaned. Her sex was swollen and throbbing still, sore from the sly smacks her husband had landed on her undefended placket at the end. The new stimulation burned through her flesh. Lancelot felt like a hot iron impaling her. She shut her eyes, gathering her strength.

Then Lancelot groaned from the depths of his chest, and she looked again. Behind her paramour she saw Arthur, straddling the knight's hindquarters, gripping his hips. Hands—she didn't know whose—pushed her legs up and out of the way. The breath was pressed out of her body by the sudden crush.

"You took what's mine," whispered Arthur in Lancelot's ear, grinding into him. "I take what is yours. That is justice, my love. Now fuck her."

Grunting with effort, teeth bared, sweat running down the curls of his black locks and dripping upon her below, Lancelot did just that, while Arthur rutted upon him. Guinevere—a man's hard length inside her, a man filling her and splitting her and stirring her—could still hardly imagine, could barely picture what her lover must be feeling: fucked and fucker at the same moment; master and servant; ravished himself even as he despoiled her. As for her, she thought if she let her breath out she would never fill her lungs again. Both men were grinding upon her, both men pinning her to the sodden counterpane. She looked into Arthur's face and saw the lust in there, for the first time. She heard Lancelot's groans, noises he'd never made for her. His eyes were narrowed to slits, his head pulled back to stretch his neck. Arthur was ramming harder and harder, his thrusts hammering through Lancelot into the woman at the bottom of the heap.

Arthur is fucking me at last, she thought, as she ignited into flames.

She was not sure what happened after that. There were groans and barking rasps of crisis, curses and panting, but she was tumbling over in a great dark sea, only half-awake and not even half herself. Something … something else had risen from the depths of her soul to claim her. Something dark and unknown and far stronger than her waking psyche. Something that reveled in her pain and shock. She thought it must be like a great wyrm that lived in the depths of her need, down there where there was no light, rising to the surface when she was with Lancelot, to devour her innocence. And now Arthur had called it forth too, and fought with it, and won.

They slid apart, lying back upon the embroidered coverlet, limbs spread as they tried to cool. Guinevere lifted her head to look at her husband. He was staring at the draped cloth overhead.

"I will not tell you not to lie together again," he said. "You'll do it, with or without my knowing."

She reached out and ran fingers through the wet hair on his chest, longing to reassure him. Arthur blinked, rolled a little to see her, and stroked her tangled golden locks.

"You may continue in your adulteries," he said. His voice was soft again, his eyes mild and warm. He was the husband she remembered. "But there's a price for my forgiveness. Always, there must be justice. For each sin you and he commit together, I will punish you both, as I did this time."

Lancelot pushed himself up onto his arms, wincing, and laughed in his throat. Guinevere thought of the way her husband had whipped her, of the terrible retribution he'd visited on her soft round bottom. Even now it smarted and throbbed.

"I'd like that," she said shyly. "Very much."

Arthur's length, fat with repletion, twitched. Like a serpent dreaming in its cavern, waiting to rise.

There lived a wife at Usher's Well,
And a wealthy wife was she;
She had three stout and stalwart sons,
And sent them o'er the sea.

—Child Ballad No. 79

The rain never bluidy stops, it just comes in at different angles. Sometimes falling straight down like God Himself is taking a pish on us, sometimes flung in our faces by fists of wind. It cascades off the slate roofs and seeps through the thatch, and turns the yard into one great basin of water. The cattle were brought in to their winter byres early, before they drowned in the swollen burns, but they're growing lame on their softening hooves and sick on the mildewed hay. It's only November and already we're eating into the winter stores and burning the wood that should have been seasoning for the long haul into spring. There's mold on every surface. You come in all clarted up wi' mud, and you can try to wash your clothes but you cannae dry them afterwards over the smoky, spitting fires, so no one bothers. Everything smells fusty. Everything is twice as heavy as normal and treacherously slippery.

It's all her fault.

She sits in her chamber, looking out of her window at the track up the fellside, the one that leads to the coast. Somewhere beyond that gray-green slope the sea waits, huge and hungry, and there are times that I imagine that the roar of the wind is the sound of its waves. That's the road the three of them took that morning, riding out so braw and handsome in their new cloaks of red wool that she and I had cut and hemmed and lined, working together through the evenings. She watches the track, waiting for them to come back.

My Mistress has the finest window in all the village of Usher's Well, there in that chamber. Near as big as a kirk window, with leaded-glass panes almost as clear as air, though the fellside is a murky, slithering green through the rain. She's got one of the few rooms that the downpour hasnae found a way into through the roof, too. No drip drip drip from sodden thatch onto the coverlet of *her* bed. Which is good for me; one of my duties is to sleep beside the widow and keep her bones warm, sharp elbows and all. In my exhaustion, I've even learned to sleep through the weeping.

Others may guess at her pain, but I'm the only one who knows for sure. She's a strong wifey, my Mistress. By God, she's had to be—bereft of a husband at such a young age, but holding together household and demesne for the three strapping sons she raised. She's as tough as a butcher's apron and as hard and true as a cleaver. No man in Usher's Well has won an inch of ground from her, nor taken a single penny that she didnae owe him fair and square. You'll never see her give way, not in public.

She only cries at night, in the dark. By day she watches, dour-faced, through her window. I try to coax her to eat. But she only obeys because I tell her she must keep her strength up, if she is to be hale and hearty for her sons' return. You see, she refuses to believe they are dead; that's the thing. She has set her will against God's, and for the life of me I cannae tell whose is the stronger.

That's the source of this terrible dreich weather.

I know that, because I heard her say it. I was there, when the messenger came from Dunbar with the news that the *Dancing*

Annie had gone down in heavy seas, not even out of sight of land. She'd been pushed south down the coast onto rocks, and wrecked there. All hands dead.

My Mistress cried out when she heard, like a lamb having its throat cut, and fell down upon the cobbles of the yard. I rushed over to help her, not having heard the words spoken from where I watched at the kitchen door, my besom in my hands.

"What's wrong, Mistress?" I asked, but she only wailed. I looked up at the messenger, a hare-lipped youth with frightened eyes. "What did you say?" I demanded.

He could only mumble, "A storm. God rest their souls."

"They are not dead!" she gasped.

I didnae understand, at first. I didnae piece it together. The weather had been blustery all week, raining on and off. "Come up, Mistress," I begged, pulling at her shoulders. "You're getting your dress all mucky." It's my task to clean and mend her clothes, you see. "Come inside—it's horrible wet out here."

"May it never stop raining, Meg," she said, in an awful, cracked voice that made the hair stand up on my neck. "May the winds never cease. Not until they blow my sons home to me, safe and sound in their earthly flesh and blood."

That's when I understood. It hit me cold and keen, like a knife in the belly.

We got inside, and the heavens opened. It hasnae stopped raining since. We havnae seen sun since that day, nor heard silence. Nothing but the sluicing of water and the hustle and blare of the wind, blowing from the east; from the sea. Always a murky dark, even at noon. The musty stink indoors, and outside the numbing cold and the tang of salt. The sky pressing down over our heads like a roof.

Nine bluidy weeks.

The world feels like a lead coffin, one that's half flooded, and we're sealed inside being rattled about on the back of a bier. There's nowhere for the water to go, it cannae drain out, so it just keeps hitting us.

They're starting to leave, the other servants. They're vanishing one by one, down the fell-track to Dunbar. Looking for employment or to sign on to a ship, or going back to family crofts—anything, anywhere, that might be drier and less uncanny than this place. They say we're cursed.

I *know* we are cursed.

My Mistress is wrestling with God, and will not give an inch.

I watch her from the floor of her chamber, as I squat over the fireplace trying to get the logs to blaze properly. We're using birch because it's the only thing that'll catch when wet, but it burns through so fast, and with so little heat, that I'm forever traipsing up and down the stairs with the log-basket on my back. She's wrapped in a fur-lined pelisse to make up for my lack of success. Her face, thinner now after all these weeks of half-starving herself, catches the gray light along her cheek bone.

Oh Lord, but she looks like Finlay from that angle. My heart clenches inside me, a spasm of loss.

Finlay. Sweet Finlay with the curly brown hair and the fluff of beard on his lean cheeks. Finlay who would follow me into the dairy and press me against the shelves and call me his sweet Meg, his pretty Margaret, his windflower and his kitten and his little white dove. Who'd kiss my hands and my lips and hold me close, nuzzling my hair. Who swore he loved me, even when I laughed him off and pushed him away.

Gently. I was gentle with him. I didnae want to hurt his feelings. He said he loved me and would marry me and we would have beautiful bairns together, three of each, and the lassies would look like me and the lads would look like him.

It was all lies of course—no, not lies, but thistledown dreams. He was the smart one, the son who had learned his letters. He was destined for Oxford University far away down south, and so to take Holy Orders. He would never marry anyone. Besides, my Mistress would never countenance any one of her sons marrying a mere serving maid. Marriage is for equals, and I'd never be theirs.

That hadnae stopped Finlay's older brother Rory tumbling me of course—and taking my maidenhead, in fact. Rory was a big, straightforward fellow with a boisterous, ever-eager cock. He rummaged his way through every wench of beddable age in the household, but I doubt that anyone resented him for it, for he was always generous with his coins, and an easygoing master who often intervened with his mother to make sure there were extra portions at dinner for the servants, or to turn away her wrath at some domestic transgressor. Unlike my Mistress, Rory never complained that I was late lighting his fire in the morning, or slow serving at the table. He would only wink and smile at me and pat my rump, and when he came upon me in private he'd pull up my skirts and bend me over a press and slip me his length, strong and easy. On feast days he'd dance me on his broad lap until his prick was as hard as a pole and I was red and flustered, and then he'd touch me secretly under my skirts until I was running as wet and slick as a crock of butter left too close to the oven, and ready to do anything he wanted. That was how he had me, the first time.

"Are you a woman, yet, Meg?" he'd murmured in my ear as he dandled me. He could have shouted it and no one would have heard over the ruckus.

"No, Master Rory," I'd said, blushing, feeling my blood soar and my skin flame and my bones loosen.

"Are you ready for me to make you one?" His fingertips had stroked my purse until it gaped, begging for him to steal what lay within.

I'd moaned then, and shuddered on his lap.

"Och, this medlar is ripe, I think," he'd said. His other arm was around me, his other hand stroking and squeezing my maiden breasts through my bodice. I was losing all sense; nothing in all the world mattered as much as that devastating tease between my thighs.

"Aye," I'd whimpered. And as that wicked fingertip had circled the plump little pip of my medlar, I'd said "Aye!" again and shut my eyes and pressed my face to his neck as I'd slithered helplessly over into paradise—right there in front of the whole household, his brothers and his mother and all the guests. I didnae cry out, but I heard the catch of Rory's breath and then his long exhalation. I dinnae ken if anyone paid any attention. Well—I know that my Mistress saw, because she shot me a narrow-eyed glare as Rory eased me from his lap, patted my rear, and pushed me out of the hall in front of him

It was the Midsummer feast. Rory led me out into the unmown hayfield and laid me down in the long grass, lifting my skirts. His length looked smooth as wood in the moonlight. He wet his thumb in my juices and placed it over my pip, and he kept that there, pressing and stirring, as he laid his cock to my gates and broke them down.

He was heavy, and the smell of wine and crushed grass made my head spin. I wondered why anyone did anything else but this all their lives.

My poor Mistress at the window there disnae look like

Rory, and never has. I suppose he takes after his father, who was dead before I came to this place. Certainly he's her favored son.

Was her favored son. It's hard sometimes to remember that he's dead, she denies it so adamantly. They're all dead, drowned in the deep.

Damn, but what was she thinking putting all three on the same vessel?

Ach, I suppose she must have asked herself that many a time, poor thing. It had seemed wise enough when they took their leave, to travel together and look after each other—Rory to journey all the way to London and take up his father's affairs at the guildhall, Finlay to attend classes at Oxford, Allan to spend time on board one of the family ships as he longed to do, learning a captain's trade from the master of the *Dancing Annie*.

The youngest of the three brothers, Allan, was different again to his siblings. Sharp-nosed and almond-eyed, he always found the walls of this house too constraining. From an early age he was out every day, riding the fell ponies or disappearing down to Dunbar, where we heard he liked to hang about on the docks and talk to the ships' captains and pilots. He had a taste for Dunbar women, and the dowdy servant girls back home never interested him much. I lay with him only once, when he was brought to bed with a fever for a few days. The doctor his mother had summoned told him that he must on no account rise and exert himself, and the poor lad went nearly mad with boredom. I was sent in to change his bedpan but I ended up riding his narrow hips, and sucking his slender, red-crowned cock until he filled my mouth with brine.

Allan I barely knew. But I liked Rory. He was a fine and pleasant man. And always, when I had an itch, I knew Rory would be there to scratch it, so long as I could sneak away from my Mistress to creep into his bed. He would have made a fine Master, had he lived.

Finlay … Finlay I liked very well too, but there was a pang there. Perhaps I liked him too much. He made me want things I couldnae have, so I turned him down every time.

I wish now I hadnae. He was a virgin when he left us, so far as I know. Too shy for his own good, that lad—one who thought with his head and not with his body, unlike most, and got trapped in there. Damn it. He should not have drowned unloved; that straight young body untasted. I wish that just once before he left …

Ach, it's too late for regrets. The ache under my ribs does no good. The milk is spilled, and all the wishing in the world will not put it back in the pail.

Though my Mistress is of another opinion.

◆ ◆ ◆

It fell about the Martinmass,
When nights were long and dark:
That carlin wife's three sons came hame,
Their hats were made of bark

◆ ◆ ◆

"Meg," she says, suddenly. I look up from the pan of ashes I've been scraping together.

"Mistress?"

Her voice is low and hoarse. Wind and rain have worn it away. "They're here."

I rise from the hearth, knuckling my aching back. She disnae sound excited, or happy, so I dinnae feel anything but my normal weary pity. I wander over to the window where she sits, and look out over her head. I dinnae expect to see anything.

There: there on the crest of the track, as it rises over the pasture field. Three figures, side by side, pale against the rain-slicked road. They dinnae appear to be moving, and through the rippled glass and the falling eve it's impossible to make out any detail. Nevertheless, a chill slips through my layers of woollen cloth and brushes my spine like the touch of cold fingers.

"It's them!" My Mistress sounds surer of herself this time, though her voice is still weak. "They've come home!"

"No, Mistress," I say, laying my hand on her shoulder. My own voice is perhaps a little unsteady. "Dinnae get your hopes up. It's … it's too far to tell at this distance."

"Then we must go see!"

I nod, dumbly. What else am I supposed to do? As she gathers her skirts I light a candle from the hearth fire, to illuminate her descent down the stairs. And I precede her through the shadowy interior of the great house, holding my skirts with one hand so she does not tread on my train.

At the front door the porter Jacob is sitting in stockinged feet, hacking caked mud off his boots with a knife. He glances up.

"Jacob, open the door! My sons are returned home!"

I see the whites of his widening eyes. For a moment he stares, and then he crosses himself. "Mistress?"

"Open the door!"

He looks at me, for confirmation. I say, with a creeping reluctance I cannot quite admit to myself, "There are men on the road."

"Mistress, it's near dark. I've just shut the outer gate. No one of good intent will be abroad at this hour."

She draws herself up. "Open the door, man!"

He moves slowly, drawing the heavy bolts. He shoots me a loaded look as he lifts the latch; I know he means me to run through to the hall and gather the menservants at the first sign of trouble.

The pale gloaming evening sifts into the porch. For a moment I cannae work out what's wrong, what's different. Then I realize that it's *not raining*. The evening hangs like silk, and not a breath of wind stirs in our faces.

It's stopped. *Not until they blow my sons home to me*, I think, suddenly far colder than even the November air warrants.

Across the wet yard comes the clang of the bell at the outer gate.

Furtively, I take my turn to cross myself.

"Go out and open the gate, Jacob," my Mistress commands.

He looks at her, and out again across the cobbles at the arch silhouetted against the last glow of the sky. "No," he says flatly.

She stares. I think I see the old fire kindling in her eyes. Jacob feels a sudden need to justify himself.

"Not on my soul, Mistress. This is the uncanny hour, when the Good People are abroad. I'll not dare it."

She looks down at her own feet, clad in their tiny slippers, and then turns to me. "Meg?"

The bell sounds again, a flat mournful noise. I dinnae know what to do. I dinnae want to wade through the puddles to confront … I hardly know what … out there in the weird half-light. I'm scared. I shouldnae be. I'm not afraid of anything—not of the bullocks on the hillside nor of the men in the hall when they've had a skinful of ale. I'm the only servant girl who'll walk round the house at night in the dark, not even taking a candle to light my way. I'll even go after nightfall into the buttery, which the cook and all the other womenfolk swear is haunted by a boggart.

I shrug. "I'll go ask who it is, Mistress," I say.

So I do. The water is up to my ankles in parts, but I set my jaw and slosh through to the yard gate. As I reach it the bell clangs for a third time, a noise that now makes my teeth grate.

"Who's there?" I call loudly. There's a spyhole hatch in the plank, but it's made for a man's height and so above my head.

There's no answer. I put my hand on the slippery wood, then find the crack between the door's two leaves and peer through. It's not yet proper dark out there, but my field of vision is no wider than the edge of a knife. Something moves—something white—crossing from left to right too swiftly for me to focus.

"Let us in." The voice is deep and masculine, and so close that I think for a moment that it's been uttered in my ear, and I jump back startled.

"Who's that?" I demand.

"Meg?" It's a different voice this time—softer, but still a man's. "It's me: Finlay. Let us in, lassie."

The breath leaves my lungs, steaming. "Finlay," I whisper soundlessly. It *is*—it is his voice. I remember it so well, whispering those sweet, meaningless promises between his kisses. My heart is clanging louder than the gate bell did.

"We came back, Meg. Let us in. We came home."

A small sound is born in my throat, but dies before it can escape. "Truly?" I whisper.

"Truly." He has heard, somehow. "It was a long walk, Meg. Let us in."

I realize I'm crying—though I only know because the tears feel scalding hot on my cheeks. I brush numb hands across the wooden planks. I want to know if it's true, I want to know who it is standing on the other side. But I dinnae want to see.

There are no more calls for access. Nothing but silence—

no muttering, no knocks, no impatient shuffle of feet. Absolute silence. Like the grave. Then behind me, the Mistress's faint call: "Is it them Meg? Is it my lads?"

Taking a deep breath, I seize the beam and lift it from its bracket. Then I step back from the door as it swings open.

They stand there, the three of them: Rory and Finlay taller than the whippety Allan. They wear white now, not red; stiff white cloaks, and broad-brimmed white hats that drip with the last of the rain and cast deep shadows. Their breath, if they have any, disnae steam as mine does, and their indistinctly visible faces are pale.

"Meg." The broadest one, Rory, steps forward. "Where is my mother?"

"In the house," I manage to whisper. "She's waiting for you."

One by one, they walk past me and cross the yard. They move slowly, like men who have walked themselves into exhaustion. They must have come a very long way indeed, I tell myself—from Purgatory they've come, or the depths of the sea— and without thinking I glance down. Through the puddled water Finlay's feet gleam, bare and fish-belly white.

Then they have passed me and are filing toward the lit doorway. I catch a whiff of dank, malodorous air, but it is too late now to refuse them. All I can do is trail at their heels.

Their mother is waiting by the door. As they approach she lets out a squeal and runs forward, heedless of her fine slippers of Spanish leather in the wet, and she throws herself onto Rory's broad chest. I can hear her laughing and sobbing and trying to talk, all at once and all tangled up. "You're here! You're back! I knew you were alive! I knew it!"

Rory puts one hand on my Mistress's head, a little

clumsily. My stomach feels like it is full of shale; the Rory I knew would have caught her up and hugged her and whirled her around him. This one just waits, submitting to her hugs and her cries without reaction. I think even she realizes that something is wrong, because she draws back suddenly and stares up into his face. For a moment her expression goes blank, and then horribly awry—and then she laughs and squeezes his hands in hers, and turns away to her other sons. They stand like pillars of salt, almost motionless under her embraces.

"You look so ill, my poor laddies! Come inside, come inside! Your hands are like ice, Allan! Come in before you catch your—Come and warm up."

I follow them inside, into the candlelight and the comparative warmth, where there are layered rushes underfoot to soak up the worst of the mud, and familiar faces to greet them. Rumor has brought every remaining servant into the hall, to see for themselves the return of the three brothers. They stare, eyes glistening, mouths open or set in twisted lines. There's a susurrus of disbelief, an indrawn under-the-breath hiss of dismay. Hands flicker: head to chest, shoulder to shoulder. Figures that have pressed in close to see start to retreat, sidling or pushing backward.

"Meg, help them off with these … things. I suppose they wear them onboard ship, do they?"

I reach up, obediently, to take Finlay's curious white cloak from his shoulders. It's made of bark, I work out: great papery pieces of birch-bark, crudely stitched together, but clearly from a birch tree bigger and whiter than any I've seen in my life. Their hats are made of the same material. As Finlay doffs his and passes it to me, I see his face clearly for the first time.

He's *dead*. There's no doubting that. I've helped lay out a few corpses over the years and I know that look. His skin is utterly bloodless and has an ugly glisten to it, and his eyes are sunken in bruised hollows. Only the flicker of the candlelight gives him any semblance of color or life, and I can imagine he would look much worse under daylight. And he *smells*, I notice now—they all do: a smell like the kelp piled on the beach below Dunbar after a storm. He smells of the sea.

He looks at me for a long moment, and I feel like my heart has stopped too. His pupils are so dilated that the darkness seems ready to pour from them.

How are we to bear this? How? I have caressed this young man and I have felt the ache of his leaving and I've wept for his death. I have—

in bed, at night, while my Mistress slept and the hours seemed to yawn like the depths of the sea, I have—

—I have touched myself and imagined it was him, come back to me.

Oh God.

"Such strange hats," my Mistress gabbles shrilly. "Where did you get them?"

"There is a tree," says Allan. His voice is flat and soft, devoid of feeling. Not one of the three has shown any hint of emotion. "It grows outside the gates of Paradise. That was as far as we could get. We couldnae go past."

"Well, I am sure they are very practical for keeping off the rain. You wouldnae believe the awfy weather we have had here since you left, my boys. The neeps rot in the fields."

"Mother," says Rory, in that same even tone. "The rain—"

"Let's get you into some dry clothes; you're drookit. And och, look—you've all lost your shoes. How did that happen, you foolish laddies?"

"When the ship went under," answers Allan quietly, but my Mistress is clearly, *determinedly,* not listening. She turns away, just in time to see the servants scattering down the hall.

"Blankets!" she calls, angrily. "Build up the fire in the Great Hall, and lay the table, and mull a pitcher of wine! Draw fresh water so they may wash their hands! Fetch them dry clothes and boots! We will have a feast tonight, all of us! My three sons are hale and well, and back safe from the sea!"

Finlay is still watching me with his black, black eyes. No breath stirs his chest. His curls hang in wet ringlets, and he would break my heart with his wistful, familiar beauty … if it were not for the fact that he is dead.

I longed so much to see him again. I watched him ride away up that track with such pain. And now here he is, right in front of me. I could *touch* him, if I dared.

"Come in, my bonny lads," their mother urges. "Come sit by the fire!"

I take the chance to flee to the kitchen, obeying orders.

❖ ❖ ❖

Then she made up a supper so neat
As small, as small, as a yew-tree leaf
But never one bit could they eat.

❖ ❖ ❖

The three sons are cold company, as might be expected. My Mistress has got them sitting down at the head of the table when I return, with their backs to the fireplace, but they've no interest in what we put before them. I cut them the finest white bread, whilst the poker warms in the embers until I can dip it into the spiced wine with a hiss. But they eat nothing, and sip not a mouthful of that good hot mull when I place the goblets on the table.

My Mistress hardly seems to notice. She's pulled up a bench and she sits facing them, her hand on Rory's knee, and she disnae stop talking. She prattles on about the weather, and the farms, and the servants. Nine weeks of gossip. And when she runs out of that she talks about their childhood adventures, and how Rory fell out of the Great Pine that day when he was eight and broke his arm, and how Allan tried to ride the Roan Bull but only provoked it to break the fence so that the kine were scattered for miles across the fields, and how Finlay shamed the priest on St. Swithin's Day by correcting his reading from the Psalter.

I want to stop my ears with my hands and block out her blether. But silence, I know, might be much worse.

Poor woman. She cannae see what is in front of her.

They watch her, and listen politely, and hardly speak a word. Their clothes steam as the heat from the fire builds. At one point Jacob comes in, grumbling and squinting and laden down with dry clothes from their bedchamber presses, but they decline to change into new attire.

"Thank you, Mother. But we dinnae feel the cold," says Rory softly.

As I'm standing behind them pouring the unwanted wine, I notice that there's a piece of seaweed caught in Finlay's hair, its little brown bladders pale against the wet curls. It makes me shudder. But the worst moment is when the other servants come in to pile steaming hot food before the three brothers: pottage of neeps, and peppery haggis-pudding, and slices of mutton. They dump the food and scuttle away as if they'd been forced to serve lepers. The three men look down at the meal without interest. Then my Mistress, without apparently thinking at all—she's in the middle of a soliloquy about who was wearing what at the

Sunday service in the village kirk last week—pulls Rory's plate toward her and cuts up his mutton into tiny pieces, as she must have done for him when he was a wee bairn.

I dinnae think she even sees what she's doing. But it's terrible to watch. I feel my throat swell, and I turn away. I wish I could leave. I wish I could shake her by her thin shoulders until she sees what it is happening before her eyes.

Then, abruptly, I notice the lull in her exhausting monologue. I turn in time to see my Mistress rise to her feet. Desperation is etched around her eyes, but there is a smile scrawled across her lips where none should be.

"My poor laddies," she says. "You are so tired after your journey that you cannae even eat. I'll go see that your beds are made up."

"We are tired," Finlay admits, but is instantly contradicted by his older brother.

"We cannae sleep."

"We have tried," Allan says. "But the rain …"

She stretches her horrible smile. "The rain has stopped. You will sleep sound tonight, now that you are safe home. I will go prepare."

"Let me help you, Mistress," I offer quickly.

"No, Meg. Stay here and serve at table. Bring them anything from the kitchen that they choose. My sons are to have all they desire, tonight." She turns away, her movements stiff, and walks off down the hall, leaving me alone with the dead men.

There's a long, unpleasant silence. I know there's no point in offering them food. The three men watch me from eyes filled with the grave's darkness.

"So Meg," says Rory quietly, pushing out his chair. "Will you sit on my lap, for old times' sake?"

His thighs are as broad as ever, though his slowly drying clothes are stained with salt. I remember his playful embraces and the rasp of his hairy skin, rough as bark, against mine. I shake my head. "I think not, Master Rory. Your lap has grown cold since last I knew you."

He disnae react, except with the slightest inclination of his chin. He disnae even blink. Not one of them has blinked since they arrived, I'm suddenly sure.

I fold my hands before me, determined to wait it out. The platters of wasted food steam.

"Pretty Maggie," says Allan, with something approaching expression in his voice and—to my horror—a movement of his gray and bloodless lips that approximates a grin, "will you play at bob-apple between my thighs once more, for old times' sake?"

Oh how well I remember the fever-heat of his lithe body beneath mine, and the unaccustomed narrowness of his bucking hips, and the urgency of his thrusts.

"I will not, Master Allan," I answer him. "That's a fruit that does not keep well in salt water."

He nods.

Finlay presses his hands to the table and bows his head, and then lifts it to look at me directly. "Will you kiss me, my Margaret?" he asks, his voice as stripped and thin and strange as sea-worn driftwood. "For auld lang syne?"

Oh Lord, help me.

His kisses had always made me blush, unaccountably. They'd been nothing like his brother's straightforward pecks, but instead gentle, lingering creatures of breath and warmth, caresses bestowed on my mouth and throat that seemed to have no other purpose than their own pleasure. They'd made me feel almost uncomfortable. I feel a tear escape and run down my cheek, which I dinnae doubt is as pale as theirs.

"The taste of your clay-cold lips would be awfy strong now, Master Finlay," I say. My voice is hoarse, but I try to speak gently. "It would do me terrible harm, I fear."

He disnae reply, but his expression holds me. I dinnae know what to read in his still, harrowed face. It seems to me that there is pain there behind the mask of cold flesh: an ache that cries for respite. But whether it is the fires of Hell or the gnawing cold of the sea that torments him, I cannae tell.

I want to stroke back his damp locks. I want to see peace in those troubled eyes.

"I'll go fetch more wine," I mumble, though they have done no more than touch their full cups to their closed lips until now. But I cannot bear this. I have to get away. My insides are knotting under my ribs.

I get as far as the passage to the kitchen before my Mistress blocks my way. "Meg!" she cries forlornly. "Their bedchambers are damp and drear—the rain has entered and ruined the linen. I didnae know!"

"Wheesht now," I say, daring to place my hand upon her arm. "It's the weather; it's not your fault."

"But I should have seen to it—I should have been ready for their return."

"They took us all by surprise, Mistress," I assure her. I'm relieved when she nods, shocked when she steps forward into my embrace and lays her head on my shoulder. I feel her narrow frame shudder, and I dinnae think it's the cold to blame.

"I cannae find any of the other servants. I wanted them to change the mattresses, but … I cannae find them anywhere. Even Jacob."

Cowards.

I pat her awkwardly, stroking her shoulder. "It's alright, Mistress. We'll get it sorted."

"I wish them to sleep in my own great bed tonight," she says, a little muffled against me. "That bed is warm and dry. I laid my fur pelisse upon it. They're so cold."

My eyes half-close in dismay. The bed is big enough for three, certainly, but—*Her own bed? For her dead sons?* The thought of what might await her in the morning makes my skin crawl. "Is that … right?"

"We will make shift elsewhere tonight." Her voice, so weak and plaintive, becomes suddenly stronger as she pulls away and looks me in the face. There is something in her eyes— something that burns, that hurts, and that frightens me far more than the darkness in the open, watchful eyes of the dead brothers. "Go pile the fire in my room high, Meg. Dinnae stint with the wood. I want them to be warm."

No, I want to say. But she is my Mistress, and she is so alone, and love has broken her heart and her mind. I bite my lip and I nod. And I go out to the woodpile.

Up the dark stairs with the log-basket on my back I go, as I have done a thousand times. But not like this night. When you lay a corpse out for a vigil you normally keep the room cold, for obvious reasons. But not tonight.

On my knees in the split ashes, I build up the fire, coaxing the flames with my breath until they roar. The blaze scorches my pale cheeks. My insides are in turmoil. I dinnae know what to feel. I am torn between horror and exultation at this dreadful miracle. I am torn between pity and a wicked, secretive pleasure I will not confess to anyone until my dying day: the joy of looking upon a face thought lost forever, a face longed-for and hotly desired. I am outraged that God has let them walk again—and yet, in my deepest core, sick with gratitude.

I am so afraid.

But not just of the dead.

Then I hear their feet, heavy and measured, upon the stair, and my heart nearly climbs out of my throat and bolts across the room. *What do I do?* I cast about myself in panic. I dinnae want to be cornered here in their bedchamber. But to go to the top of the stairs as they ascend—to see those corpse-faces looking up at me through the darkness, while they tramp slowly toward me—that I cannot bear. There's no other way out, only a door to the tiny garderobe. I might go hide in there all night, crouched over the drafty, stinking hole. Would I be safe in there? I'm as sure as I can be that they have no need for such facilities.

Ach—I have dithered too long. Their tread is at the door. I lift my sleeve to shield my face from the fire and I busy myself tidying the ashes, pretending not to have heard. My heartbeat punches me in the entrails, over and over and over.

The door creaks and falls back with a slam.

I look up. I have to. All pretense is over.

The dead men stand, all three of them, beyond the foot of the bed. Finlay is a little to the fore, his brothers to either side. There is no sign of my Mistress; perhaps she kissed them goodnight downstairs. They are still as posts, still as earth. No breath, no flicker of an eyelid.

My legs nearly give way beneath me as I stand, and I have to clutch at the bed for balance. Finlay's head turns a little, following my motion. My Mistress's fur pelisse is soft under my clutching hand; she has spread it as a counterpane upon the blankets.

I regain my composure, a little. Perhaps I can walk to the door. They are not blocking it. True, I will have to walk around them, but they offer no threat, yet.

Their stance is menace enough. Their mere existence.

I look into Finlay's face, searching for expression. It is a mistake. There is such loss there, such regret and yearning etched into every haggard line. It draws me, like a dark candle flame. Before I breathe another breath my palm is upon his cheek. He feels just as I imagined: as damp and cold as a slab of meat.

But I've grown used to damp and cold these nine weeks.

"I'm sorry," I hear myself say. Tears are burning at the back of my eyes. Closing them, I stretch up and kiss his lips.

The two other brothers sigh. It must be hard work that, with no air in their lungs. Finlay does not exhale as his ice-cold lips press mine. But his hands steal to my waist and draw me close.

"Will you wed me, my sweet Meg?" he murmurs. The same question he'd asked in the dairy, back in the long-forgotten summer.

I'm trembling now, uncontrollably, but I make a fair fist of saying, "Ah, no, my brave laddie—it's too late for that."

"There's so much … Too late …"

I stroke his face, though it is blurred by my frightened tears. "Not too late to love," I tell him.

His arms slide around me, pulling me to his cold frame. The strength in his limbs is startling, but the thick knot of his groin is familiar. The seaweed perfume fills my head.

"I missed—" he says, uncertainly. "I wanted—"

"I know." I nod, pushing my fingers through his hair, feeling the sand all gritty there. "Dinnae worry. It's fine now."

He stoops to kiss my lips again, and wraps one icy hand about my throat in a caress that makes me shake. Shudders course through my flesh as he stokes down to my bosom. And then suddenly, soundlessly, his brothers are there too, flanking me. Their hands are on me. My bodice laces at my back, so that normally my Mistress unties it for me. Now their dead hands pluck at the knots and draw the long laces out through their eyes with a hissing sound. I'm crying now: sobbing through my kisses. It is fear, but not simply fear. It is just that this is too much to support without something breaking.

Bodice, overdress, shift and petticoat. Tugging and pulling like some underwater current, slipping beneath the cloth, kissing my warm places with chill.

They strip me, the three of them. I am naked and glowing in my living heat, my skin stippled with crazy goose-flesh that will not die down, my nipples hard as sea-shingle. Their hands trace my curves and hollows and I know it is memory they seek: the memories of warmth and life and blood-blushed skin, lost to them now. Across the surge of my ass Rory chases the scent of crushed grass and beer and revelry, the giggle of a lassie trying to crawl into his bed without waking him, the splayed thighs and wet welcome and the gasp of shock as he entered me. In the cleft of my breasts Allan gropes for the galloping rattle of his fever-bed, the rush of relief as I pulled up my skirts for him, the smells of sweat and cunt and spilled gruel, and the squeals of delight vibrating through his teeth as he nibbled the teats hanging in his face.

Over my lips and waist and breasts, reaching down between my thighs, Finlay searches out his own memories: whispered giggling intimacies, the summer scents of cow-breath and milk, the thrill of a nipple half-willingly exposed; a dress eased awry, an areola crinkling under a tender fingertip. Lips to throat, feeling the racing pulse. The slyly teasing pressure, momentary and perhaps unintentional, of a hand or hip against the tumescent bulge at his crotch. Sighs and giggles and murmurs of arousal—followed always by gentle slaps of rejection that were almost caresses.

I never let him. Now I can curse myself for being such a fool. I should have spread my legs and let the young man mount me; I should have let him lay me down on the dairy table and rut deep and long until we both screamed for pleasure. I should have let him know the taste of my sex and the heat and the grip of it. I should have sucked his beautiful silken balls empty of seed, and spread my ass-cheeks with my hands to expose the winking invitation of my nether hole.

I should have given him everything, and taught him every joy and every solace a woman is able to offer a man before the long night of Death. Before he left us, and the sea took him.

For now he is back, and he still desires all that he hasnae had.

Oh Lord, save me: I am drowning. The tide is rising in my flesh, lifting me from my feet. I reach out with desperate fingers and find Finlay's jutting spar. I grab it instinctively, through the damp wool of his trousers, and he helps by tugging at laces and toggles until it spills out suddenly into my bare hands. I never beheld it in life. It is thick and hard, more like horn than flesh— Och, it is cold, but it is something solid, something to cling to as their hands ebb and flow, sweeping me up in an undertow that I know will drag me off my feet.

Then they do it. Rory and Allan break from our cluster and pull me away, lifting me and laying me upon the great bed. I feel the warm silky brush of fur beneath my back. I look fearfully at Finlay, who stands where we abandoned him. His expression has not changed.

Then Allan goes over to help his brother off with his

doublet and shirt. And my vision is occluded by Rory, who puts both hands between my thighs and spreads them. Then he reaches for my sex.

Cold—cold—his hand is cold. But I have warmth to spare for him, and wet too. Two fingers, at least, are slid inside me. I remember Rory's fingers well: thick and leathery with knuckles like the knots on twigs, the creases ingrained with dirt. Now they curl inside me, and I buck my hips in welcome, unable to help myself, and let out a small cry.

It's been nine weeks since I was ridden. Rory was the last man to touch me, when he put me down over the wall of the sheep-fold while everyone else was loading the ponies—around the corner from them, but barely out of sight (the man was never shy)—and gave me a good seeing-to from behind, slapping my bum as he spent. Afterwards he gave me a kiss and a hug and a silver penny, muttered, "I'll miss that sweet cunt of yours, Meg," and walked away. As I watched the brothers ride off up the fellside, Rory's seed was leaking down the insides of my thighs, beneath my skirt. Well he knew me.

Now he knows, if there is any calculation going on behind those sunken eyes, that my sex is soft and ready and eager. It opens easily to the spread of his thick digits. In the old days he would have grinned at me, but not this time. His face is set, his eyes milky.

Then Rory looks back over his shoulder at his brothers, and nods. He moves aside, his fingers deserting me. For a moment I feel empty, like a dropped glove. I look down once more and see Finlay standing at the foot of the bed, naked and ready, his cock as engorged as a hanged man's. How his skin glistens! Thank God—the sea hasnae bloated him, though he bears great dark bruises across his belly.

Biting my lip, I raise my knees, like the raising of the portcullis at the town gate. My wet sex is an open invitation. And as he comes forward to accept, I lift my hands to him.

Ach. The first moment you step into the sea, it is always a shock. He washes over me like a winter wave, stealing my breath. His body is hard, with the leanness of youth, and his erect cock hardest of all. Cold impales heat. His back slides beneath my hand. His brothers are standing above us, watching, but I barely see them; in my inner sight nothing but a stake of burning cold, plunged into a hot and molten core. Moving. Sliding. Stretching me in ways that I desperately need. His death-mask face over mine. His shoulders knotted. Curly hair coarse with salt; salt crusted on his skin, salt on my lips. The sea is bitter-salty, and I think that perhaps that is where all the tears wept in the world end up: filling the oceans.

It is a wonder that there is any dry land left for us to stand upon.

Dear God, but his cock is beautiful in me. This foul thing, this walking corpse—he is beautiful. My own tears rebuke me, but they cannae quench my heat.

I fear that this time, our first, it will be over in moments. But I'll tell you this much: the dead are not quick. Finlay, pinning me, moves with the slow brutal surge of the beating surf. There is no haste. Every wave lifts me higher, drops me deeper. One gelid hand clutches my left breast, squeezing tight. His lips brush my temple. I am sliding into the depths, losing my footing, kicking out but finding no purchase for my feet. I am finding it hard to breathe. Cold slips inside me, into my lungs. Dark water closes over my head. I look up and see the flickering glitter of light, but I know I'm sinking and cannot rise.

They say that, as you drown, the panic and the terror

drifts away and that you feel, at that last moment, a kind of pleasure.

> Drowning, I dissolve in delight.
> He is everything I have longed for.

❖ ❖ ❖

> *Fare ye well, my mother dear,*
> *Farewell to barn and byre*
> *And fare ye well, the bonny lass*
> *That kindles my mother's fire!*

❖ ❖ ❖

I wake next to a dead man and sit straight up, gasping. The cockerel outside in the yard crows a second time, its voice hoarse and bitter.

A glance about me reveals that the fire has died down and gives no light but a tiny glow; it must be hours later. But there is a kind of light in the room; I can see a man silhouetted against my Mistress' great window. His outline is entirely black, like a cut-out piece of darkness, but the world beyond is a faintly luminous gray.

He shifts, turning. I discern broad bare shoulders. "It's time we were away," he says, and I recognize Rory's voice. "The gray rooster crows. Dawn comes across the sea."

"The worm frets," says a second voice. "If we are missed from our places …"

I look to the other side of the room, but I can make out nothing more than a standing figure, pale from head to toe. No mind: it is Allan, judging by the voice. That means that the slab of meat at my side must be Finlay.

"Brother, rise up," says Rory softly. "We must leave."

Without a grunt or a word, Finlay sits up from the hips.

It's too dark to see him, but he puts his arms around me. "My pretty Meg," his whispers.

I close my eyes, recalling what was done last night. The memories are fragmentary, and I am deeply grateful for the lack of clarity. What I do remember is shame enough. My calves are stiff, my lips bruised. My whole body aches with delight.

They say that kissing a corpse upon the lips means you will die within the month. If that's true, then I am damned and more.

"Remember me," murmurs Finlay. "But dinnae weep, my sweet one."

The three dead men move about the room. They need no light. I am next to blind, though, and it takes me a little while to realize that they are putting on their clothes. Then someone moves over to the door, and throws it wide.

There is light outside: only a single lantern, burning low, but I've been in the dark so long it seems to flood this shadowed room. My Mistress sits in the passage outside, curled up in a blanket, and her blinking, confused face must be a mirror to my own. She's been there all night, guarding her sons' chamber. Rory reaches down and pulls her to her feet. He's gentle, or as gentle as his stiff limbs allow him to be.

"Mother," says Allan, "we are leaving now. We must be back by dawn."

She starts to shake her head.

"Mother," says Rory. "You must let us be. You know that."

"You are keeping us from rest," adds Finlay. "Please, Mother. We cannae sleep while it rains."

My Mistress bows her head in her hands. For a moment all three sons surround her, and then they break away and head for the stairs. Their footfalls sound like the dull knocks of nails driven into wood. Finlay is last to leave. He pauses at the door and looks back—not at his mother, but over her head, at me. As if he's trying to take one last memory with him.

But he says not a word.

Then they are gone, and I'm sitting up in the middle of my Mistress's bed, naked and shivering, and our gazes lock. Her jaw sags and her eyes grow wide. I see, with a cold pang, that she didnae know I was in here. She must have assumed that I'd fled like the rest of the servants. *She didnae know.*

I reach out and snag the crumpled fur pelisse, drawing it up to cover my nakedness. As if it could hide what I've done.

The smell of the sea is terrible.

The drop pilot is a blocky woman with a thatch of curly gray hair—the bleaching's a side-effect of the uppers they keep pilots on, Peyton has heard. Certainly she looks too young to be naturally gray. She casts Peyton sidelong glances as they watch the five men load into the drop capsule.

"What's it like?" she says.

"What?" Peyton doesn't take her eyes off the marines. The bolt-gun at her hip is new and feels incredibly heavy. She wonders if she's going to be sick.

"What's it like being inside their heads when they die? D'you see anything? Is there, like, a tunnel of light or whatever?"

Peyton's mouth tastes metallic and she realizes she's bitten the inside of her lip. "I don't know," she rasps. "Never happened."

"You guys that good?"

The quiver is involuntary. "My first drop."

The pilot doesn't answer, but her eyes widen before she turns away.

Fuck you, Peyton desperately wants to tell her. *You don't ever have to touch the dirt. You don't get anywhere near the Spiders.* But this is her cherry jump and she knows she's the one who has to prove herself.

"Peyton!" Sergeant Jomoa lifts his hand. "Saddle up! Now!"

She scurries to obey, reaching up to the hatch. He puts one hand on her ass and boosts her up into the interior so powerfully that she nearly falls into Rialto's lap. Everyone laughs. A couple of hands land slaps on the curve of her butt. She's wearing the thin, skin-tight leather-look jumpsuit of a Pslider and it doesn't do much to shield her from the sting.

"Want to sit on my dick for the drop?" suggests Hayes.

"Keep your cheese-stick inside your armor till this is over," growls the sergeant, scrambling in through the hatch. "Unless you're going to use it to fuck a Spider. Then, be my guest, Hayes."

Trying to ignore the sniggers and the gropes and the whoops—they like her new uniform, it seems—Peyton pushes through to her seat just behind the forward bulkhead and straps herself in. The men sound confident and eager. Maybe, she thinks, they won't need her much. They've all done this before, many times. They know what they're about. All she has to do is watch and learn, with a bit of luck.

She pslides behind the sergeant's eyes.

—SHE'D BETTER BE UP TO SCRATCH OR WE'RE ALL FUCKED SIDEWAYS SENDING US A LITTLE FUCKING GIRL WHAT THE FUCK IS H.Q. THINKING OF??!!!

Shocked by his thoughts, she pulls out. There's no sign of any emotion at all on the man's broad, scarred face. He isn't even looking at her. She makes a show of checking her webbing, aware that she's suddenly hot and sweaty.

I can do this. I've been training for this for ten years.

As the pilot's voice comes over the intercom and the pre-flight checks start, she takes a tentative look inside the minds of each of the marines, like she's checking her pockets just to make sure she's not left her keys at home.

—SHE'S GOT GREAT TITS I WANT TO GET MY COCK BETWEEN THOSE PUPPIES AND SCUZZ ALL OVER HER FACE OH YEAH MAMMA I COULD JUST DO THOSE JUGS RIGHT NOW HEY HEY HEY GOTTA STIFFY OH YEAH IT'S THE ONLY WAY TO FLY

That's Hayes. No surprises there.

—SHE'S NOT ORIEL OH FUCK ORIEL WE SHOULD NEVER HAVE BROUGHT HER INTO AN UNSECURED ZONE IT HURTS LIKE A MOTHERFUCKER JUST THINKING

Eriksen, of course. Peyton feels guilty even touching his mind. It feels raw and angry, like a picked scab.

—LEFT FIELD CHECK THE LEFT ALWAYS YOUR BLIND SPOT PISSING GUN MOUNT THEY NEED TO REDESIGN THOSE THINGS SPIDERS COME OUT OF THE LEFT LIKE BLUE NINJA COCKROACHES

That's Brannon, his thoughts so focused that she feels like she can't breathe inside his head.

Rialto isn't articulating any thoughts at all: from him she just gets a blurred picture of a courtyard with a wisteria creeper hanging over the wall and woman—a big soft woman in a bright print dress—popping beans out of their pods.

Testing, she says into his head. *Can you hear me?*

Rialto glances at her and nods. The mental picture goes blank and is replaced by a wall of LA LA LA LA. They can shield themselves from her if they concentrate. She blushes, feeling like she's been caught spying.

Then the engines catch and roar, and she knots her fingers together and stares at them, fighting her surge of panic. *I can do this. I'm trained. They need me. They're relying on me. I will do it. Oh … shit. I've known them ten days and now their lives depend on me getting it right.*

◆ ◆ ◆

Ten days before, Lieutenant Vanderhuys had escorted her to the barracks to meet her squad for the first time. Peyton had always found Vanderhuys intimidating—she was a tall, proud woman in her forties, who wore her Pslider leathers even off-duty and walked with long strides even in high boots. Peyton was wearing regulation gray panties, a sleeveless top and little flat pumps; she didn't even have a bra on. Her breasts felt free and uncomfortably vulnerable, bobbing behind the tightly-stretched cotton, and she was struggling to keep up with the older woman's clicking heels.

She'd been ordered to don only those clothes and put her hair up in a plait that morning, after her daily medical. She remembered the doctor turning to Lieutenant Vanderhuys with Peyton's vaginal juices still glistening on her latexed fingers.

"Hormonal levels are optimal, Lieutenant," she'd said. "All bio-signs excellent. I'd say she's ready to go."

"Good," said Vanderhuys. "They've been waiting."

That was it, after a decade's training in military tactics and communications. Hour after hour spent on the combat simulation games, co-ordinating a virtual five-man squad in conditions ranging from trench warfare to infiltration of a Spider hive. Physical fitness training. Psionic exercises—she'd excelled at Precog. And in her downtime: the fuck-machine, pushing her body to the limits and honing her orgasmic responses. Ten years of training and pills and injections and tests, changing her from a normal human girl to a woman with a specific and extraordinary talent. All for this day.

Peyton had been feeling pleasantly horny this morning when she awoke, but she didn't now. She just felt dizzy with anxiety. Following at the lieutenant's heels down the drafty corridors of the Base, she felt as if everyone they passed was staring at her— wearing only her underwear, and pale with anticipation. They all knew what was going to happen to her, didn't they? Today she was finally going to be imprinted on a marine squad of her own. Today she was going to qualify as a Pslider.

Vanderhuys stopped outside a broad door with an "L" engraved on the metal, along with some sort of bird with its wings spread. "Here," she said, with a cold little smile. "Unit L for Lammergeier. They're good men. Three years combat experience, on average. This is the first downtime they've had in four months. They'll be very pleased to see you."

Peyton felt as if there were no bones in her legs. She wobbled suddenly, staggering a little.

"Something wrong, Corporal?"

"No, Lieutenant." Peyton bit her lip. She'd been given a rank, but it was courtesy only: her background wasn't strictly military. She'd been raised and trained in the confines of an EFORCE school. "I'm … nervous," she confessed.

"Nervous?" The lieutenant's eyes widened. "You think this is hard, what's expected of you?"

She nodded, relieved to be understood.

"Hard?" Vanderhuys moved in closer, her eyes narrowing to slits. "Have you been listening to dissident propaganda or something? Fuck that shit, Corporal. If you had a cock you'd be out there in some Kazakhstani shithole fighting Spiders right now. An eighty percent chance of injury in your first tour: seventeen percent chance of coming home in a plastic bag. Whereas these—" she grabbed both of Peyton's nipples between thumbs and forefingers, pinching them tight and tugging them through the cloth—"These afford you the remarkable privilege of serving your species in relative safety. You've only got a twenty percent chance of injury or death in your first tour of duty. It *is* a privilege, corporal. Do you understand that?"

"Yes, ma'am," Peyton gasped, feeling the pain of her trapped nipples like a red flame in her flesh.

"So are you ready, Corporal?"

"Yes—Oh!"

Vanderhuys gave them one last twist and let go. "About turn."

Peyton swayed on her feet, but turned to face the door. Her nipples burned as the pain receded, the twin points swelling angrily now and poking up through the cloth of her top. Vanderhuys put a leather-gloved hand on her ass.

"You lubed up?"

"Yes, ma'am." Tears prickled behind her eyes, but she blinked them back. They'd pumped so much antiseptic grease into her that she'd felt it ooze out of her clench as she walked.

"You'd better be." Vanderhuys flicked her ID over the sensor by the door. The red light turned green and the metal plate slid back. "Report to me tomorrow, 08:00, Corporal."

Peyton stepped into the room as a fug of warm air rolled over her. She was looking down the length of a small barracks chamber. She counted five men in regulation khaki T-shirts and shorts, some sitting, some sprawled out on the beds. They all looked up and stared at her. The musk of smoke and male bodies took her breath away.

One of the men rose slowly to his feet. He was twice her size, easily, and looked as if he were made of bronze that had been beaten until it cracked into scars. He removed the cigarette dangling from his mouth and sucked his lips.

She'd never been allowed to smoke. It was a privilege accorded only to combat personnel.

"Sergeant Jomoa," she said weakly, drawing herself up straight. The door hissed shut behind her. "Corporal Peyton reporting for duty."

❖ ❖ ❖

The drop-capsule falls like a lead coffin, all exterior

power off so as to maximize the time they'll have undetected by Spiders. When the 'chute canopy opens, the sudden deceleration smacks Peyton forward and back in her harness so hard that she squeals in pain. The men, used to this and better braced, laugh out loud.

"Thought you liked it rough, Peyton?"

"You should be used to being banged around by now!"

But the moment they touch dirt, all levity stops. Orders are snapped, weapons are hoisted, vizors are dropped to mask faces. The rear doors yield with a metallic groan.

"Deploy," says the sergeant. "Now." Then they're gone, out into the yellow dust, and Peyton is alone. Except that they are still with her where it really matters: inside her head. And there she can feel everything: the constriction of their plasteel armor, the trickle of sweat inside a helmet, the race of adrenaline. She's with them—and before them—and around them. She's their comms link and their surveillance camera.

It's a rescue mission. Not one to rescue people, of course—even if the population of this city hadn't been wiped out months back, there isn't enough room in their capsule for more than a handful of extra human bodies. But there's something that HQ wants picking up—a sealed capsule from a lab on the third basement level. Peyton doesn't know what's in it and nor, she suspects, does the sergeant. But it's something worth risking the lives of a squad of marines for.

◆ ◆ ◆

"Corporal Peyton?" The big man stubbed out his cigarette on the top of a metal locker. "Welcome to Lammergeier Squad."

There were noises from the others—jeers and whistles. "Take a look at that!"

"They sent us a brunette. Fuck, man—I wanted a blonde this time."

"Think the paperwork got mixed up?"

"Shuddup, Rialto. You'll make the 'ickle girl cry."

"Huh. Bet she'll be crying before we've finished with her."

She didn't look at them. She didn't dare. She kept her eyes fixed on the sergeant, and when he beckoned her forward she obeyed. He pulled a hard chair out into the center aisle between the beds and sat upon it, which put his eye-level just—only just—below hers, and then he looked her up and down thoroughly.

"So. You're pretty," he announced. "Looks like we got lucky, boys."

"I'm ready to get lucky!" laughed one of the men, swaggering in from the side with his hand already rummaging vigorously down his shorts. Peyton glanced sideways at him just as he popped his cock out. The tip looked ruddy and glistening. She shied away, her cheeks filling with blood.

"Stow that, Hayes," the sergeant grunted.

"Sarge!" he complained.

"You'll get some, don't worry. All in good time." His gaze flicked back to Peyton, weighing her up. "You never seen a man's dick, Corporal?"

"Yes, of course," she said huskily.

"Of course?" His eyebrows shot up. "Lots of them, then?"

"Well … pictures. Vids."

He grinned, and there was laughter all round. It wasn't very kind laughter. She wavered, heavy-limbed with dread. She'd been brought up by women, among women. Men were all in the military. There was precious little opportunity to meet any man who wasn't crippled, aged or an officer, even if she had been allowed to socialize freely; even if potential Psliders weren't kept confined in their training schools, their lives regulated around the clock. These men felt almost as alien to her as the Spiders. Their bulkiness, their rowdiness, their loud voices … even the smell of them was unfamiliar. It made her hair prickle and her palms sweat.

"Vids, huh?" The sergeant patted his thigh and she stepped in closer. "You like watching them?"

Watching them was a compulsory part of her training. Why then, did she squirm inwardly as she answered him? "Yes, Sergeant."

"Well, that's something. Let me see those tits, Corporal."

So, this is it.

She pulled up her gray cotton top, so that her breasts jutted out from beneath. Her aching nipples were hard as bullets now, and aimed right at his head. She saw him lick his lips, and for a moment he seemed lost for words.

"Fuckin' A," said one of the others happily. They were all on their feet, all watching. She felt the flush steal down from her cheeks over her breastbone. Her tits quivered with every breath.

"I want me some of that!"

"Fuck yeah. It's been … too long."

"Come on, Sarge!"

"Shush." Sergeant Jomoa put his warm and callused hand between her knees and drew it up the inside of her thigh, all the way to her cotton panties. Gently, he pressed the edge of that hand up against the cloth. "So you never been fucked?"

"I … uh." The gentle rubbing of his fingers along her shielded pussy seemed to rob her of words. The cloth was moist with sweat and lube and anticipation, and clung to her as he pressed it in. "I've trained on the machines … Sergeant."

"Oh?"

She cleared her throat. "You know."

"Yeah, I know. We've got our own machines." His fingers slid under the fabric of her panties and found her wetness as he added, with a hint of bitterness, "We're not permitted any real women other than our squad Pslider."

"Uh," she whimpered, his slick touch on her clit making her squirm. "I excelled on the machines, Sergeant. Extra credit."

"That's good." He withdrew his hand, an appraising glint in his dark eyes, and sat back in the chair, spreading his thighs. The fabric of his shorts was stretched tight, the fly already gaping to reveal a great curved mass of flesh rising beneath. "So show me. Show me how you earned that extra credit, Corporal."

Pleasing him was her only way forward. She dropped to her knees and, fumbling a little with the unfamiliar clothes, freed his cock from its constraints. But all her hours of diligent study hadn't prepared her for this, though she'd worked her way through every color and size of dildo presented as an option. The real thing wasn't just *big*; it was *hairy*—nested in thick curls, hairy around the balls, hairs even growing up the shaft from the root, like outriders for an army. And it was hot, and a little sticky, and it had a taste totally unlike the plastic and disinfectant she was used to, and it moved—responding to her touch like a live thing, which she supposed it was, in a way—twitching and swelling and stiffening. Making her mouth wet, she engulfed it, and the sergeant put both hands on her head and pushed deep into her. She felt his bulk nudge the back of her throat and she heard the rumbling sigh of his satisfaction.

"Not bad, Corporal," he said, as her head rose and fell

in his lap, and she licked and sucked with each stroke. His deep voice had dropped to a huskier note. Then his fingers tightened in her hair. "But if you want to graduate with honors, you need to do this …" he added, pushing her down hard on his erect cock, shoving right into her throat.

She opened up to him. That was something she had practiced. She let him do the work and slide her up and down, fucking her throat. His cock was so thick that she knew her jaw would be aching before he was done, but that was a pain she could cope with. Her head whirled with the scent and the taste and the heat of him—so much so that she hardly noticed her panties being pulled down to half-mast behind her or the stiff dick slapping against her splayed bottom. The voices above her were made indistinct by the sergeant's palms over her ears. Not until her ass-cheeks were parted by rough hands and that dick bounced into the cleft between, rubbing up eagerly against her, did she whimper anxiously.

But the sergeant noticed. He stopped her mid-stroke, allowing her to draw breath through her nose. "You ruining my fine view, Hayes?" he asked.

"I couldn't help it, Sarge. She was winking at me—look!"

Hayes demonstrated by poking the whorl of her butt-hole with his fingertip. Her ass was well-lubed and exceptionally well-trained, and that digit sank into her without resistance. The sensation—that electric ripple of invasion—was in no way diminished though, and Peyton uttered a muffled squeal around the thick length of NCO rod in her mouth.

"I think she likes it, Sarge," said Hayes, circling his finger in her anus and making her wriggle.

"You're no gentleman, soldier," the sergeant growled. "You haven't even been introduced and you're up her ass." He sat up, pushing Peyton off his cock. She gasped for breath. "Line up, you dirty horndogs, and stand to attention."

Peyton heard the men hurrying round behind her, but her concentration wasn't allowed to stray that way; the sergeant reached down between his spread thighs, grabbed both her nipples in a firm pinch and rolled them until she squeaked. "You got fine titties, Corporal," he murmured. "You like it when I do that?"

"Yes, Sarge," she said helplessly, her eyes fluttering half-closed.

"Good girl." He used her captured nipples to draw her to her feet, and then he turned her, settling his heavy grip on the back of her head instead, pulling her hair tight. "Meet your squad, Corporal Peyton."

They stood in a line, hands by their sides, and they were all naked now. Naked and muscled and hairy and tattooed, in that way that no blandly pornographic video or aseptic sex machine had been able to prepare her for. Each of the four men had one of those lammergeier vultures emblazoned across his chest, and their limbs and torsos were canvasses of complex inscriptions and pictures. None of them had a body as big as the sergeant's, but still they towered over her. Some smirked, some frowned, but all watched with eyes dark with lust.

"These are your privates, Corporal," rumbled the sergeant jovially, pushing her forward to face them. "I'm glad to see these unruly motherfuckers are saluting you."

They were all erect. Four cocks—varying in angle and size, certainly, but all thick and hard and pointing at her with frightening intent. Four pairs of balls bunched high under those lolling, twitching shafts. While another cock, the biggest one of all as befit its bearer's mass, pressed up against her back.

"You've met Hayes," said the sergeant.

Hayes grinned. He had the exaggerated biceps and bulging pecs of a soldier who spent his boring hours off-duty in the Base gym, and his cock had the same twisted sense of humor he did, swaggering with a cheeky curve off to the right.

"Now get down and salute that flagpole, Corporal," the man behind her said, pushing her to her knees. He kept hold of her head as she tipped her mouth over the swollen cock-tip and swallowed the length in as deep as she could take it.

"Fuck yeah!" Hayes groaned, arching his back. "Oh fuck yeah girl! Oh, you do that!" He tasted salty. Peyton's mouth made undignified slurping noises as she sucked, bobbing up and down on his cock. But as soon as Hayes' meaty thighs went taut enough to tremble, the sergeant wrenched her off, trailing strings of spit.

"Shit!" the marine complained.

"This," he said, pulling her to her feet and ignoring the bereft and swaying Hayes, "is Eriksen."

Eriksen was sandy-blond and had full, pouty lips that exaggerated the sullen look in his pale eyes. Maybe, she thought, he didn't like what he saw of her. Certainly his cock was only semi-hard as she fell to her knees before him; but then it stiffened up and filled out, as if making up for lost time, as she sucked on it. His balls were hairless, like those of the shaved actors in the vids, and he didn't move at all in response to her ministrations, or make any sound.

Rialto was just the opposite: darkly hairy all over, even up to his throat, so that his tattoos looked blurred. Scars cut through the fuzz of his closely-cropped scalp like paths through a scrub-belt. His eyes and lashes were so dark they looked like they'd been outlined in kohl, and would have seemed feminine if it were not for the craggy face they were set in. His cock was stubby but thick, a knobbled club of a phallus. "Uh," he grunted, working his hips in a steady rhythm as she sucked him: "Uh. Uh. Uh."

"God, I've missed that," said Hayes sarcastically, from down the line. "The sound of Rialto getting his rocks off … You wait till he comes, girl—he roars like bear."

"You fucked many bears, Hayes?" asked Rialto, through clenched teeth. "I thought it was usually sheep."

"Shit—would you make a noise like a sheep, dude? That'd really turn me on."

"Shut the fuck up, you two," the sergeant growled. He prized Peyton, open-jawed, from Rialto's glistening cock, and swung her up to face the last man in line. "Brannon," he announced.

Brannon sort of scared her. He didn't frown like Eriksen, or smirk like Hayes and Rialto. He stared at her, his face completely blank and only the jut of his engorged cock and the sweep of his eyes across her breasts betraying his interest. He didn't look into her face at all. As the sergeant brought her within arm's length, he reached out without warning and grabbed her breasts, lifting and squeezing them together, thumbing her nipples roughly.

"Oh," Peyton cried softly, caught between the two men, unable to pull forwards or backwards.

"Don't damage them, Brannon," the sergeant warned. "She doesn't carry spares."

Brannon let go of her aching tits and put his hand round the back of her neck to pull her to him. For a moment she felt like she might be snapped in half between the two men, and then she was sliding down Brannon's sinewy body, face pressed to the scars and the ink, over the ridges of his hard stomach and down onto a long cock marbled with blue veins. She gobbled at it gratefully, glad for the respite from those hungry hands. He had come so close to hurting her … and now her breasts buzzed and stung with need, and the ache was sinking right down through her body to her sex.

But Sergeant Jomoa didn't give her long to analyze her feelings. As Brannon started to spring a sweat, he snagged his fingers in her hair once more to free her from the prick that pinned her in place.

"Fuck," said Brannon softly, grabbing his cock.

"Now," the sergeant said, turning her head to look down the line. "You've met the squad. Your turn to choose. Which cock do you like the look of best, Corporal?"

She licked her lips, trying to think. Not Brannon—too intense. Not Hayes—too boisterous. The sergeant—but he was so big, she wasn't sure she could cope right away. She went with her instincts—precognition by any other name. "Eriksen," she said. He was the only one who'd showed real restraint.

The sergeant's brows rose in surprise, but he nodded. "Eriksen: forward," he ordered. "You're first."

◆ ◆ ◆

She doesn't feel the EMP. She just realizes that the exterior bulkhead doors aren't responding when she hits the button to close them. Throwing herself at the handle of the manual close, she begins to turn it frantically.

Sarge! Door circuits down! We've got Spiders close by!

—THAT'S OKAY PEYTON JUST SECURE AND STAY COOL IT'S WHAT WE'D EXPECT SNAFU

They're drawn to electrical signals. It's like throwing chum into seawater. They'll come in all their glowing long-legged beauty, and they'll fry any electrical equipment that isn't caged or hardened, and they'll fill the radio frequencies with such interference that comms are fucked and the human race is reduced to shouting and semaphore. That's where the Psliders come in, of course.

—POSITION PEYTON! WE'RE GOING IN—WE NEED YOU ONSIDE! His voice is clear in her head. She's got a mental picture too: a plaza with a colonnaded walkway. She's studied the schematics of the building until she knows every square foot. She knows where they're heading. It's her task to keep them in touch with one another. Psliding from head to head, relaying information and orders, watching everyone's back. Keeping them all safe, so that when pickup sweeps through and snags the capsule, they'll all get home together.

◆ ◆ ◆

"Shit, man. Not fair."

"Don't be a dick, Hayes."

"I just like to go first. It's tighter, you know."

"That's because yours is like a cocktail sausage."

Ignoring all this, Eriksen stepped forward and caught her by the cotton vest still bunched up at the top of her breastbone. There was no sign of pleasure on his face at having been chosen; if anything the blue-ice glare deepened.

"By the numbers, Private," said Sergeant Jomoa dryly, wandering off a little to light another cigarette.

"Yes, Sarge." Twisting the cloth until it pulled uncomfortably tight under her arms, he passed his other hand over her exposed breasts, petting and rubbing, petting and rubbing … and then breaking off to tug experimentally at her hard nipples before going back to stroking her. If he'd squeezed her roughly it would have just been a grab, but these caresses heightened her breasts' sensitivity almost beyond bearing. Peyton couldn't have hidden her response if she'd tried; the rush of sensation made her close her eyes and bite her lip, though that couldn't stop the little breathy moans escaping.

"Oh fuck yeah," murmured Hayes.

Then Eriksen trailed his fingers down her body, right into the soft and hairless split of her sex. Standing on tiptoe, it wasn't particularly easy to open her legs wide enough for him, but obedience was ingrained. As his fingers slithered around in the copious wet he found and delved into her passage, her pussy tilted instinctively and ground into his palm. She'd never been touched by an actual man down there—but when he held her sex in his hand, it was like she was made to fit him.

It was almost enough to make her protest when he withdrew his fingers. But then he lifted them to his face and inhaled her bouquet, tasting one fingertip and then another.

"Ah, fuck," said Rialto in the distance. "Real pussy. None of that machine shit."

All the time Eriksen was watching her face, as if assessing her reaction to being played with. *No*, she thought—*not assessing. Judging*. No imprinting was needed to recognize the disapproval that burned in his cold eyes. She had a sudden panicky moment as she thought she'd picked the wrong man entirely.

So it took her by surprise when he swung her around by her shirt and sat her on top of the nearest foot-locker, pushed up her thighs—and then sank down to a crouch between them, burying his face in her open pussy. She lost her balance and tipped back with a cry, her head and shoulders flopping down onto the hard military mattress of the bed behind. The machines—the vids—the doctors—none of them had prepared her for this: the feeling of a man's hot face between her thighs, the scour of his stubble, the hungry sucking play of his tongue. It was almost too much, just for that first moment, and she cried out and kicked, her legs finding no purchase on the air. But Eriksen grabbed her calves and pushed her legs right up and back, pinning her in place. And after that it wasn't too much. She only wanted more.

"Shit, man," Hayes complained. "Hurry up, my balls are blue here. Fuck that romance shit. Do it later."

"What, after you've spunked all over it?" Rialto asked.

"Hey. Maybe he'd like a little gravy on his meat."

Eriksen emerged for air, leaving Peyton bereft. "She has to come. That's the point, isn't it?" He had some sort of European accent.

Brannon grunted. "She'll come. Look at her. She's a real pslut." He said it without rancor. "Just fuck her."

The thing was, he was right and Peyton knew it, though she'd never been with a man before this day. EFORCE had trained her mind for psliding and her body, with equal thoroughness, for orgasmic response. Once aroused, she could be pushed into climax over and over again—until she was beyond satiation, until she was no longer able to think, until she was weeping with exhaustion between bouts, but burning for another one the moment it began again. It was what she *was*. How else was she to bond with her squad? Or endure the life she'd been assigned to?

"Don't take all day, Eriksen," said Sergeant Jomoa mildly.

With a grunt, Eriksen heaved himself to his feet, though he looked down at Peyton as if she were a piece of meat. Only his massively stiff cock betrayed any emotion. Draping her heels over his shoulders, he muscled up against her pussy, slid one thumb over her clit and slipped his length inside her. Contraception wasn't an issue—her eggs had all been harvested already. He didn't hurry. He didn't push deep before he partly retreated, waited a moment and then slid in again just as slowly. It was as if he didn't want to commit any other part of him than his cock to this enterprise.

But it was enough for Peyton. The slip of his thumbpad over her aching clit, the girth and pressure of his shaft—and then, the slight tightening of his jaw, the grimace of effort around his cold eyes. That was enough to tear the ripcord and let her first orgasm tumble out in a red silk explosion. She arched her back as it billowed through her, and wailed.

"There you go," said Brannon.

For a few seconds Peyton simply soared on the pleasure. Then she started to hear it, like the sound of a radio gradually being tuned in to a clear station: broken snatches of a voice in her head.

—RIEL … UT THE … TIGH … WHAT IF SHE GO …?

It was Eriksen. She'd been told all about this moment, but the sensation was still eerie: *In the moment of orgasm your mind will open to the person you are in congress with, and you will imprint upon him.* She could hear his thoughts … not just the unarticulated words, but the great mass of emotion behind.

—BASTARDS FUCKING BASTARDS SENDING US THIS WHOREGIRL WHAT AM I DOING THIS IS ALL FUCKING WRONG SHE'S SO

Peyton whimpered. Behind that studied indifference, Eriksen was burning with rage. She could feel his coagulated resentment, thick as blood clots.

—NOT THE SAME FEELS SO GOOD OH I FUCKING HATE THIS SOMETIMES WISH I WAS DEAD LIKE HER I SHOULD HAVE BEEN OH FUCK THIS WHOLE SETUP IS SO FUCKING WRONGWHATINEEDWRONG OH ORIEL

She stared up at him, aghast. His face was slackening now, his eyes no longer focused, sweat beaded on his temples. He'd forgotten her clit at some point; now he was just gripping her hips and thrusting into her, like his cock was a weapon and he was stabbing her to death. She could feel his suffocating hurt, and his desire to pass that hurt on. She could feel the rising darkness of his orgasm, pushing him forward on every stroke. He was ramming hard and fast into her pussy, looming forward, juddering all the breath out of her.

—OH FUCK OH FUCK ORIEL ORIEL ORIEL!!

Then he was coming, and she caught a blurred mental glimpse of black curling hair before his climax came crashing through her mind like a grenade going off, blowing everything else away, words and images blasted to pieces. He came, and so she came too, sharing the jagged white-hot release.

When she regained her senses she reached up and touched his face, stroking the sweat from his skin. He caught her wrist and pulled her up so she was sitting on the locker. Breathing hard, they stared into each other's eyes.

"Who's Oriel?" she whispered, a moment before thinking better of it.

A steel shutter came down across Eriksen's mind. Without a word, he yanked out of her and stalked away.

◆ ◆ ◆

—CORPORAL YOU IN POSITION? WE'RE IN THE LOBBY.

She is. With the building schematics arrayed around her on both internal monitors and backup paper maps.

I'm good. I'm good Sarge. I can see you. Take a left through those double doors. You're looking for stairs down.

It's like her training exercises—a bit, although instead of alternate headcam views on her screen, she has five heads to pslide between. She can hear what they hear and what they're thinking, she can relay information silently between separated marines, and she can even see through their eyes as long as she concentrates. That's the hardest part: building an accurate idea of who's where, doing what, while each individual is in constant motion.

—SHIT NO LIGHTS IN HERE

That's Brannon. There's a pause as chemical glowpacs are lit and one tossed gently down the corridor. They can't carry battery flashlights, after all.

—WE GOT STAIR DOORS

That's Rialto, taking point. Peyton squints through his eyes, her own closed so she can see the markings in his mental image more clearly.

That looks right. You want to head—WAIT! Hold on! Anxiety makes her broadcast so loudly that everyone in the squad hears her at once.

—OW! DON'T SHRIEK GIRL complains Hayes

Precog makes her skin tic, the nerves jumping. *There's a truckload of Spiders in the stairwell,* she tells them urgently. *A whole nest. You can't go that way without a major firefight.*

—YOU GOT AN ALTERNATE ROUTE CORPORAL?

Yes, she says. *Yes. Hold on.*

◆ ◆ ◆

Peyton put a hand over her mouth and looked around. Somehow, without moving, it was as if the other four men had taken a step back.

"Corporal Oriel was your predecessor," said Sergeant Jomoa. She thought he looked disappointed. "You do know the privacy protocols, Corporal?"

"Yes Sergeant. I'm very sorry."

What happened to her? she wondered.

"Let's hope that's the last dumb-ass mistake you make. Rialto, you're up next."

Rialto uncoiled from his perch on another locker and

stepped forward, his mouth pulled sideways into a grimace. "That was sloppy, girl," he told her in a low voice.

She looked away, nervously. She had hardly gotten her breath back and this big hairy man stooping to loom over her—this condemnation—felt like too much to cope with. "Honestly, I'm sorry," she repeated.

"Luckily for you," he said, plunging his hand between her thighs to grope the gash Eriksen had opened and then abandoned, "I don't mind sloppy so much." He showed his teeth. "That's one slippery snatch you got there. You ready to read my thoughts, girl?"

Wide-eyed, she nodded, stifling a whimper. His fingers were thick and callused.

"Gotta warn you, girl; they're pretty fucking dirty thoughts. Hope you're not shy." He pinched her clit accurately between two fingers, and Peyton found herself suddenly incapable of stifling any noise.

"Ohhh!" Her cry made the men around her snicker.

"That's good. I like a girl who lets it all out." He grinned. "When I make you come, I want that dickhead Hayes to know it, right? Every time."

She didn't know what answer to give to that, but luckily he wasn't waiting for one. Grasping her thighs, he tugged her forward and lifted her bodily, big hands sliding under her ass. She clung to his shoulders, but she needn't have bothered—he held her with as little effort as he might have held a plasgun.

"Open wide," he said, lowering her down his torso to spear her with his cock.

Peyton squealed in shock at the invasion—gratifying Rialto no end, judging from his expression. He let her sink right the way down onto his length, all the way to the thick root, and leaned backward. Suddenly he spread his arms wide. Impaled on his stake, her weight entirely on his pelvis, Peyton clung to him as he found his balance.

"Look! No hands!" he announced happily.

"What are you, man—a circus act?" Hayes complained. Even Eriksen, sitting on the edge of a bed and lighting a cigarette, was watching. Brannon snorted.

"Go on. Give it to her."

Rialto obliged. Grabbing her ass again in both hands and setting his stance broad, he began to jerk his hips rapidly, pummeling Peyton's crotch while his member rammed her core. It felt like the breath was being shaken from her lungs. It felt stupidly, horribly, freakishly arousing, having her deepest parts brutally rattled like that, feeling her whole body centered on his cock. She was trapped there, skewered, and every little thrust stabbed her deeper and split her wider. Her wriggling efforts to lift herself, to escape even one inch of her impalement, gave way to a stiff-legged tension. Her mouth formed and locked in an O of tormented pleasure, and as her climax tore her open she threw back her head and let loose a wail that went on and on, like a siren. She forgot to hold herself, forgot to worry about the watchers, forgot how precarious their upright stance was— she arched her back and let the light arc through her, until the darkness that came after nearly swept her away.

—THERE THAT'S RIGHT OH YES JUST PERFECT FUCKING BEAUTIFUL

Rialto's voice burst into her head loud and bright, as warmly colored as firelight. There was no sense of anything held back, nothing but avid appreciation. When he lifted her from his stiff cock and let her slide to her knees before him, his fingers wound in her hair in a manner that was nearly a caress. "There's a good girl."

—SHE'S LIKE A DOLL SO FUCKING TINY PRETTY LIKE A DOLL LIKE A SEX TOY GONNA FILL HER WITH CUM LOOK AT THAT DOLL MOUTH JUST RIGHT FOR MY COCK

"Suck it," he rasped. "Come on, girl."

She blinked back into focus, finding herself face-to-face with his stiff and waving erection. Despite the ease with which he'd lifted her before, his body was now glistening with sweat. And his whole crotch area, she saw, was greased and slippery with a cocktail of her sex juices and Eriksen's semen, which much have gushed out of her pussy as he pounded it. It streaked his thighs and blobbed like pearls in the dark hair of his rucked balls. She could smell it, grass-green and musky. Her mouth watered at the scent.

Peyton loved the taste of cum. She'd had the harvested spunk of soldiers dripped onto her tongue by syringes as she'd reached her machine-orchestrated climaxes in the fuck-engines— just so that she'd grow used to the flavor and associate it with her own pleasure. And she'd been thoroughly trained in the sucking of cock. She remembered hour after hour of oral exercises: strapped into the machine with one dildo pumping her pussy, she'd had another fed to her lips, and her reward for making the artificial penis spurt salty ersatz-jizz each time had been the brush of a vibrating pad to her engorged clit, allowing her to come.

Now she had the chance to prove herself with the real thing, and the prospect made her pussy ache with emptiness. She opened her mouth to Rialto with a will.

—OH FUCK YEEEEEES AT LAST AT LAST SO WARM AND GOOD LIKE A OH GOD IS THAT HER TONGUE? HOW DOES SHE DO THAT?!! IT FEELS LIKE FUCKING ANGELS DANCING ON MY COCK SORRYHOLYMOTHER SHE SUCKS

LIKE A FUCKING ANGEL CHRIST EVERY BIT AS GOOD AS
POOR ORIEL I LOVE THIS DIVISION SOMETIMES IF YOU
CAN SAY ONE THING ABOUT THIS WAR IT'S PRODUCED
SOME AMAZING COCKSUCKERS AND THEY LOVE DOING
IT THAT'S THE THING THEY JUST LOVE IT LOOK AT HER
DOLL MOUTH WRAPPED ROUND MY DICK HOW DOES
SHE GET IT SO DEEP THERE'S NOTHING TO HER SHE'S
TINY WHERE DOES IT ALL GO? I'M GOING TO DIE AND BE
BURIED IN THERE AND I DON'T CARE THIS IS FUCKING
HEAVEN. JESUS. JESUS. I'M GOING TO COME. JESUS. OH.
OH. OHHHHHHHHH YES THERE OH HOLY FUCKING
CHRIST OHHHHHHHH FUCK SHE'S COMING TOO LOOK
AT HER LOOK AT HER SHE OHHHHHHHHH

OH
YES

◆ ◆ ◆

Lammergeier Squad reaches the basement without loss
and without having to toast more than a couple of wandering
Spiders. The acrid stench of the burned aliens is new to Peyton,
and even experienced through Brannon's senses it makes her
sneeze.

—ARE WE CLEAR CORPORAL?

She stares at the security door through the sergeant's
eyes, alert to the spike of precog dread. *Clear, Sarge.*

They have to use plAcid to burn out the fused lock. As
Hayes shapes the putty the others take cover and keep watch.

Spike.

Eriksen—behind you! Above aboveaboveabove!

As Eriksen swings round she sees a glittering blue Spider
crawl out from the gape of a ventilation shaft, legs aglow like
neon tubes. The surge of Eriksen's ire is scarlet in her mind,

indistinguishable from the roar of his flamethrower. The Spider falls, curled in a crispy ball.

—GOOD CALL, the sergeant tells her. From Eriksen there's no word.

Alone in her drop capsule, Peyton bites her lip and smiles.

◆　◆　◆

She kept Rialto's cock in her mouth even after sucking it dry, even as it started to flag. She didn't want to let it go. The afterbuzz of his orgasm was like a bonfire.

"Holy shit, girl," he said faintly. "That's not bad. You got a talent there." They'd been right; Rialto did roar as he climaxed.

Then a hand seized her braided hair, pulling her off his fat length. "My turn," said Hayes.

Rialto bristled. "Fuck, man—you don't interrupt!"

"You're finished. I'm having her now."

For a moment the two men glared at each other over her head. Peyton could taste Rialto's atavistic instinct to keep possession. His hand was heavy on the top of her head. Then suddenly he laughed and withdrew that hand, slapping Hayes on the shoulder.

"You go for it, Hayes. Bang her good."

Hayes grinned. "I'm gonna bang her brains out." He used her plaited hair to lift her to her feet. "That's what you want, isn't it, pslut?"

"She's a Corporal, Hayes," said Sergeant Jomoa lazily from his seat. "Address her properly, marine."

Hayes didn't even blink. "That's what you want, isn't it—Corporal Pslut? You want this,'—he rubbed her hand over his hard hard cock— "to fill your ass with hot Lammergeier lead, don't you?"

"Yes," she whimpered, as her hand automatically

caressed his shaft. And it was true. She wasn't afraid anymore; all that had been swept away by the tsunami of orgasm. She was nervous still—nervous of what these big rough men were going to do to her—but it wasn't a blinding, debilitating fear. She wanted, now, to *know*.

Hayes glanced down at her little hand grasping his big cock. "Oh yeah," he said happily. "I think you're going to fit in here, Corporal. Now, let's see where *I* can fit in."

Towing her over to the nearest bed, he turned her and pushed her onto the mattress, spanking her rear. "Hands and knees, let's see that … Oh. Yeah."

Hands and knees, ass presented to him, thighs apart. Nothing hidden. The blanket was rough under her knees. She heard the other men shifting position to get a good view. Hayes ran his fingers down her crack, prodding the lubed pucker of her anus and raking through her open, puffed-up sex. She knew she must be glistening and shiny all over. He touched her clit and she quivered, moaning her gratitude.

"Now, this is a hell of a choice," Hayes mused. "Pussy or ass. They both look pretty fucking fine from here. Pussy or ass." He climbed up on the bed behind her, his thighs hot and hairy where they rasped against her own. "Pussy …" He dipped his cockhead into the well of her cunt. "Or ass …" He nudged up against her whorl, pressing to find the point at which she yielded.

"Ohhhh!" she groaned, her splayed thighs trembling.

"Pussy …" Back again.

"Hey, fucker, don't be dirty," Brannon muttered. "You ain't the last to go. And I like a clean ship."

"But it's so hard to choose! So …" Hayes sighed, and then suddenly seemed to commit himself—sliding his cock full-length into her sex. But he hadn't abandoned her rear entirely.

She felt his fingers press to her anus, inveigle their way in, and then straighten to become a manual phallus. It was two fingers at least, judging from the girth of his invasion.

Peyton made a desperate squealing noise as he shoved all the way in.

"I think she likes me," Hayes announced.

Peyton certainly liked anal. She could come and come if her rear passage was being stimulated, and she knew that right now she didn't stand a chance against Hayes. Gripping her hip with his free hand, he began to piston into her ass, driving his fingers in as deep as they'd go. She was desperately grateful for the peppermint lube the doctor had pumped her full of that morning. And it might sting her pride, but she was grateful to the boorish, boyishly-cruel Hayes too. His big fingers spread and flexed and curled, sending shockwaves of unbearable sensation all the way from her ass to the top of her head. She began to make *uh-uh* animal noises, unable to voice in any other way the feeling of delicious violation. Her body felt like it wanted to split in half. His cock ground into her pussy, though without the vigor he was devoting to her ass.

"Please!" she cried, breathless. "Not so—not so—oh—oh—Please!"

"Please what?" asked Hayes, but his voice was drowned by her shriek as she climaxed.

His inner voice too, it turned out, was disinclined to articulate anything sophisticated. —FINE FUCKING ASS OH YEAH OH YEAH LETS DO THIS THING BITCH!! I'M GONNA UNLOAD FILL YOU WITH JIZ TIL IT RUNS OUT YOUR FUCKING EARS were the first words she heard, and he kept on repeating the *Oh Yeahs* as he thrust harder and harder with his cock and eventually forgot to thrust with his hand at all, just holding on to her from inside and out as he slammed home. Peyton had to grip the blanket and bury her face in its scratchy fibers to stop herself being shoved down flat and crushed. But his hand in her ass kept her coming and coming; four or five times before he found his own tipping point. His orgasm was bright and came in discrete staccato pulses, like tracer fire against a night sky.

He came down from his high faster than she did.

—HUH ONLY THREE FINGERS SHE'S NO ORIEL. I USED TO BE ABLE TO GET MY FIST UP ORIEL.

She felt inexplicably hurt.

❖ ❖ ❖

Scan. Fire. Move.

Spiders fall, skitter and thrash across floors, burning as they writhe.

Eriksen watches Hayes' back. Brannon is shifted forward to pair with Rialto.

Peyton is losing touch with her own body, more there with her men than here in the drop capsule. She hardly registers the coffined interior of the craft, the glow of the monitors, or the tick-tick-tick of probing claws on the outside of the craft. She pslides from mind to mind, circling the group, feeling everything. The pinch of minds narrowed down to points of watchfulness. The smell of unburnt fuel and burnt Spiders. The itch and soar of adrenaline. It's almost a game: points scored for each hit, allies and enemies, no room for anything but winning. But it's a game with death as the stakes.

They love it. This is what they were made for. They don't think of home or family or what will happen when this is over. They don't notice the discomfort or the effort or the ache of their muscles. In fact they hardly think at all. They want to kill Spiders. They want to protect the man next to them. They want to win. Above all, they want not to let their squad down.

They're in the zone.

◆ ◆ ◆

Brannon came to her while she crouched on the bed, her front end collapsed onto the blanket and her butt stuck up in the air, her asshole and pussy now plumped and blowsy like blown roses. He lifted her effortlessly, pulled off the sleeveless shirt still rucked up under her armpits—*Am I still wearing that?* she wondered, as it was taken from her—and used the garment to mop Hayes' semen as it oozed out of her split. He threw the top away.

"Don't hurt her too bad, Brannon," said Rialto. He sounded jocular.

"Hh." Brannon waved his hand in front of her eyes like a stage hypnotist. "Look at her—she's in the endorphin zone. Flying. She's up for anything." Then he sat down on the bed and pulled her into his lap, straddling his thighs. His cock was as thick and hard as ever, but it slid into the juicy depths of her sex with so little friction that she only sighed.

The others gathered in a loose circle to watch.

"Pass me my bag of tricks, guys," Brannon said, looking down at her breasts with such cool appraisal that even through her fog of arousal Peyton felt some apprehension. He wasn't leering, despite the stiffness of the length he had up inside her; he was calculating. She could almost hear the cogs turning in his mind.

Someone dropped a bag on the bed at his right. He rummaged inside, and she stared at his averted face, trying to guess what lay behind the cropped fuzz of his hair, the blue vein at his temple.

He found what he was looking for. It was a can of sanitizing gel. He squirted some into his left hand and then sploodged a large dollop onto the wet, flushed slope of her breastbone. It felt icy cold and had the same familiar peppermint scent as the lube they'd stuffed up her ass before all this started. She squirmed as he used both hands to massage the goo over her breasts, paying particular attention to the puckering halos of her areolae, and twisting her nipples until they were drawn out into hard points again.

I am flying. I am. Oh please. Keep doing that.

He couldn't hear her yet, of course.

She had just about gotten her breath back after the previous round with Hayes. She found it coming short and shallow once more, the pleasure heady but spiked with nervous anticipation. There was no mistaking that he was preparing her for something.

"D'you know what these are?" he asked softly, holding up two objects from his bag. They were identical: black plastic, almost small enough to hide in his palm, with open jaws.

She shook her head.

"They're piercing crabs. For putting in piercings. Rings, bolts, whatever you load them with. They're very fast and they'll punch a hole *anywhere*. One snap and …" He smiled, and Peyton felt the blood drain from her cheeks. "Just so you know: every time we come back from a mission, I'm going to put a little silver ring down there on your pussy lips."

Oh … shit! She crashed down from her cozy high into chill, shivering dread.

Brannon brushed the back of one finger over the point at which their bodies joined, sending a thrill through her clit. She squirmed, trying to draw back from him, and she felt the cock inside her give a kick and swell a little bigger. "Pretty soon you're going to have a whole row of rings down either side," he said, his voice husky. "That's if you're any good as a Pslider Op, of course."

She bit her lip. She wanted to look away from him, to look to the others for help, but for once they had fallen silent and she could not break free of his gaze, any more than she could escape that big cock impaling her core. And she did not dare pslide into any other head and find out what they were really thinking right now.

"You got a problem with pain, Corporal?" Brannon asked, gently. She knew now how deceptive that gentleness was. "You won't make much of a soldier if you're scared of pain."

She couldn't answer. She nodded convulsively, in acknowledgment.

"Still, you don't have to worry about these just yet." He laid the piercing crabs aside on the bed. "First things first. You need inking up."

"What?" she whispered, as he produced something else from the bag. It looked like a big fat pen.

"Lammergeier Squad. You've got to wear the crest." He caressed the top of her breastbone. "We all wear it."

She whimpered; and though nothing showed in his expression, she felt again the throb of his cock.

"Now, I'm fast—but you need to hold still. This burns a bit. You wriggle, and it'll fuck up the art. I don't want that to happen." His gaze flicked to the men behind her. "You guys better hold her still."

Hands gripped her shoulders. One slid over her throat, pulling her head back. She found herself pinned, leaning back in Brannon's lap, braced against someone's hairy body—Rialto of course—Brannon's cock like a stake inside her. There was a very faint buzz, like a moth burring against a lamp. Someone took her right nipple between thumb and finger and began to pinch and tug the nub of flesh. She couldn't see who. She could only see the top of Brannon's head, his scalp shiny through the fuzz of hair, and Rialto looking down on her. In desperation she pslid into his mind.

—SHH BABY HOLD STILL IT'S OKAY

She was shocked. She wanted to tell him she was scared, that pain horrified her, that she didn't want this. But she didn't dare. She was their Pslider. She wasn't allowed to be scared.

—ITS ALL GOING TO BE OKAY BABY FUCK YOU LOOK HOT

Someone else took her other nipple and began to roll it skillfully, sending sparks of pleasure cascading through the fog of fear. Then Brannon began pressed the pen-tip to her skin, and began to ink.

He'd told the truth about two things: that he was fast—almost as fast as someone drawing with a pen on paper—and that it burned. As the sting hit her, her whole body jerked and quivered, taut as a bowstring. She clenched her teeth and didn't cry out, but she felt the rush of sweat to her skin as the pain marched into her head like an occupying army, huge and jagged, blotting out Rialto's voice. Somewhere she was dimly aware that Brannon's cock was swollen still further, and that her jerking hips must be encouraging that, but she couldn't care. She strained against the hands holding her, glad of their strength, glad that she couldn't ruin everything.

The pain was fierce, but it wasn't actually unbearable. As the inking went on she had time to come to grips with that thought. It was pain, but it was other things too. Her whole body seemed to catch fire from the heat of the ink, burning and soaring. Her nipples in particular—she knew her nerve endings there were artificially enhanced for optimal pleasure responses, and the stimulation to her captive buds took the edge off the agony and seemed to transmute it.

So when Brannon began to sketch down the slope of her right breast, closing on her nipple, everything was somehow changed. The pain was a ladder now, something she could climb rung by rung toward a numinous goal. She arched her back, pushing her breasts up instead of trying to pull away from her tormentor. She began to keen in her throat, and Rialto's hand tightened. Her whole chest felt as if it were being lashed by black fire.

And then it stopped. Brannon had reached the border of her areola and halted, lifting the pen. Peyton opened her eyes, astonished and bereft, and for a moment he raised his head and looked deep into them, as if searching for something. Her panting was loud in the silent barracks, as if everyone else had ceased breathing.

Then he looked down and started again, on her left breast.

This time there was no stopping her. Inch by inch he worked his way down to her nipple, and rung by rung she climbed that dizzying ladder. The black fire lashed her aching breasts. His engorged cock slithered in her churning cunt. As he reached that most sensitive apex of her flesh she began to come at last, juddering wildly and screeching; riding the pain with joy.

—WHAT A LITTLE FUCKING BEAUTY LOOK AT THAT SHE'S HIGH AS A FUCKING KITE SHE LOVES THE RUSH I COULD DO ANYTHING I WANTED SHE'D LET ME GOTTA BE CAREFUL HERE SO EASY TO BREAK HER

It was hard for Peyton to grasp it all at once; Brannon's raging erection inside her coloring everything crimson with lust; the oblivious, instinctive focus of his cool hands; his analytical inner voice with its terrible underlying need.

Then:

—YOU CAN HEAR ME NOW CAN'T YOU? CAN YOU HEAR ME? CANYOUHEARME?

Yes. I can hear you. He must have latent Pslider genes, she thought; his inner voice was astonishingly clear and assertive. She opened her eyes. He nodded.

—WANT TO SEE WHAT I'VE DONE TO YOU?

He didn't wait for an answer. He just called out for a mirror, and while he wiped her burning sweat-slicked chest down with an antiseptic towel, someone brought a steel-backed shaving mirror and held it over Brannon's shoulder so that she could see his handiwork.

There was the lammergeier emblazoned across her breastbone, wings fanned in beautiful detail. Just like the tattoos they all bore, except for this one difference: in the vulture's claws was a taut chain, one end stretching down her right breast, one down the left, as if pulling upon her nipples.

"There. You belong to the Squad now."

The other men made approving noises.

—YOU'RE OURS said Brannon's private voice. WE OWN THAT ASS AND THAT CUNT AND THAT MOUTH. THAT PRETTY LITTLE BODY. WE *OWN* YOU.

She shivered, watching tears slide down her cheeks and drip on her reddened breasts, but feeling no sorrow. Just relief.

"There's one last finishing touch," Brannon announced. He held up the piercing crabs again. "Gotta get it looking right."

Hayes whooped.

Peyton shuddered, but lowered her lids, accepting.

—YOU KNOW WHAT I LIKE DON'T YOU?

You like pain.

—OH YES

His excitement was vast, like a thundercloud. She could feel the clench of the ball-sac between his legs, the pulse threaded up the length of his cock, his orgasm massed and teetering. None of it showed to anyone outside their shared headspace. When he placed the crabs over her nipples and thumbed over the safety so that they caught and pinched the stiff points, his hands were rock steady. He looked from tip to tip, making sure the alignment was correct.

—THIS WILL HURT REAL BAD. ARE YOU AFRAID?

Yes. She didn't try to hide it from him. How could she hide, when they were in such intimate proximity? He wanted her to hurt. Just the thought of her pain was enough to nearly send him over the edge. She was shaking now.

—YOU CAN SCREAM. I'D LIKE THAT.

"Come here," he said in a low gruff tone, and used the crab claws to pull her close. His mouth moved over hers. Then he pressed the triggers.

White light arced across her breasts. She gave him what he wanted, and screamed. But she didn't have time to feel real pain, because a split second later his orgasm hit her like a volcanic eruption, and then they were burning together, locked in a private inferno.

When she came round his arms were about her, holding her upright in his lap. Her tits felt like they were on fire, but Brannon was slippery with sweat and clammy cold and quaking with aftershocks.

OHFUCKOHFUCKOHFUCK   Brannon's   voice gabbled. OH FUCK OH FUCK.

And she could feel his gratitude.

◆ ◆ ◆

The capsule is a sealed gray box which it takes two men

to carry. Peyton doesn't recognize any of the ID numbers printed on the side and registers no stab of recognition from the marines, but then it isn't like any of them are valued for the depth of their technical know-how. Eighteen Spiders have fried in unwitting defense of a box they've no conceptual grasp of either.

As far as anyone knows, the Spiders are individually non-sentient. True to their invertebrate form, they function like a swarm of insects, crossing the vacuum of space in cocoons. Peyton has heard it postulated that they possessed a hive mind, diffused across the mass.

She feels now that the Spiders might not be the only ones. Lammergeier Squad move, fight and function like a gestalt entity. Psliding from head to head, she finds it hard to distinguish between the individual men, so focused are they on their task. Hayes isn't joking any more, and Eriksen isn't grieving. Rialto is no less ruthless than Brannon. Only the sergeant stands out, because she can taste his sense of responsibility—for the mission, and for his men.

❖ ❖ ❖

Brannon lifted her from his lap at last and plopped her down on her knees in front of him. Peyton found herself eye-to-eye with his slick, lolling cock. The thing flopped about like a drunk and she wondered if she should lick it clean of her pussy juices. Then Brannon stood up, patted her on the head and wandered away, taking his tackle with him. She watched him saunter over to where a tin of the usual weak military beer awaited him in Hayes' hand. He cracked it and took a swig, glanced back idly at her, smirked to see her watching, then turned his shoulder.

Hayes slapped him on the arm, congratulating him on his work.

"You okay, Corporal?"

That was the sergeant, still sitting in his plastic chair with his knees spread insouciantly. Still wearing T-shirt and shorts, the last person in the room with any clothes left on, although his cock was standing clear from the fly of his khakis, caressed lazily in one big hand. He looked like a god, she thought; a huge bronze idol, impossibly broad-shouldered.

"Yes Sergeant," whispered Peyton, not daring to wonder whether she *was* in fact okay. She looked down at herself—at her delicate breasts now tattooed with the signs of her captivity, and at the twin steel horizontals through her nipples that the sketched chains seemed anchored to. Her orbs quivered as she fought to control her breath and hold back sobs. Her face burned with shame and shock.

She could feel them all, massed at the borders of her mind, their inner voices loud and raucous. All but one. She bowed her head.

Then, on hands and knees, she crawled away from the bed until she had a clear line to Sergeant Jomoa. He crooked a finger, beckoning her to pay homage at the altar of his crotch. Instead, she turned her back, bowed her forehead to the floor and lifted her ass high. The invitation could not have been clearer if she had had it announced over the Base P.A.

The sergeant chuckled. Someone whistled, low and mockingly appreciative.

Peyton pressed her hot forehead to the tiles, glad of the cool there. Her aching breasts hung, their tips heavy with the new metal but not quite brushing the scuffed surface. She could feel the first seep of Brannon's spilt cream from her well-used sex, the puffiness of her labia, the slippery clench of the rear passage that had been opened but not filled by Hayes. Her clit throbbed with need. The hormones of arousal flowed through her bloodstream, making nerve-endings blossom like flowers begging to be pollinated. Making her cunt pulse and dilate hungrily.

Looking down between her splayed thighs, she saw a long slow drip of viscid moisture appear at the curve of her mons and hang, stretching. Brannon's cum. Or Hayes'; or Rialto's. She was so full of their semen that she was overflowing. She whimpered; she did not feel full, she felt horribly empty.

"What d'you want, Corporal?" Sergeant Jomoa rumbled.

She wanted his cock.

Slowly, ass high and thighs wide apart and head still low, she began to creep backward toward his voice. It was a long way on cold tiles; every shift of her hips an offering to him of shameless naked need. Her bum swayed. Her nipples burned. The iris of her rear felt like a hypnotic eye straining to open and stare him down. He was huge, and his cock was huge, and she wanted that.

Touch me, she told him, though he couldn't hear her. *Touch that, the deepest part of me. Fuck me.*

It was her job to open them up to psi-comms. But all she wanted was for big Sergeant Jomoa to open her.

"Oh fuck, man," Hayes groaned. "Look at that."

"That is fucking sweet."

"Go on Sarge. Fuck's sake. Take it."

She was, she thought, a meter or so from his chair. She stopped there and writhed her ass from side to side. "Please," she whispered to the tiles, reaching behind her with both hands and pulling her cheeks apart.

Sergeant Jomoa grunted. She saw his flicked cigarette land and bounce on the tile almost at her nose. It lay there, the smoke wreathing up in a gray line from the tip. Then the chair creaked. Peyton looked over her shoulder then—she couldn't help herself. She saw the big man hunker down behind her, his knees splayed so he could straddle her ass. The male musk of his body reached her even through the cigarette smoke, and she could feel the warmth radiating from his flesh. He moved silently, without haste or effort; laid one hand across the small of her back as if measuring its span, prodded his monstrous cock to her whorl and pushed. Even untrained and unlubricated she would not have been able to resist anything that hard. And Peyton was slither-slippery and very well trained indeed: the gate of her ass stood no chance against the invader, despite its prodigious girth. She cried out as she yielded to him.

The sergeant took her by the hips and pulled her right onto the length of his cock.

"Shiiiiiiiit," said Hayes, wincing theatrically.

Oh god that felt *good*. The stretching, and the pain, and the way the pain dissolved into pleasure, and the way the hunger flared in her ass so that it felt like she was sucking him in, deeper and deeper, pulling him inside. It felt good to be sodomized, good to be split in half by that massive tool, good to be watched as she panted and writhed and submitted. It wasn't just the NCO with his cock in her ass; it was the whole of Lammergeier Squad. She was giving it up to all of them.

She began to cry, not holding back her wails.

"Oh man," Hayes said. His cock was already hard again and he was holding it like a weapon. Brannon, eyes narrowed, ran his tongue across his lips. Rialto was touching himself, squeezing his balls gently, stroking a semi that was filling out with every second. Even Eriksen, lurking at the back of the pack, was moving round to get a better view of the action. And Sergeant Jomoa fucked her slowly and very thoroughly, which was just what she needed. It allowed her to come time after time, one hand stretched back between her legs to play frantically with her clit. It allowed her to sob out all her anxiety and her pain and her confusion between orgasms. And when he finally quickened, hands gripping her hips like he would crack her pelvic girdle, his huge cock powering deep and hard into her ass and flooding her with his spunk, she made her gratitude very vocal.

Only when she'd stopped making her own noises did she hear his, inside her head.

—WELL FUCK SHE MIGHT DO YOU NEVER KNOW SHE MIGHT HAVE MORE SURPRISES SHE MIGHT DO.

◆ ◆ ◆

They run the last few hundred yards to the drop capsule. She can see through Brannon's eyes the bulking metallic haven. And she can see that there are Spiders all over it. Dozens and dozens, scratching and rapping at the panels, trying to pick their way in as if it's the carcass of some huge beetle.

—BURN THEM!!

They close, fanning out with their flamethrowers. Even enclosed as she is, she hears the roar, faintly. Spiders dance and explode, soft interiors boiling to steam.

—MORE COMING UP BEHIND US

That's Eriksen. She sees a blue mass swarming out of the doorway they've just escaped from, even as she relays the warning to everyone in the squad.

—OH FUCK HERE WE GO

—MOTHERFUCKERS MUST HAVE HEARD

—SHIT THOUGHT WE'D GET AWAY CLEAN THIS TIME

—HURRY THIS UP MEN!!

Peyton plunges for the wheel that manually operates the exterior doors. Her heart is banging in her breastbone.

Flamethrowers don't make quick clean kills; enough Spiders and her squad will be overwhelmed.

—PEYTON WE'RE CLEAR OPEN NOW!! GET A MOVE ON BEFORE THE REST GET HERE!!!

She pumps the rotating handle wildly, feeling the grip slip in her wet hands. The doors are huge and respond slowly, with a noise of squealing metal. Her arms are aching. She can hear shouts from outside now. She can't register any words. She's not out there with the men any more, she's in here with the wheel and the effort and the pain, her muscles straining.

The hydraulics reach the trip point and snap the catch open. She hears the sprung door bounce.

—IN IN INSIDE EVERYBODY INSIDE HOLD THE LOCK GET IT SHUT NOW!!!

Peyton sags. There's a twin wheel inside the airlock: the men will be able to shut the outer door from there. She leans against a panel, trying to get her breath back. The acrid taint of their stress is overwhelming, drowning everything else—even her precog alarm.

—OKAY PEYTON WE'RE IN OPEN THE INTERIOR DOOR

She hits the button.

—WAIT!! WAIT!!! THERE'S SPIDERS IN HERE WITH US SONOFABITCH!!

It's too late. The interior door hisses open and something blue and long-legged, as big as she is, scuttles in onto the roof. She can hear everybody shouting, all at once, but she can't see jack because all the interior lights have gone out, all the monitors and the LEDs too. All she can make out is the faint blue glow of splayed Spider legs, and it's getting closer.

She throws herself backward down the interior, falling over seats, scrabbling wildly toward the front bulkhead. The

Spider sparks miniature lightning like a Van de Graaff generator as it moves. It illuminates the dead instrument panels as it passes across them, jerkily. It's seen her.

Shit! she thinks, in pure panic. She can hear the men shouting and crashing about, but she can't see them and they can't see her. And they can't use flame in here without killing everyone.

The spider gathers itself, hunching. She pulls the bolt gun from her hip-holster and slaps the safety off, her hands feeling as slow and clumsy as lead mittens. It seems to weigh a ton as she lifts the muzzle. One shot, captive bolt. She has to have it pressed to the Spider's body before she pulls the trigger.

It leaps, knocking her backward. Electricity bites her flesh. She has no choice about pulling the trigger: her hand spasms and the bolt goes off. Everything is pure white pain.

And then dark.

❖ ❖ ❖

When she comes round she is looking straight up at Eriksen, who has his hand on her throat.

"She's alive," he grunts—and then snatches her up bodily, crushing her against his armored chest. She doesn't want to pslide into his head, not now, but she can't help hearing the leakage from his inner thoughts:

—ALIVE ALIVE NOT THIS TIME ALIVE OH THANK GOD

"Ow," she says weakly, and they laugh, their voices booming over her head. Eriksen stops crushing her ribcage and pushes her to arm's length so he can look her over. She realizes the whole cabin is lit by chemical glowbags.

"Are you hurt?"

"Sore," she says, amazed as much by the way he's looking

at her as by her own survival. Her whole body aches. "But okay."

"Doing better than that fucking Spider anyway," says Hayes, kicking the curled alien corpse.

"You sure made a mess of that one," Brannon agrees, pointing to a plume of blue innards splattered over a seat.

"Not bad, Corporal," says Sergeant Jomoa.

Rialto leans over. "Come here, lucky girl," he says, hooking Peyton out of Eriksen's arms and pulling her to her feet. He kisses her, hard and warm. In his plasteel armor he feels like some sort of cyborg. She winces as her breasts, still tender from their piercings, are squashed against his breastplate.

"Hey," says Eriksen, standing up behind her. "Gently. It's her first mission." He slips a hand round her waist to pull her out of Rialto's embrace, so she ends up with her back to his chest. His other hand cups the mound of her sex as if to protect her chastity. Rialto laughs. Peyton manages her first look around the capsule; the men are unbuckling armor and stowing weapons in lockers. They're all here. No losses. Sergeant Jomoa looks round from the door in the forward bulkhead.

"Brannon, get your ass up here and check this thing's still got fly-by-wire capability."

"Can it wait, Sarge?" he grumbles. He's looking at Peyton in Eriksen's arms.

"What, you think she's going somewhere? Eyes on the mission, Brannon."

Brannon curls his lip but obeys, deliberately squeezing between Rialto and Peyton as he passes forward. "You got Spider blood on that nice new uniform, girl," he points out.

"He's right," Rialto says. "We should do something about that."

"How about this?" Eriksen asks, reaching round to hook

down the main zipper of her flightsuit. It's a very tight costume and her breasts spill out luxuriantly. "Any better?" he asks Rialto, and stoops to lick Peyton's ear. His breath is hot. He smells of sweat. They all do.

"That is *way* better," Hayes concurs from her right, dumping his groin and thigh armor with notable alacrity.

Rialto grins happily, and flicks both of Peyton's nipple-bars with the tips of his finger. Her breasts feel huge and hot. "Gotta agree. What do you think, Sarge?"

Sergeant Jomoa slams a locker shut, his eyes narrowing as he looks her way. "You okay after that Spider, Corporal?"

"I think so—Oh!" She loses all words as Eriksen has given her mons a good squeeze.

"We should give her a full medical examination," Hayes suggests. "Inside and out." He opens a pocket on his jacket. "I brought lube."

The sergeant shakes his head, rueful, and grins. "I guess we got time."

"Hear that, lucky girl?" Rialto's voice is low, his lips close to hers. "You're just about to get lucky again." He's cupping her breasts, vibrating the bars, making her squeak and shiver. But she can't pull away because Eriksen is embracing her from behind. Then Hayes pushes in.

"Stand back: I've got first aid training." He's also got his cock out already, erect and optimistic as ever. "Just open wide and say *Ah*, Corporal." With that instruction, he pulls her over from the hips, pressing her face to his groin. Peyton sort of expects Rialto to object, but he steps aside and she finds herself bent double, her mouth full of Hayes' cock and her ass planted firmly in Eriksen's crotch.

Then Eriksen finds the other end of the long double

zipper, at the small of her back, and draws it down—right over the curve of her ass. She'd thought the zip was that long to facilitate her using the toilet in her uniform: it hadn't occurred to her that it provides excellent access for her fellow squad members. She feels a draft of cooler air as her ass-crack and pussy are bared, but by then she's concentrating on sucking Hayes' impatient cock. The smell and taste of him is rich from confinement in his armor.

Hands—multiple hands—play with her pussy, teasing it open, slapping her gently. She says "Ah" around Hayes' length, but it's rather muffled. She can't see anything beyond his hips. She can't hear anything except the slurp of her own mouth and the rasp of his hands over her ears. Then without warning someone—and she can't tell who, most probably Eriksen or Rialto but she doesn't know—is sliding his cock into her pussy. It's that sudden. No messing around. They want to fuck her.

They desperately, urgently, want to fuck her. Because they are still alive, and buzzing with victory.

So they do it quickly, taking turns, no man finishing before he pauses for breath, pulls out and passes her to the next guy. Brannon comes back in from the forward compartment, says, "We're good to go," then sees what's happening and adds, "But there's no hurry," before joining in. They pick her up and turn her round, spreading her wide, doubling her up, stretching her out. She's surrounded by cock, filled with cock, choked by cock; thick and meaty and hard with the knowledge of mortality. They fuck her on her back, on her front, upside down. They fuck her face and her cunt and her ass—all three, each man in turn, until she understands that this is a ritual. At a couple of points she finds herself with three men in her at once. She has never felt so safe, or so needed. It doesn't take long before she's coming, and coming hard. Her screams fill the small chamber. They're probably attracting more Spiders, but no one cares. They can burn those off at launch.

When they've all had her in every orifice, Hayes directs them to hold her face up, at thigh level. He straddles her chest, presses her aching, burning breasts together, and ruts along the sweat-slippery cleft between, his purplish cockhead aimed at her lips. When he comes he lets fly all over her throat and face and tits.

The others take their turn after that to ejaculate on her breasts. Fists blur, pumping. Balls clench. Semen spurts and flies and slops. They cover the lammergeier tattoo in their pale cum, until she finds herself kneeling in the center of the circle with jizz running down her breasts and dripping on her pubic mound and spread thighs. Their hairy, muscular legs are like pillars surrounding her. The smell of sweat and sex in this enclosed space is almost suffocating. She runs her fingers through the mess of semen, smearing it over her sore nipples, rubbing it into the lammergeier tattoo, then catching it up and sucking it greedily from her fingers, looking up at them as she does so.

The mingling taste of them is harsh and salty. She knows it is a taste that will be hers, and hers alone, for the rest of her life.

—YES YES FUCKING YES EAT IT ME US

—ALIVE WE LIVE THIS TIME THIS TIME ONE MORE TIME

—GOOD GIRL OH YOU GOOD GIRL

—OH YOU BEAUTIFUL BEAUTIFUL DIRTY WHORE NOTHING BETTER NOTHING

—OURS OURS OURS NOW FOREVER OURS WE OWN YOU WE PROTECT YOU WE LOVE YOU WE NEED YOU OURS OURS

She is their fuck-doll and their lifeline. Their sex-slave

and their guardian angel. She is *theirs*.

Their Pslider.

A Man's Best Friend

The dog liked him on sight.

That in itself was a surprise; Xhai was used to village dogs running out to challenge him aggressively as he walked by, which was why he carried a staff. When he heard the clop of horse hooves on the stony path behind him, he turned to see a girl on one of those thickset ponies they had round there, and two herd dogs trotting alongside with their curled tails arched high over their backs. There was no man with her, but the women of the Dog People were notoriously independent. She was riding, for a start, rather than sitting in a litter as a woman of any pretensions to respectability ought to do.

But then, Xhai was a long way from the Imperial Court now, and a long way from any aspirations to respectability himself. His garb was faded from months of travel, and his boots worn down at the heels. It was not just village dogs who had taken to eyeing him suspiciously.

Xhai stepped well off the path, partly to demonstrate that he had no hostile intent, partly so that he'd have a good defensive stance if the hounds decided to go for him. The young woman rode on, one hand on her hip. He was careful not to stare, but he couldn't help seeing that she was young, and that her blue jacket had slipped to reveal the sweep of one bare shoulder.

It'd be unthinkable anywhere else in the Empire, he told himself, smiling inwardly as he watched the two hounds run forward. But here in the hinterlands of the Dog People, women breastfed their babes on the street and did their laundry stripped to the waist in the rivers, while men only looked on and grinned.

One of the dogs looked away from him and trotted on

down the path. But the other did something he did not expect: it started to wag its tail furiously, its backside waving too in its enthusiasm, and then it scampered up the bank with tongue lolling and bowed before him, before jumping around as if greeting an old friend. As it dunted his hand with its head, begging for a caress, Xhai glanced up at the woman on the horse.

He only meant it to be a friendly, reassuring smile that he gave her, but it turned into something else. She was looking down at her hound, lips parted, with an expression of surprise. Her long hair was blue-black in the sunlight and the skin of her shoulder was as soft and golden as a peach. He'd been wrong in his estimate of her age; she had a maiden's figure but an adult's face, lively and full of character.

Xhai's smile grew warmer, without his meaning it to.

She met his gaze and instinctively smiled back, before looking away, abashed. The exchange took only a moment—and then she was riding on past, whistling for her dog, her face a little flushed. The animal licked Xhai's hand furiously, turned after its mistress, stopped to look back, ran in a small circle, and then followed on. As Xhai watched the trio disappear down the path, he saw that dog stop several times and look back up at him, as if in longing.

It wasn't the only one smitten. Xhai stood without moving for some time, rather shocked. Warmth tingled through his whole body, and her smile seemed painted on his memory. Her pleasure, so quickly hidden, at his gaze—it was like a glimpse of something private and precious, more erotic than the exposed shoulder. His stones felt heavy. One look at that passing herdswoman and life had surged into his cock.

He hadn't reacted in that way to a woman in months … no: years, he noted ruefully. He wasn't a youth any longer, to fall in love with a pretty face at a moment's notice. And he hadn't felt lust, real lust, since …

Since the Battle of the Red River. Since Liwan died.

Xhai shook himself from his stupor. This was no time to fall into reverie; he was nearly at the town of Three Cranes. Nearly there. Soon he could rest, and find something to eat. Soon he would have reached his goal of his three months' journey.

He couldn't imagine what would happen after that. It was like a great black fogbank across his mind.

❖ ❖ ❖

He picked his way down off the hill-path into the dusty town by the river ford. You could tell, he thought, that it was a town built by nomads. Half the houses were nothing more than round felt yurts. The rest of the buildings were wooden and ramshackle; it looked as if you might wake up in the morning and find the whole thing gone. But the market was extensive and lively. Dog People in their blue silk jackets predominated, but there were people from every corner of the vast Empire, and even a smattering of yellow-garbed imperial soldiers.

Xhai turned away from those, not wanting to see. It was not so long since he had worn imperial yellow, and the memories made his stomach clench.

He bought pork dumplings on a street stall, washed them down with tea that the vendor had adulterated foully with milk, in the local style, and went looking for an old woman. Among the Dog People, he knew, the men were warriors and herders, but all the animals and the tents and everything the family possessed were passed down the female line. A man married into his wife's family—and then spent the rest of his life trying to keep out of his mother-in-law's way, Liwan had told him, laughing. It was the women who would know where to find the family he was looking for.

Xhai went to the food market, and among the women who bustled back and forth buying and selling, found an elder with a twinkly eye who seemed both impressed by his ability to speak her language and much amused by how tall he was. After he had bowed to her and called her Grandmother in the polite manner, and accepted another tiny cup of the rancid tea, he broached the subject of his quest.

"I'm looking for the tents of the family Ghan. Do you know where they are this season?"

The old woman squeezed his thigh in an alarmingly familiar manner. "They are out of town, up in the hills. Why are you looking for them, Easterner?"

"I have a message to deliver, from a friend."

"You've come a long way to deliver a message."

He did not rise to the question. "I have, Grandmother."

"Well, you are in luck. See over there, by the crate of ducks? The woman with the blue hairsticks and the red boots? That is Ghan Tsulin. She will be able to show you the way."

Oh gods.

It was the woman from the footpath. Xhai recognized her the moment he looked, and every muscle in his chest seemed to spasm.

He had no idea what it meant, to have seen her without knowing. To have looked upon her and felt … As if he knew. As if somehow, he *knew*.

"Are you feeling well, Easterner?" The old woman stared up at him, frowning. "You look terrible."

He made his excuses and stumbled through thanks. Then he set off toward Ghan Tsulin, who was haggling over a trio of green apricots. He stopped behind her, well out of reach.

He'd been half-a-head taller than Liwan, who was not short by the standards of his tribe, and he positively loomed over women of the Dog People. Scabbarded over his back, too, was a sword. He didn't want to seem threatening; that could easily start a riot here, where they were surrounded by her tribal kin. And then he'd have to use the sword.

"Ghan Tsulin."

She turned, looked up at him with widening eyes, and then glanced about her sharply. Xhai realized she was looking for her dogs, but they weren't around.

"I have a message for you. I …" All his rehearsed words had deserted him. "I've walked from the Imperial Capital to tell you."

"Who are you?" she asked, one fist moving to her hip, staring up at him boldly with none of the shyness of civilized women. She had tiny freckles all across her cheeks and the bridge of her nose, he saw. Freckles were considered a terrible flaw in Court circles. He didn't understand why he was noticing this. His eyes seemed to be disconnected from the clenching pain in his gut, as if they belonged to someone else entirely.

"My name is Lin Xhai." His voice sounded like sliding shale. "I knew your husband, Ghan Liwan."

She understood. She saw it in his face, and he watched the comprehension dawn in her expression in turn. It was like seeing someone fall from a high cliff; down and down and down.

❖ ❖ ❖

The yurts of the Ghan family were nestled in the grassy foothills north of Three Cranes. There were dogs roaming loose all round the felt huts and, accompanied by a youth with wispy mustache riding a pony, they ran out to greet the woman on horseback and the walking man. While Tsulin conferred with the boy, Xhai eyed the dogs. Some stood well back, barking at him. Others came close, nosing him eagerly.

"Strange," said Tsulin as the youth rode off to the yurts. She hadn't wept as they traveled home, not a single tear, but her face looked haggard nonetheless.

"What?"

"This one, Snowgoose, she knew my husband," she said, pointing at the bitch that'd accompanied her into town and been so friendly to him. "And this one, this one; all of these. Those"— she pointed at the barking dogs—"are all too young to remember him. It's like some of them know you."

Perhaps they smell Liwan on my clothes, he thought, but didn't answer.

By the time they reached the center of the encampment, men were emerging to meet them. Men only. There were no women or children in sight. Xhai thought this an ugly sign, but suddenly an older woman stepped out of a yurt and came forward, shaking her head sadly.

Tsulin introduced him to her mother, and then to her brothers and brothers-in-law. Everyone looked sombre, but there were no passionate displays of grief. Of course, Liwan would not have been related by blood to any of these people, who were his wife's kin, and it must have been years since they last saw him.

Xhai could follow only some of the conversation, which took place in the Dog People language and ran too fast.

Finally Tsulin turned to him. "You bring news of a death," she told him. "So you must be cleansed. Follow Felung." She walked away into a nearby hut, alone.

Xhai considered it politic to obey.

The boy with the wispy upper lip took him into a sweat-tent made of skins. The two men spent the next hour or so in the suffocating steamy gloom there, naked around a low fire and a brazier of hot stones, which Felung tended with charcoal and ladles of water. Xhai felt no desire to converse; it was almost too much effort to breathe. He shut his eyes and listened to the hiss of steam and felt the sweat rolling down his skin like tears. Finally, when it felt like his head would burst with heat and that he was close to passing out, the flap was lifted and the two of them were released. Felung led the way. Naked, he walked out onto the trodden grass and knelt. Instantly several men poured water over him.

Forewarned, Xhai didn't yell when it was his turn for bucketfuls of what felt like ice-water to drench him from head to toe. It was in fact almost pleasant, once he'd got over the shock, to be relieved of the heat and the stickiness. His skin tingled. He crouched with head bowed as they sluiced him clean, his long hair hanging like a black curtain, watching the water soak into the grass and vanish. *The earth eats us all*, he thought, *sooner or later*.

Then a pair of red boots moved into his field of view. Startled, he looked up. Tsulin stood before him, a heap of folded clothes in her hands, her face masklike. She was wearing coarse white cotton herself now: the color of mourning.

"Those aren't my clothes," Xhai said, grasping for words and coming up with the first thing that seemed safe. He greatly disliked being seen by her like this—naked, kneeling, his scars visible. He had to remind himself that the Dog People had fewer reservations about showing their bodies.

"We burnt those," she said, holding out the bundle.

Xhai bit back a protest. One-handed, he took the clothes from her, while his other hand shielded his crotch. He was ashamed that her presence had given him an awkward, unwieldy erection, and was glad when she walked away. Clumsily, still damp, he managed to drag enough clothes on to make himself decent. Dog People clothes. It was only as he stood up properly and surveyed his ankles—the trousers were loose, to his relief, but too short in the leg—that it occurred to him that they were probably Liwan's old clothes he'd been loaned. His heart gave a lurch.

Felung had vanished. The old woman was nowhere in sight. Tsulin was waiting, sitting by the round wall of her yurt. He had nowhere else to go to, so he strode across the dusty grass toward her. All around, men were taking down walls of felt and loading struts onto carts.

"What's happening?" he asked Tsulin, as he reached her. The only structures that weren't being dismantled were, it seemed, the sweat-tent he'd come out of and this yurt where Tsulin waited.

"They are moving camp down the valley. They won't go far … but I am a widow now. I cannot live with them. For a year."

"*What?*"

"I'm unclean. I must not come into contact with any child, or any woman of childbearing age. I cannot go into the city." She tilted her head, sounded resigned. "Don't worry. The men will bring me food."

He was appalled. How could she be safe, living on her own without her family around her? For a moment he wanted to express his anger, but then he reprimanded himself. Dog People ways weren't like the ways of the rest of men. Liwan had taught him that.

"I … have something to give you," he said, discomfort making him gruff. "Did you burn my backpack too?"

She shook her head, pulling a shape with her mouth that might in better days have been a smile. Rising, she led him round to the door of the yurt. Snowgoose padded along behind them.

Inside, the room was dim and a little stuffy. The floor was heaped with carpets, the walls a lattice of wooden struts supporting the felt. There were heaps of belongings piled randomly about the room, as if someone had just moved in. One of those heaps was Xhai's backpack, his sword laid on top. He unsheathed it just to check that no fool herder had used the watered steel to chop logs while he wasn't looking, but it was undamaged.

He emptied the pack slowly. After three months, most of his spare clothes were so rank that he wanted to burn them himself. But worth preserving were three separately-wrapped bundles. One was flat and hard, and he laid it aside. It twanged faintly.

"What is that?" asked Tsulin, standing at his shoulder.

"My *guqin*," he said, uneasily. Just the sight of that shape made him queasy. He wondered, for the hundredth time, why he hadn't left it behind at the Imperial Palace. "A lap-harp."

"You are a musician?"

"I'm … I'm the Emperor's own bard." The words sounded awkward in his mouth. "It's my task to write songs about His Imperial Majesty's victories in the field of battle."

She snorted, very faintly. "And how did such an important man come to know a soldier of the Dog People?"

He chose not to take offence. "I heard him singing, while we were encamped. I stopped to listen, and I asked him to teach me more Dog People songs, and then your language."

She shook her head, eyes flashing mild disbelief. "He was no great singer!"

"It wasn't the purity of his voice that mattered." Xhai chewed his lip. "When the Emperor saw us together, he appointed Liwan to be my bodyguard." *And I thought that he would be safer in the royal entourage than as a lowly cavalryman.* That had turned out to be a vain hope.

"So. Did you write a song for my husband, when he fell?"

The words cut. Xhai felt his mouth fill with blood. He shook his head, not looking at her.

"Why not?"

"The words would not come. This … this is for you."

The second bundle was spherical, wrapped in several layers of cloth and tied with string. She knew what it was: she took it from his hands reverently and knelt on the rugs, setting it before her. Xhai moved to kneel facing her, across the bundle, and instantly Snowgoose came over and lay at his side, dropping her nose on her paws with a sigh.

Tsulin's hands were deft and tender, loosening the knots.

Inside the outer burlap nested layer upon layer of silk, brightly colored and embroidered. The quality of the needlework was extraordinary; the best the Imperial Palace could furnish. Red for a warrior, green for the Earth, blue for Heaven, yellow for the Emperor. The innermost layer was white for death, embroidered with the symbols of immortality. Inside that was a small cremation jar, about the size of Xhai's two fists.

"Oh," said Tsulin softly. Xhai watched her narrow hands cup the blue ceramic, and had a sudden overwhelming desire to see those hands on his bare thighs. The dissonance made him shudder. He looked away, blinking; when he looked back she had the jar open.

The contents were dry and pale, nothing but ash and crumbs. Tsulin touched her fingertips to her husband's remains, as if to prove to herself that they were real.

"I knew he was dead," she said. "Before you came."

Xhai frowned.

"Three years, he's been gone. Three years since your Emperor took him away to war. But five months ago, when the cherry blossom was out along the river … I was drawing water, when Snowgoose began to howl. She sat down and howled all afternoon, until nightfall. She refused to come back to the yurts. I went home, and all the old dogs were howling too. I cast the yarrow sticks—I can do that—and they said: *you will lose something of great value*. I went to the graves of the ancestors, and I listened to their voices on the wind. The voices said: *he is dead*." She stroked her thumb across her fingertips, the ash bleaching her gold. "When did he die?"

"Five months ago, at the Battle of the Red River," he said, the hair prickling on his neck. The cherry blossom had been falling there, so much further south and east. These mysteries were beyond him.

She met his gaze, her eyes dark and liquid. "Three years I have been alone, and I broke my heart for him. Five months ago I witnessed the signs, and I mourned him again. I thought I had done with my heartbreak. Then you turn up. Now I must sorrow again."

His eyes burned as if he'd rubbed them with salt. "I'm sorry," he whispered. "Liwan made me promise. He said that if he were to die, I must find you and let you know. He said that I must give you this, so that you might marry again, and have children before you grow old." He held out to her the third object from his pack: a small, loosely-wrapped piece of cloth. She took it from him, and uncovered a thong necklace; white beads strung along leather, of no obvious value.

"I put this around his neck on our wedding day," she said softly. "And he gave me this in exchange." She bared her right forearm, revealing a bracelet of carved white plates, like slips of ivory.

"It's dog bone, is it?" Xhai asked. He wanted desperately to touch the soft skin of the inside of her elbow.

Tsulin nodded, tears trembling on her lowered lashes. "The dog symbolizes love," she explained. "A dog will love you all its life, no matter if it is ill-treated or abandoned. It will always come home to you. Yesterday I went to the graves of the ancestors and I heard their voices again. They said: *he will come back to you*. I didn't understand it." She looked down at the pot of ashes. "Until now."

Xhai's throat felt swollen. "He loved his dogs. I mean—everyone else hated them, the ones that follow the army: they steal food and they …" He stopped. *They eat the corpses on the battlefield*. He didn't want to tell Tsulin that. The memories were still too raw. "Liwan picked up a puppy in one of the villages we went through. Everyone thought he was crazy, but he kept it in the wagon and fed it from his own ration. He told me, 'A man is not a man unless he has a dog that loves him.'"

She smiled—sadly, but the first real smile he'd seen on her face since their first meeting. "What happened to his puppy?"

"Um." Xhai cleared his throat. "I killed it and burnt it with him on his pyre. To go with him into the afterlife. That was the right thing to do, wasn't it?"

She nodded. "Yes. That was right."

He passed his hand over his face, confession blurting out of his throat: "I feel worse about that dog than about all the men I killed in battle."

For a long moment she stared at him, her eyes black pools that threatened to drown his world. Then she took the cremation pot in her hands and stood. "Come with me."

❖ ❖ ❖

She led him out of the camp, such as remained of it now that all her family were leaving, and up toward the foothills. Snowgoose and a couple of other dogs trotted alongside. The sun was setting, and the green hills were turning gold. Xhai watched her from behind, not worrying about their destination, his chest full of heaviness and his eyes fixed on her slender form. When Tsulin looked back to check that he was still following, he saw that she was clutching the blue jar against her heart, nestled between her breasts, and the sight made his blood churn.

He did not understand this, how he felt. True, it had been far too long since he had lain with a woman, and the sages say that abstinence befouls a man's soul and threatens his health—but Liwan was dead and she was his grieving widow. He should be feeling only compassion for her, and duty. Not this unspeakable desire. He wanted her. He ached for her—not simply to mount her and fill her with his seed, but to feel the silken brush of her bare skin against his, to bury his face between those gentle breasts, to feel her heart racing beneath his palm. It was as if every inch of his body had woken from a long sleep, ravenous with hunger. It was shameful beyond words.

She led him to a gate with an elaborately carved beam. It stood before a place of small hillocks and rock outcrops—a gate without a fence, black against the fading glory of the sky. Behind them the grass was short, cropped low by the goats and cattle and horses of the Ghan family. Beyond that gate, the grass grew long and lush. Xhai wondered if the herders kept their animals away, or if the beasts knew.

"Come," said Tsulin, leading the way beneath the great lintel. The dogs did not accompany them. They followed a path crushed through the grass, into a tiny valley, up to one of the jutting outcrops of stone. "This is the burial ground of my family," she told him.

"Do the ancestors speak to you tonight?" Xhai asked.

She went still, listening. The evening was without a breath of wind. Slowly she shook her head. "They are silent." Then she pointed ahead. Wedged beneath an overhang was a stone slab, painted with characters that Xhai, despite all his scholarly education, could not read. "Help me move the stone."

They knelt side by side in the grass to dig away the soil at the base and slide the heavy slab from its place. Where it had been, a black hole gaped; a natural cavity beneath the boulder, Xhai thought, but put to human use. Though the light was fading, he glimpsed several cremation urns inside.

"My father," Tsulin said softly. She reached out and brushed her fingers across the glazed surfaces. "Our children."

Liwan had never mentioned children.

"Rest with our ancestors, husband, and be at peace," she whispered, setting the blue pot among the others. Xhai stood and moved away, giving her space to pray. He looked out across the darkening landscape and the blue gloaming. Early stars were emerging in the west. The evening was still, no breeze stirring the grass. He could feel his heartbeat, thudding in his chest.

When Tsulin had finished, he helped her replace the grave slab. Her face was pale in the shadows, but he had heard no weeping. They walked away a little.

"I didn't know you'd had children," he said softly.

She ran her hand across her head. "They were both born too early, and only half-made. One the second year, one the next, and then the soldiers came and took him away for the Emperor, so I never had a chance to give him another." Her voice sounded hoarse. "I must have spoken to a widow-woman when I was small, my mother says, and been stricken barren. Now I have passed the widow's curse on, to my children. To my husband, who is dead of it."

The weight in his chest was jagged now. "No!" he protested. "You did not kill him; war took him. It is an insatiable thing. I have seen a thousand thousand men dead upon the battlefield—do you think your little curse did that?" He wanted to grab her and shake her. He wanted to seize her face and kiss it. "You did not curse him. Liwan spoke of you often, and always with love. He longed to return to you. You were a *joy* to him."

Tsulin turned to him in the blue dusk. He could hear her breath, fast and shallow. She laid a hand on his breast and his heart crashed against it. She tangled the fingers of her other hand in the still-damp ends of his long hair. He clasped her around the waist, before he could think about it, and she pressed against him, panting. His blood was roaring in his veins, and he was filled with both delight and the terror of teetering upon the edge of doing her a terrible wrong. The scent of her hair filled his head, driving out thought. Her body was pliant under his hands and he couldn't tell if he was pushing her away or pulling her to him.

Then she reached down and grabbed his cock through his trousers, and his whole world fell apart. He didn't need to see clearly to clasp her face and lift it, covering her lips with his kiss. She moaned into his mouth, her open palm writhing across the hardness of his shaft, and he staggered, pushing her back across the grass. Both her hands were suddenly at the drawstring of his trousers, pulling frantically, as he kissed her and kissed her and the breathless dusk whirled around them.

It was only when she bared him that he really believed it. Only then that he knew what he was doing. He laid her down in the long grass and yanked open her jacket to reveal those luscious breasts, soft as peaches. The scent of her skin was intoxicating; the ripe swell of her flesh beneath his mouth and the stiff pucker of her nipples drove him out of his senses. He sucked upon her even as his hands tore at her trousers, jerking them down over narrow hips, pulling off one of her boots and hurling it away in his haste to open her legs.

He found her sex, moist and open and soft. There was no question of finesse. Her hands scrabbled at his cock and balls, pulling him to her, squeezing his shaft like it was a spear and she was ready to kill someone with it. So he stabbed her to the core and felt her gasp and heave beneath him. Her heat was all around him, wet and slippery and exquisite; her legs embraced his hips. For a moment he froze, not daring to move. He felt her arch her spine, and heard her growl as she bit at his jaw.

"Yes!" she gasped.

It was like a fight to the death. Her body heaved beneath his. She was slighter and softer and so much weaker than him, but she refused to go limp. He was thrusting with all his weight, but still she fought him, her body growing more and more rigid as he drove in and out. And he didn't want to hurt her, didn't want to defile her, but he couldn't stop, couldn't tear himself away from the hunger of her mouth, and the fingernails that bit into his clenching buttocks, and the wet hot incredible need of her sex, the need of her body, the need of her lost days and her stolen love.

Until she start to shake, clamped rigid and locked around him, and she jerked and cried out like something dying, and then for a moment he paused because he thought that somehow he was hurting her, and then he knew he was going to die too; he could feel his death pouring through him like a red tide from his balls all the way up his spine. It was coming, coming, coming—

he jerked out of her, desperate to spill on the green grass, but he'd lost control of this long ago and he erupted all over her belly and thighs.

Oh, he thought, as he fell through a star-filled void. *I had forgotten what it's like. How good.*

"Liwan," the woman beneath him groaned, and began to sob for the first time—racking wet sobs that went on and on.

Stunned at first, Xhai had no idea how to react. Back home, tears were a private thing. Comportment demanded that he respect her by leaving her—but this time instinct was stronger. He rolled off onto his side and pulled her into his embrace, cradling her against him as she wept into his chest. The scent of crushed grass was like a silken shroud, draping them from head to foot.

He stroked her hair, watching the stars come out, as she cried herself into silence.

◆ ◆ ◆

Tsulin's yurt sat all alone when they got back to it, its walls pale under the narrow moon. No one from her family had lingered to say farewell, but Xhai still hesitated at the door.

"If I am found in your tent …?"

"It doesn't matter," she said wearily. "I am a widow, already polluted. A widow may do as she wishes. And any man may go to her."

No, he said inwardly, his jaw tightening. *This is not kindly. I will not allow it.*

She lit lamps of butter and hung them about the interior. Under their yellow flames her skin seemed to glow golden, and he found himself mesmerized by the play of light upon her smooth cheek. He'd expected the ache of his desire to fade now that he had shot his quiverful, but her flesh still seemed to draw at his. Xhai went to her and untied the sash from about her waist, peeling off her jacket, dropping her trousers to pool at her ankles. Only her jewelry remained: the necklace and the bracelet of bone. She did not resist him; she simply stood looking up at him as he ran his hands over her breasts and waist and hips, and only her nipples responded to his caress, tightening to points.

"You're beautiful," he said, the thickening edge of his voice betraying the urge he felt.

She shook her head, very slightly. "I'm too old to be beautiful."

Certainly she was nothing like the tottering lotus-flower beauties of the Imperial Court, with their painted, sweetly vacant faces like those of children. He had never cared much for those. But Tsulin was lithe and strong, her feet firmly planted, her breasts warm and thrilling with life. He looked into her eyes and saw watchfulness and mistrust there. *Well, and why should she not feel that way?* he asked himself. *We have known each other only a few hours, and I am not of her people, and I am a man, besides. And men, all men, lie to women. We dare not tell them what we truly feel.* "Don't you believe me?" he asked, taking her hand and pressing it to a cock that was already firming beneath the cloth. "Believe this one then."

She seemed genuinely taken aback, brows arching. "Is he honest?" she murmured.

"To a fault." Xhai's lips brushed across hers, tasting her breath, as he twisted out of his own clothes, letting them fall. She looked him up and down as if seeing him for the first time. Her fingers drifted, exploring his body: his thickening shaft, the narrow trail of hair that ascended from his pubic mat, the many scars and blemishes of a man who had been to war. Old scars, white; newer ones, still pink and shiny. Scars of sword edges and arrow points and armor buckles, the knobbled bone of a rib shattered by a fall from his horse and badly healed. He did not mind letting her see, now.

"You are not what I expected … musician."

"No?" He kissed her parted lips, pulling her up against the hot hard wall of his body.

"Such a lot of … So many …" She pulled away, looking into his face. "Tell me …"

"What?"

"Three years he lived without me. And so much happened to him. But you knew him. Tell me about Liwan. Tell me how you met." Her eyes shone with unshed tears. "Tell me how he died."

Xhai took a deep breath as the jagged weight in his chest rolled, then nodded. "Come here, and I will tell you," he promised. He led her to a bed on a low pallet, and scooped her up to lay her down upon the quilt. The sight of her beneath him was enough to make him want to spear her again, right now, but he held back. Running his lips and the very tip of his tongue up the tender valley between her breasts, he murmured again, "I will tell you."

And he did. He kissed her breasts and told her how he had met Liwan and spent the whole of that first night demanding songs from him. He circled her nipples over and over, and described his friend's audience with the Emperor, Son of Heaven. He worked his way down the trembling plain of her belly and murmured about nights in mountains under pounding rain, and days on horseback crossing black deserts, and mornings of crisp fallen snow; about charges and ambushes and bravery and long hours of waiting—for the Emperor, for the enemy, for sunrises that never seemed to come—about evenings off-duty and drinking in inns, and that one night spent pacing their tent banging his head against a wall of lyrics that wouldn't come to him even though His Imperial Highness wanted the song at dawn and Liwan could only suggest sillier and sillier rhymes until they were both breathless with panicked laughter. He told of a last, courageous battle, and of how Liwan had fallen defending him. He told her how, afterwards, the Emperor had commanded him to sing and he could not, the *guqin* lying dumb in his hands, the notes broken in his throat.

All the while he spoke, he stroked her thighs and stirred her fleece with his breath and lapped at the unfurling peony of her sex, licking her clit and sucking upon her swelling folds until she was brimming with juices. Her taste was familiar but exotic, a pleasure recalled from ages long past; soft and ripe and fragrant as a peach, making his mouth water and his engorged cock press against the quilt. He made her quiver and stretch and moan, until his words were drowned in her flesh and there was only the sound of her heaving upon the bed and gasping. Her hands clawed at the quilt and she bucked beneath him, crying out in release.

I had forgotten that too, he said to himself, savoring the sharp bite of her juices on his cracked lips, and the particular ache at the back of the neck that comes of eating a woman. *It has been so long*.

He lifted himself onto braced arms, looking down the length of her body. Her skin shone and she looked more beautiful to him than any treasure of the Imperial Palace—and it was almost more than he could bear.

He had left a great deal out of his narrative of course. All the savagery and the pointless brutality of the long campaign. Much of the stupidity and frustration and the filth and the indignity. He had not told her that after the Battle of the Red

River, when the Emperor commanded him to sing at the victory feast, and he would not, that he had been thrown into a dungeon cell. That he'd lain there for days and nights until His Imperial Majesty recalled his existence and had him brought forth before the throne once more, and ordered him again to sing. That he had croaked and shaken his head. That the headsman had been summoned forth with his great curved blade, and that only then, just before the steel was raised, had the Emperor asked him *Why?* That he had said, "I made a vow to Ghan Liwan, to tell his wife, and I have not kept it. The songs are gone from me."

That the Emperor had ordered him released to fulfill his promise. That instead of riding here with a troop of armed guards, a journey which would have taken only a few weeks, he had chosen to leave the Imperial Palace on foot, alone. That he had needed to walk.

And the most important part of all, that he had left out too.

All men lie. The unspoken words lay like a stone in his ribcage. Even as his cock angled rampant from his crotch and urged him to her unguarded gate, the real truth crushed against his heart as if to stop it beating.

Tsulin's face was open now, flushed and tremulous, her thoughts no longer hidden behind the mask. Tears glistened in her eyes. "Three years," she said. "Did he love any other woman?"

"No," he whispered, closing his eyes. "No woman but you."

The darkness swirled around him. His balls ached.

"Why are you crying?" she asked.

Xhai opened his eyes, and looked down at the tears splashed upon her stomach. "No woman," he repeated, tasting salt on his bruised lips, mingled with her honey.

"Liwan was my husband," she said, her voice rising. "Only I may weep for him. You are not his widow."

"He was my …" Xhai paused. His heart thudded.

"Your friend." Her voice was harsh; he could hear the fear in it.

"More than that."

Her mouth made a little "o". "What are you saying?" she breathed.

"I think you know."

"My husband was a man—a true man of the Dog People—and would not lie with another!"

He could not look at her directly. He remembered Liwan lolling back in the bathhouse tub, thighs spread wide, a rueful grin on his face as he surveyed the ruddy hard-on so stiff that it was jutting above the surface of the water. *Ah*, he'd cried, as if at a cheeky pup, *look at that, will you? It's been so long since I had a woman that I could hammer nails into a board with it.* His smile had been so inviting that Xhai had barely hesitated before reaching out to grasp that shameless breakwater. He could still remember the overwhelming rush of relief he'd experienced as his hand closed and Liwan grunted with pleasure. He could still picture the quizzical half-grin on his friend's face as they'd surged in the bathtub, hands sliding and tugging on each other. Still feel the man's smooth hard body against his, still smell the scent of his skin and the soap and the rice wine on his breath. The first taste of his ejaculate, soapy and sharp, was a ghost in his mouth.

"We were lovers," he said. It was the very first time the confession had passed his lips, but the words came out as if they were so heavy, his chest so crammed with their weight, that there was nothing he could do to stop them falling. He was so stunned by the eruption that he didn't see her hand moving—until the blow cracked across his face.

"Liar!" she spat. For a moment she glared at him, waiting for him to strike her back. When he did not move, she drew back her arm for another blow. This time he caught it, pinned her wrist back onto the bed, and heaved himself half over her to keep her down. She twisted beneath him, baring her teeth.

"I … do not lie," he rasped. The heavy thing in his chest was trying hard to become rage. He knew it would stop hurting him so much if he let that happen.

"Which of you played the woman's part then?" she snarled, sounding desperate. "I bet it was you. I bet you knelt to him. He would be the man."

Xhai's lip curled, but he forced himself to speak softly. "That's not how it works."

"Did he fuck your ass, Easterner?"

His cock wanted him to think about the way she was lithe and soft and helpless beneath him. His cock wanted him to drown his pain in her sex. He had to force himself to attend to her scathing accusation.

"He did." *Oh yes, he did. Night after glorious night.* "And he sucked my cock. And he lay with me in the dark and held me." He knew he was being cruel now: taunting her. "Just as I did all those things to him."

"How is that?" Her eyes shone with distress, and her pain and incomprehension distorted her voice. "He desired women! He desired me!"

"And me." Xhai remembered Liwan laughing, saying, *A man may enjoy the taste of both fish and pork.* He didn't think it a good idea to report the words to Tsulin. "He wanted me. And now he is gone …" The pain in his chest was unbearable. He wanted her to understand, but without his music he had no way with words.

His eyes burned. He felt like he was begging her. "Now he is gone I don't know what to do. *I don't know what to do.*"

She spat no answer to that. She stared at him like he was something beyond understanding: a man risen from the grave, or some bizarre creature of legend. Xhai knew that if he pressed against her any longer, he would lose control. His cock was demanding entrance, while his heart pounded with anguish. It felt like he was being mangled between two great stones. It took all his strength to make himself push back off her, kneeling up. His skin was slicked with sour sweat and his erection stood like the pole of an imperial banner, but he dared not touch it.

Tsulin undid all his good intentions by sitting up abruptly, face-to-face with him. Her eyes narrowed to dark slivers and she panted between her bared teeth. They stared and stared, as if somehow, if they did it long enough, understanding would pass between them.

"Show me," she growled.

"What?" For a moment he was utterly at a loss.

"Show me what you did to my husband." Her fingers bit into his thigh. "Do it to me."

It was Xhai's turn to be wrong-footed. "You mean …"

"If I was him, here, now, what would you do to him? I want to know."

I would kiss him. And then I would mount his ass and ride him until his legs gave way. "It'd hurt you," he warned, his cock throbbing with the surge of his pulse.

She sat up straighter. "Good."

Now *that* he understood. Sometimes there is no ease for inner anguish except the pain of the flesh. *Yes*, he said to himself: *Yes, yes.*

He nodded, then heaved himself to his feet. His cock was

like an iron bar, but he was not afraid of it now. He put his hand on the crown of her head, pressing her face to his crotch, rolling her cheeks across the rigid beam of his shaft. For a moment her breath was hot on his balls. Then he pushed her away. "Lie down, he ordered her. "On your belly."

He still thought she might refuse, but she obeyed. While she turned away he moved swiftly to find an unlit lamp. It was full of greasy brown butter that would do, he thought, very well. When he turned back she was lying on the bed, her forearms tucked beneath her breasts to hold her up, her toes digging into the quilt with tension. He knelt over her and laid a heavy hand on her head. "Put your hand down and touch your bud," he told her. "You will need that when I start."

"I want it to hurt," she said in a ragged voice.

"Is this your first time?"

"Yes."

"It will hurt plenty. Touch it. Open your legs. And let the tension go. You must be as water to my stone." As she wriggled her hand beneath her to the juncture of her legs, he pressed her head down gently but firmly to the bed, so that she was lying flat. Then he turned where he knelt and surveyed the territory he was about to invade: the twin mounds, gently curved as the hills of the Dog People; and the deep valley between. Under the lamplight she was golden-amber, and the whorl of her hole a duskier hue, a whirlpool of luscious temptation.

Oh, it had been too long, Xhai thought dizzily. His mouth watered as he stroked that pucker and felt it flex fearfully, sensitive to the lightest touch. The swollen teardrop of her sex below was still glistening from their earlier congress, so he took that wet on his fingers and stoked it up her cleft, up and down, up and down.

Tsulin whimpered, perhaps involuntarily. The sound made his cock jerk.

Oh, but she was beautiful. There was no doubt about that; no denying. He wanted to spread her bottom with both hands and plunge in, sucked down into that tight maelstrom; he longed to fill her with his fire. He could feel the seed simmering in his pouch, ready to boil over. If this was Liwan lying naked and open before him, he would breech that narrow gate like a battering ram.

But she was not Liwan. He had to be gentler.

The butter was a start, at least. He slathered his cock with it, and then he greased her crack from fore to aft, and then he moved over her, kissing between her shoulder blades as he slid a single slippery finger into her clench.

There was momentary resistance, a reflexive tightening of muscle, but he overbore that easily, inveigling his way up to his second knuckle—so hot, so tight—and beginning to stroke. Tsulin held out for a while, and then began to groan. Well he knew that sound, which went straight to his soul via his straining balls—there was nothing in the world so intimate, so frightening, so shaming and yet so freeing as the feel of one's anal passage being entered. He didn't know what it was like to have a cunt, but he could not believe that even that orifice held as much mystery or pleasure. He'd seen whores lying distracted or bored as men rutted in their female parts; he'd never seen *anyone* react with indifference to being sodomized.

Tsulin's hard ring of muscle clenched and then dilated. Xhai rewarded that by biting gently at her shoulder, and her noises became a low throbbing thread of sound that made him smile. He worked his finger in and out of her, round and round, circling and caressing, until she was soft and pliant. Then he pulled out and did it all over again—with two fingers.

And so, slowly, he opened her.

He was happy to take his time. Now that his focus was on his hand, the urgency of his own need was reined back. Her reactions filled him with delight; the trembling and the crying out and the delicious yielding of her tightly guarded places, the opening up that was as much a surrender of her rage and resentment as of her body. The muscles of his forearm grew hot, but it was the good ache a warrior knew well. He found that the nape of her neck was pleasingly sensitive and that it only took the lap of his tongue there to make her pant.

When he had three fingers slipping easily in and out of her hole, right to the root, it took only a momentary withdrawal and a small shift of his weight to bring his cock into play, taking the place of his hand. He pressed in and began to push, feeling her envelop him, and it was like entering the gates of the Western Paradise. Waves of pleasure rippled through his whole being. She was deliciously tight, yet completely yielding. And as he worked his hips, slow and shallow, trying not to crow with delight, she shocked him to the core by jerking desperately beneath him and spasming in uncontrollable waves of orgasm.

That's … not what I expected. He went still as she did, watching as she slackened her tearing grip upon the quilt and gasped wetly into the cotton.

As Heaven was his witness, he was barely within the outer rings of her portal. The twin globes of her bottom had proved surprisingly muscular when tensed … and women have more ass to get in the way than do men. Xhai wiped the sweat from his forehead onto the bed and decided to change angle.

Easing from her twitching iris, he rolled her onto one hip and pushed her upper thigh up toward her chest. Tsulin looked up sideways at him looming over her; she was flushed and wide-eyed, but her hand was still tucked down at the front of her sex and that was what he wanted to see. Kneeling up, he scissored up between her thighs. Her hole was still soft and open and accommodating; he took advantage of the welcome by pushing his cock in past the flexing portal and right into her depths.

From that position, he could sheathe himself all the way to the root in a few firm motions. And now that he was in, he found he could thrust good and hard without damaging her. He gripped her hip and shut his eyes and surrendered to his own need, shafting the widow's ass straight and true and deep.

He wanted to imagine that this was Liwan he was balling; Liwan's hard body beneath his own. *I came to you because you are all I have left of him. Be him for me, now. Be …*

And for a moment he did see Liwan—the cavalryman lying on his side on the battlefield, unmoving. Xhai was running over to him, and at first he thought his friend was only unconscious because there were no great wounds, no hewn limbs or hacked flesh, just a man lying quietly as if in sleep, and not even any blood visible. Until he rolled the Dog Man over and saw that the ground beneath him had drunk all the blood, the dry earth too thirsty to even let it pool out from the deep puncture wound beneath his arm.

Xhai's eyes shot open. He looked down at the woman—and she was a woman, not Liwan at all, and his cock was still pounding her ass—and as he watched she came again, crying out *Oh* in fear of the pleasure that washed over her, tears running down her face. He passed his hand from her shoulder to her hip, leaning low, drops of sweat running down his hair and falling on her. He was very close to his own climax; it gathered like a storm behind the first heralding drops of rain. In the rush of his ecstasy he thought, *She is not Liwan that I have come to find: I am Liwan come home to her. Come home to lie with the wife that I have longed for.* He could feel Liwan in him, looking out through his eyes; a husband borne home thousands of miles, on foot, by a man who was far more than a friend, so that he might love his wife again.

She called his name, over and over.

He has not left us, Xhai thought, as the storm broke.

◆ ◆ ◆

In the morning, Xhai woke first. He was lying on his back, Tsulin snuggled up under his right arm, and it took him a few moments to recognize the radiating roof-poles of the yurt, and remember where he was.

He'd slept without dreaming. For the first time in five months.

His bladder was full and nagging at him. Gently, he disengaged himself from the sleeping woman, but as he slid out from under the quilt she opened her eyes sleepily and caught at his thigh, holding him.

"Shush," he murmured, wondering if she remembered him, or took him for another man. He bent and kissed her temple, filling his lungs with the sex-heavy scent of her. "Go back to sleep."

Her eyes were dark pools under the disorder of her hair. She looked straight into his face, but he couldn't be sure whether she was awake or not. Especially when she shut them, sighed, and went limp once more.

He wondered what they would have to say to each other later, yet that thought gave him no pain. The weight in his chest hadn't gone, but it was so much smaller that he felt like he was floating. He slipped quietly across the yurt, not bothering to put on his clothes, but taking up a different cloth-wrapped bundle.

The four dogs sleeping in a heap just inside the tent flap rose and stretched and preceded him out into the cool dawn.

He made water at a decent distance from the yurt, the only man in the whole wide landscape, while the dogs trotted around sniffing the night's scent trails. The hills where the ancestors' graves nestled looked very green under the pale sun, and an eagle was flying wide circles over it. When he returned to the hut he had his *guqin* unwrapped. Sitting down cross-legged before the entrance, he took his time tuning the strings.

Then, slowly at first, he began to play.

The Merry Maid

Once upon a time there were three brothers, who resolved to set out into the world together to seek their fortune. They went to their father to bid him farewell. To the first he gave a small purse.

"Here, my eldest child. You have always been the one to look after your brothers, so I give to you this magical purse, my greatest possession. Every morning you will find in this purse a silver coin, neither more nor less. With caution, there is enough here to keep you all from starvation as you seek your way in the wide world."

To the second brother he gave a wooden spoon.

"Here, my second child. You have always been the one with the quickest wits and the most cunning. I give to you this magical porridge spoon. I know not that it has any great value, but if you place it in a pot and cry "Stir, spoon, stir," it will do so of its own accord, and never stop until you say "Stop, spoon, stop.""

To the third he said, "Alas, my youngest son! Though you have always been the kindest and most open-hearted of my children, I have nothing left to gift you but my blessing, which I bestow now." And he did this, with a kiss upon the youth's forehead.

Then the three went out into the wide world, and they traveled many leagues through forests and fields, and they crossed rivers and passed through towns. Wherever they went they stayed together. They found work where they could, and when there was none they relied upon the magical purse to buy their food. Once or twice, when they had no money, they begged shelter or a bowl of soup in exchange for demonstrating the magical porridge spoon, for it was a rare and comical sight to see it stirring a cooking pot all on its own, with no hand to guide it.

One day they came to a land of green fields and fat cows, where the people were contented and peaceful.

"Have you ever seen such a land as this, my brothers?" asked the Middle Brother. "The women are the comeliest I have ever seen—tall and well-built, with plump and rosy cheeks and dresses of bright new cloth. The men walk everywhere with smiles upon their faces, and I haven't heard a cross word from anyone since we entered this kingdom. Every the beggars seem happy. Surely this is the place to find our fortune."

They carried on until evening, when there came to small farm and saw there a young woman driving her cows home for the night, singing to herself. While they watched this happy sight, one of the bull-calves broke free of the herd and skipped away across the meadow, so the three brothers ran down and rounded it up, ushering it back to the byre where its owner waited. She was a merry-looking maiden, with a broad smile and knowing eyes. She thanked the three brothers and, looking them up and down boldly, said "For helping me with the stray beast, you have earned yourselves supper. If you chop the wood and feed the beasts and wash the pots, then you will earn a roof for the night too. Come into my house."

Her home was clean and tidy—not large, but well stocked with food and surprisingly well-furnished, with many comforts. When the work was done she sat them down upon cushioned benches and laid before them a hearty supper—cheese and new-baked bread with churned butter, cold mutton and a loaf with dates and nuts therein. While the four of them ate, not one of the brothers could look away from her, for her brown eyes were as playful as the teasing bull-calf's, and her breasts were ample and smooth, pillowing up from behind her low-cut bodice.

"Is your husband home tonight?" asked the Eldest Brother, as they finished.

"Nay," she laughed. "I am not married."

"But you are too young to be widowed, surely?" said the Middle Brother gallantly.

"I am not married *yet*," she corrected herself. "The women of this realm do very well for themselves, with or without husbands, according to their abilities." Seeing their mild frowns of confusion, she added, "Do you not know the custom in this land?"

"No. We do not."

"Ah." She laughed, and stretched like a cat, and they all found their eyes drawn as if under compulsion to the ripe quiver of her bosom. "This is the land of the merry maids. Here a woman's most secret place is accounted a prize to be held safe for her husband and no other man."

"As it is everywhere," said the Eldest Brother, while the Middle Brother frowned and the Youngest Brother blushed.

"But here a woman, maiden or married, may give her mouth to pleasure any man and all men, and it is not counted a shame to her. The custom is only that the man must offer her a gift of some kind that she finds acceptable."

Suddenly each of the brothers felt as if there were wood between his thighs, not flesh. Where they came from, the maidens lived in terror of giving up pleasure to those who wanted it, and any such quest required wooing and persistent cajoling—and more often than not, with nothing to show for it at the end of all efforts.

She ran her tongue across her plump upper lip, enjoying

the expression upon their faces. "So: you are three fine young men, and I would be hard-put to say which of you is the most handsome. Which, if any, of you wishes to make me a gift and enjoy my mouth?"

There was a moment's silence. Then, "There are three of us …" the Eldest Brother said cautiously.

Her teeth flashed white in merriment. "Three is nothing, my sweet! Why, the Prince himself rode past here last year with a whole company of hussars, and I serviced each man there. They paid a silver coin apiece, dropping it into the cleft of my bosom, and by the time I was done my bodice was so full the laces were straining."

"Oh," said the Eldest Brother.

"That's … most impressive," said the Middle Brother.

"I wish I could have seen that," said the Youngest Brother wistfully.

She dimpled prettily at the compliment. "Well then?"

"If you accept silver …" The eldest brother fished out the magical purse. His face fell a little. "I have only one coin, I fear."

"And you?" she asked the Middle Brother.

Abruptly it seemed to him that possession of a magical spoon was a very small thing in comparison to the delights promised by those full carmine lips. "I have a spoon," he said, drawing it from his belt. "Do not laugh— it is magical. Without any effort on your part, it can stir your pot all day so that nothing sticks or spoils."

"If only I could find a man so useful," she said, with a wicked twinkle in her eyes that made the blood surge to his loins. "Very well then—a magical spoon. What about you, my sweet?"

The Youngest Brother looked downcast. "I have

nothing," he admitted.

"Nothing? I cannot give it away for naught. That is not our way."

"That was all our father gave us when we left—a purse of coin, a porridge spoon. That was it."

"Oh—you are brothers, then?"

"We are brothers," said the Eldest heavily. "And if one of us must go without, then I will refrain too."

She pursed her lips, then looked back at the Youngest with something like concern. "Had he nothing to spare for his third son? That seems cruel."

"There was nothing left! Nothing, except his blessing and a kiss." Tentative hope flared in his blue eyes. "I could give you a kiss, Merry Maid."

For a long moment she looked at him, a half-smile on her lips, speculation in her eyes. "Show me your limb," she said softly, "and I will consider."

With clumsy, eager hands, he unlaced his hose and let his cock bounce free. She leaned over the side of the table to watch. Though he was a slim youth, and the curls of his first blond beard were still soft and sparse on his jaw-line, the growth of other parts seemed to have been out of proportion. His ruddy length waved like a drunkard at her. His hands were shyer, nervous as they stroked his shaft and cupped his hairless balls for her to peruse.

"My, yes," she said in a gentle voice. "That is a fine young bough, full of sap. I will accept a kiss, for that."

His grin was like the sun coming out.

"Shall we move the table back?" she asked them all. "I'm not crawling under there."

"What—we are not …? I mean—your room …?" The Eldest asked.

"Are you shy? You are lusty young men—you must have seen each other's limbs many a time."

He grimaced.

"We are not ashamed, here."

"We see that," said the Middle Brother, scrambling to his feet. The two older men took the oaken trestle board and stacked it against the wall, while the Youngest Brother stayed on his bench, nursing his hard-on as if it were an animal that might leap across the room and bite someone if he were to let it go. The maiden waited, a soft smile playing on her face, until all was cleared away. Then she approached the Eldest Brother.

"Ah," said he, as she put her hand upon his crotch. It was months since they'd left home, and in all that time they'd hardly had a woman glance at them.

"I think they will enjoy watching," she whispered. Then she slid gracefully to her knees, her face to his groin as she tugged at the lacing of his hose. He was a man full-grown, the Eldest Brother, with a blond beard—and a blond bush of hair, no less vigorous, at his crotch. His cock stood out from that like a roof-beam hewn of oak. The maid looked it in the eye and blinked, almost cross-eyed herself at that proximity. And then she opened her mouth and sucked that thick knot of a cock-head right in, swallowing it.

"Uh!" grunted the Eldest, his eyes rolling back in his head.

The Middle Brother, staring, realized that he must be patient, and backed off to a bench to sit down hard, rubbing his own strop through his clothes and tugging at the toggles. Age brought precedence. He and his brother could only watch, hardly remembering to breathe, as the Merry Maid worked their brother's cock deeper and deeper into her mouth, making little

"Um um" noises of appreciation, until she had it all, to the root. Then she pulled out, in a long slurp, and they simply could not understand where she had put that whole glistening length. There wasn't room in her mouth for such a thing. She must be taking it right the way down her throat—without protest or gagging. In fact she seemed to be enjoying it, judging from the way her hips worked and her eyelids fluttered. Her barely-constrained breasts threatened to tumble from her blouse and bodice.

She licked and she kissed and she sucked—and then she did it all over again, and this time they saw the stretch of her throat as it opened up around that solid girth.

Setting his feet apart, the Eldest Brother put both hands on her head, in the manner of a priest giving a blessing, and began to stroke in and out. The rhythm was mesmeric. His breathing became harsher. She urged him on with muffled moans and quick sudden gasps as she rose for air. His thighs braced, straightened, braced again—and then suddenly he was thrusting, every muscle in his body in motion, every part of him pushing toward his goal. Crossing that line, he roared as he emptied his balls down her throat.

She sat back slowly, wiping her mouth, looking every bit as a satisfied as a cat who'd just stolen the cream from the dairy. Then she hitched up her skirts and turned to the Middle Brother, who sat waiting with his eyes wide and his legs spread. Kneeling before his open thighs, she looked down at the erect cock in his fist with clear appreciation.

"I can tell you are brothers," she said, smirking. "That's one gift you all share."

"I … Will you … Would you take off your blouse for me?"

That amused her. "Do you like to see my breasts?"

He nodded vigorously, words eluding him for once.

"Fine." She took her time, tugging loose the lacing of her bodice, while the Eldest Brother collapsed on to a bench to watch, and the two younger ones polished their staves in anticipation. Pulling bodice and blouse straight off over her head, she shook her breasts, reveling in their freedom. She had big firm orbs, each bouncing proudly as she arched her back to display them for approval. The line of sun-darkened skin ran just above her nipples, which hardened to points even as the men watched. "Like that, my sweet?"

"Oh yes!"

"Now let me see to that big hard limb of yours."

"Please—!" He stopped her with a gesture. "Please just … lick it. I want to see."

"Heh. If that's what you want."

This time was completely different. There was no urgency, just the opposite in fact. The Middle Brother was trying to draw his time out as long as possible, and she was in no hurry. Instead of swallowing his shaft and urging him to plunder her throat, she kissed and licked his private parts instead, stones and shaft and head, nibbling and sucking and playing with him as if it were all a game. Perhaps it was, of a sort: a contest in which he had to try to resist, and she teased and provoked him to the edge of endurance. Gradually she reduced him to heaving, sweating, trembling helplessness, and when finally his balls tightened and the surge came, she angled herself and his cock so that they could all see him spurting onto her tongue. There was more to his gush than she'd anticipated though, because he flooded her mouth and she tried in vain to stop it escaping, spasming as she choked and swallowed and licked at her second load of cream that night.

"Do we taste the same?" the Eldest Brother asked, as

she wiped at her chin. The Middle Brother was in no state to ask anything: he was still gasping and groaning.

"No," she giggled. Then she turned to the Youngest Brother.

He handed her his cup of ale that had languished, forgotten, during the performance, and she drank from it gratefully. "Before we begin," he said, "I would like to give you the kiss I promised."

"Very well."

"Sit you upon the end of this bench, Merry Maid."

But when she did so, looking at him a little askance, he went down on his own knees before her and threw up her skirts over her thighs.

"Oh! I see!" said she, as he parted her legs. Then "Oh!" again as he pushed her back upon the cushion and went nuzzling up under her skirt, pressing his lips to her virgin puss. And "Oh!"—far longer and more drawn out—as his kiss struck home. To the bemusement of his brothers, their youngest sibling did not cease in his kissing, and the Merry Maid did not resist his blandishments. Her bare breasts heaving, she lay back upon the bench's length, wriggling her hips with joy. Slowly it dawned upon them that her secret treasure, that thing that must remain inviolate until her wedding day, was more than capable of being pleasured without being entered by any cock. This sight was no hardship for their eyes either, nor for their nether parts, which despite being so recently drained were a-twitch with interest. The two brothers watched, grinning, as their youngest sibling gamahuched away.

At length the Merry Maid gave a great cry and arched her spine and then collapsed, babbling and giggling. The Youngest Brother looked up from under her skirts with a big grin and a slick of juice plastered across his face, appearing for all the world as if he had been eating a basket of ripe plums.

"Oh!" she said. "Oh, you have earned your pleasure with that kiss! Come here, my sweet, that I may repay you!"

"But—No," he said. "Not yet. I would rather do this …" And with those words he plunged back into the fray, and set to once more upon her virgin treasure with his lips. At first the Merry Maid shrieked and made as if to wriggle from his grasp, but as he persisted she surrendered in very short order, with many sighs and yelps of pleasure. This time, too, she caught her own breasts in her hands and pinched her own nipples.

That was too much for the Middle Brother. Rising from his seat, he found the pot of butter that had been on the dinner table, and scooped out a big blob upon his fingertips. He used this to baste the maiden's bosom, slathering her all over until her breasts were two slippery orbs that he could mold and press and squeeze together. She seemed most grateful for this attention, willingly giving up to the task to him. In fact she smeared butter from her skin onto her hand and used it to grease up his tool, working it with a firm grip.

That was enough to bring the Eldest Brother back into action. Coming round the other side of the bench, he took his turn tugging upon a slippery nipple. Eagerly she grabbed his cock too. They arranged themselves either side of her head, and as the Youngest Brother ate her puss, they plied their trade upon her breasts as if milking a fine cow.

"Yes!" the maiden groaned, pulling upon their cocks—lengths that were showing surprising solidity and girth, considering what they had already been through. She rolled her face to one side, urging The Eldest Brother's length toward her open, hungry mouth. With one knee on the bench edge, he discovered her could crouch at the right angle to feed his bell-end to her lips. Her tongue darted out, lapping him. For a moment he rediscovered paradise—and then she rolled away, to the other side, searching out the Middle Brother's cock in turn.

That was how they brought her off for a second time, between them—slippery tits, slippery cocks, a kiss upon a wet and slippery puss. Turn and turn about, two stiff members to suck, back and forth between them, tasting butter and sweat and salt, until she opened up once more and, with a squeal, came. By that time she had worked their limbs so hard and so surely that it was not difficult for both the elder brothers to take themselves in hand and squeeze out their seed in slopping spasms into her open mouth.

As they staggered back, the Youngest Brother rose at last to claim his own. Coming to the maiden's head, he straddled it and aimed his turgid length down her throat, laying himself upon her to tuck his head back down between her thighs yet one more time. The Maiden began to gobble and the lad began to thrust. The Eldest Brother laughed in disbelief. The Middle Brother laughed as a wicked thought occurred to him.

"Take her leg," he told his older sibling. Then he took up the magic porridge spoon and smeared it copiously with butter. Going round to the Merry Maiden's bottom, he lifted one of her thighs as his Eldest Brother lifted the other. Right underneath the Youngest Brother's laboring face was the maiden's brown wink. Sliding the handle of the spoon into it took no effort at all.

"Stir, spoon, stir," said the Middle Brother.

So it did.

With the Youngest Brother spurting his hot seed deep into her throat, and his mouth upon her pip, and the magic spoon swiveling in her ass, the Maiden roared a muffled roar and came one last time.

The next morning the three brothers sought her out in the yard where she fed the chickens.

"Marry me," said the Eldest Brother.

"Marry me," said the Middle Brother.

"Marry me," said the Youngest Brother.

She laughed then, a little, but looked thoughtful. "I would marry," she said. "And all three of you are handsome and hard-working and will make fine husbands for maidens hereabouts. You," she said to the Eldest Brother, "are strong and would care for me as you care for all your family. You," she said to the Middle Brother, "are clever and quick-witted, and will likely go far."

Then she turned to the Youngest Brother. "But you," she said, "have a merry mouth and a generous heart, my sweet, and for that I will marry you."

The Youngest Brother kissed her. "I hope you will always welcome my brothers, though," he said.

"You mean in our home?"

He touched her lips tenderly. "I mean right here."

"Of course," the Merry Maid answered with a laugh and a wink. "They are welcome and more than welcome. My mouth is a harbor wherein they may berth their vessels whenever they desire."

"I think we shall all live happily ever after!"

"And," she added with a twinkle, "I can't wait to meet your father."

Janine Ashbless

NAMED AND SHAMED

Once upon a time, a naughty girl called Tansy stole a very precious manuscript from a kindly antiquarian. But all of the world's ancient and powerful magic, lost for centuries, has returned and now there is much more at stake than a few sheets of parchment!

Thus begins a rude and rugged fairy tale the likes of which you NEVER read when you were little! Poor Tansy is led though the most pleasurable trials and the most shameful tribulations as her quest unfolds before her. Orgasmic joy and abject humiliation are laid upon Tansy in equal measure as she straddles the two worlds of magic and man.

"The most amazing book that has graced my e-book reader in a long time. 5/5 for story, 5/5 for kink"
BDSM Book Reviews

"Named and Shamed takes other erotic literature and beats its backside black and blue with bramble branches. 10 out of 10."
Cara Sutra

"From the vivid description, through the strong characterisation, through to the plot that makes you want to stay awake into the early hours of the morning – *Named and Shamed* is one of the most fun reading experiences you will have this year."
Erotica Readers and Writer's Association

Vanessa de Sade

IN THE FORESTS OF THE NIGHT

In the Forests of the Night is a darkly sensual collection of erotic fairy tales. Each story blends the magic and fantasy of the traditional fable with the carnality and lust we've come to expect from Vanessa de Sade!

In the timeless tradition of the storybook, each tale is vividly illustrated by Vanity Chase. Beautiful, visceral and devoutly debauched, Vanity's illustrations bring the book to life and explore a much more grown-up side of fantasy. The seven sexy stories within these pages offer up a mind-bending, pulse-quickening twist on a classic genre.

If you think you know how a fairy tale is supposed to end, this book will make you think again! Sexual and cerebral, magical and modern, In the Forests of the Night is the ultimate collection of sexy, adult fables!

Also available from Sweetmeats Press

Kyoko Church

Diary of a Library Nerd

That's what this will be. A safe haven.
A place for no holds barred ranting.
A place for secrets. And drawing. Even if it's bad. Even if it's wrong.
No one will see here. No one will see this.
This is just for me.
Charlotte has secrets.

Charlotte Campbell no longer recognizes her life. Once a shy, married librarian, she now finds herself jilted, holed up in her deceased father's run down cottage, and demoted to working in 'The Dungeon' with only an automated book sorter for company.

Then there's the drawings she does. They are not what her work colleagues might expect. And there's Nathan, a young patron at the library—the reason for her demotion and the inspiration for her art.

When Nathan's emails reveal a startling truth, Charlotte discovers a new dimension of her sexuality. But unsettling dreams from her past continue to plague her and Charlotte is eventually forced to confront her most deeply rooted fears.

Part Bridget Jones' Diary and part Story of O, Diary of a Library Nerd is the Wimpy Kid for adults. Compelling, erotic and accompanied by the drawings from Charlotte Campbell's very grown-up mind, this private memoir of exploration and discovery is not to be missed!

Kay Jaybee

MAKING HIM WAIT

Maddie Templeton has always been an unconventional artist. Themes of submission and domination pulse through her erotic artwork, and she's happily explored these lustful themes both on and off the canvas.

But, when Theo Hunter enters her life, she is presented with a new challenge. Maddie sets out to test his resolve as she teases, torments and toys with him. However, as Maddie drives Theo to breaking point, she soon becomes unsure whether her own resolve will hold out!

At the same time, Maddie must put on the exhibition of a lifetime. As the hottest gallery in town clamors for her best work, Maddie pushes her models harder and higher until they are physically, sexually and emotionally exhausted. Will Maddie's models continue to submit to her, or will she push them too far? And will she be ready for the exhibition in time?

The only way to find out is to wait and see … and the waiting only makes it sweeter!